DEATH SURGE

DEATH SURGE

A DI Andy Horton Mystery

Pauline Rowson

This first world edition published 2013
in Great Britain and 2014 in the USA by
SEVERN HOUSE PUBLISHERS LTD of
19 Cedar Road, Sutton, Surrey, England, SM2 5DA.

British Library Cataloguing in Publication Data

Rowson, Pauline author.
   Death surge. – (A DI Andy Horton mystery; 10)
   1. Horton, Andy (Fictitious character)–Fiction.
   2. Missing persons–Investigation–Fiction. 3. Police–
   England–Portsmouth–Fiction. 4. Detective and mystery
   stories.
   I. Title II. Series
   823.9'2-dc23

ISBN-13: 978-0-7278-8321-6 (cased)

All Severn House titles are printed on acid-free paper.

Severn House Publishers support the Forest Stewardship Council™ [FSC™],
the leading international forest certification organisation. All our titles that
are printed on FSC certified paper carry the FSC logo.

MIX
Paper from
responsible sources
FSC   FSC® C013056
www.fsc.org

Typeset by Palimpsest Book Production Ltd.,
Falkirk, Stirlingshire, Scotland.
Printed and bound in Great Britain by
TJ International, Padstow, Cornwall.

For Chrissy with much love

ACKNOWLEDGEMENT

With grateful thanks to Haslar Marina staff and Sir Robin Knox-Johnston

ACKNOWLEDGEMENT

ONE

The gentle wind propelled Horton's yacht along the coastline, past the Victorian colour-washed houses which lay staggered up the steep hills from the small bay of Ventnor to St Boniface Down on the Isle of Wight. He barely glanced at them. His eyes were focused ahead on the vast expanse of silver sea that stretched across to France but his mind was back in the Castle Hill Yacht Club in Cowes which, three hours ago, he'd left with the stink of deception in his nostrils and fury churning his gut.

He mentally replayed his conversation with Lord Eames. He'd been over it a hundred times and he could go over it a hundred times more but it still wouldn't change the fact that Lord Eames knew something about the disappearance of Jennifer Horton, his mother, in 1978, and that he was going to keep silent about it. Why? Because he worked for the intelligence services. Not that Eames had admitted it, but Horton could smell it. He could feel it and taste it and it made him sick to his stomach. How the intelligence services were involved in his mother's disappearance, or why, he didn't know, but he was determined to find out. Equally, he knew they would be determined to stop him.

He scoured the horizon. Not a boat in view, but the throb of a distant helicopter caught his attention. He peered up at the pale blue sky but couldn't see it. It was probably the coastguard or a naval helicopter from one of the ships docked in the Portsmouth Naval Base that now lay several miles behind him. He thought of his CID office in Portsmouth and the paperwork piling up on his desk but it was Saturday, he wasn't on duty, and his boss DCI Lorraine Bliss wouldn't be working either; the station was usually as barren as the Sahara at weekends when it came to a head count of senior officers.

He ran a hand over his chin. God, he was tired. This last week of researching into the disappearance of his mother and being caught up in a major murder investigation was taking its toll both emotion- ally and physically. Maybe it was time to call it quits as far as his mother was concerned and let go of the past before it became an unhealthy obsession. Or had he already passed that point?

He put the helm on autopilot and retrieved the black and white photograph from the pocket of his trousers which had led him to Lord Eames. He had no need to study it again because he knew each of the six men's features by heart; he'd looked at the wretched thing enough times since discovering it on his yacht six weeks ago. It had been left there by a man named Edward Ballard, who, he'd since learnt, didn't exist, at least not on any databases he'd checked – and being a copper they were pretty extensive. Ballard's prints and DNA, which Horton had lifted from a can of Coke when he'd come on-board in June to thank him for his help after an alleged assault at Southsea Marina, hadn't matched anyone of his age: early to mid sixties. The only Edward Ballards Horton could find in the UK were either dead, over eighty, or under five. And Horton didn't think Ballard was any nationality other than English, but he could be wrong.

His mind flashed back to that night in June. Ballard had barely stayed five minutes on-board and had hardly touched his drink, but after he had left the marina Horton had discovered the photograph pushed down behind the seat cushion where Ballard had been sitting. That, and the recall of a distant memory of a man handing his foster father a tin, which Horton had later been given, containing a photograph of Jennifer Horton along with his birth certificate had sealed the connection. Horton knew the assault had been fabricated as a means to make contact with him. Ballard was telling him something by leaving this picture taken in 1967, but what, for God's sake?

The wind suddenly sprang up out of nowhere catching the sails. He could see clouds beginning to form to the west; ripples appeared on the sea, and almost instantly it changed colour. One moment all was calm and looked set to stay that way and the next everything changed. Just like his life, he thought, correcting course. At the age of ten, with his mother's disappearance it had altered irrevocably.

Ahead, far on the horizon, a container ship came into view. The throb of the helicopter faded into nothing. The silence was soothing, and yet at the same time it was a torment. No, the torment was inside him. After years of trying to forget his mother he now so desperately wanted to know why she'd abandoned him. He could no more call it quits than give up breathing. He had to know. It was like a sore that constantly itched and yet the more he scratched the more it irritated him. Why had the investigation into her disappearance been cursory, to say the least? Why had all her belongings and photographs been destroyed? Why had . . .? His phone rang.

He swore softly. He should have switched it off. He hoped it wasn't Bliss, who for once had decided to work at the weekend to earn extra brownie points in the promotion stakes, wanting to bawl him out for not writing up his reports of the last murder investigation. But with relief he saw it was Cantelli. And the sergeant was the one person he would never ignore. Cantelli had stood by him through all the mess of those false rape allegations twenty months ago when he'd been working undercover, which had cost him his marriage and stalled his career.

'Andy, thank God.'

'What is it?' Horton asked with concern hearing the anguish in Cantelli's voice.

'It's Johnnie. He's missing.'

Horton's heart lurched; he knew the fear and panic that word evoked. Johnnie Oslow was Cantelli's nephew, who Horton had helped steer away from a path of criminality seven years ago, when he'd been sixteen and in trouble with the law, following an arson attack on a sailing club in Portsmouth. Horton had introduced him to sailing via a charity that rehabilitated wayward boys and girls. The lad had never looked back. From there he had got a job as a crew member on a Greek millionaire's personal yacht and also as a team member on one of the same millionaire's many racing yachts.

'He's been missing since Wednesday,' Cantelli said, 'but it's only just been reported. He's meant to be at Cowes Week, racing with a guy named Scott Masefield.'

'Not Andreadis, his boss?' Horton asked, puzzled.

'It doesn't sound like it. I've only got sketchy information. A Nat Boulton, who said he worked for Andreadis, called Johnnie's mum, Isabella, an hour ago to ask if she'd heard from him. She said she hasn't, not since last Tuesday. As far as Isabella is aware, Johnnie was due at Cowes on Friday, but this Boulton said he was meant to be there from Wednesday. They tried Johnnie's mobile phone but got no answer. Isabella tried it and the number is dead. She phoned me. I got the same result. So I called Cowes police station and got an idiot who sounded as though he should either be committed or in nursery school. He said this Masefield guy reported it and it's been logged. Logged!' Cantelli cried in disgust. 'I'm on the ferry on my way over to the Island to see Masefield and find out what the devil's going on.'

And that showed just how concerned Cantelli was, because nothing short of a direct order from Bliss would get him on water. The sergeant got sick just standing on a pontoon. Horton was perplexed by the local station's response because Andreadis, Johnnie's boss, was very wealthy and influential, so surely reporting one of his crew missing would have been enough to have summoned the National Guard, if they'd had one. But 'logged' meant no further action had been taken. Horton didn't blame Cantelli for being furious.

'Doesn't Andreadis have any idea where he might be?' he asked.

'I don't know. I haven't got his telephone number or this Nat Boulton's. And I can't speak to this Scott Masefield because he's racing,' Cantelli added scathingly.

Horton switched the autopilot back to manual. 'I'll meet you on the promenade at Cowes by the Castle Hill Yacht Club. Do nothing until I get there.'

'Thanks.' The relief in Cantelli's voice was palpable.

Horton started the engine and swiftly turned the boat round, cursing the fact that he was so far away, but with the engine running, and wind and tide permitting, he'd be there in about thirty-five minutes. The ferry crossing would take Cantelli forty minutes and then the drive to Cowes another fifteen. With luck and the elements with him Horton thought he might get there first, especially as Cantelli would find the narrow streets of Cowes slow to navigate because of the holiday traffic and the annual sailing event, and he'd have to find somewhere to park. Horton would need somewhere to moor the yacht, though, and that would be a problem as all the moorings would be taken. He rang Sergeant Elkins of the police marine unit.

'Dai, where are you?'

'In the midst of mayhem,' Elkins answered somewhat wearily.

Horton could hear the wind whistling down the mobile line, which meant Elkins and PC Ripley were at sea and probably close to the racing. Horton swiftly relayed what Cantelli had told him, ending with a request for a mooring on the pontoon near the yacht club and promenade.

Elkins said, 'Take ours, we'll moor up alongside you. I'll clear it with the harbour master and the Commodore of the yacht club. We'll head back to help you.'

'Find out if Andreadis is at Cowes. And who this Scott Masefield is and where we can locate him.'

The sooner they spoke to Masefield and Andreadis the better, he thought as the Portsmouth landscape of tower blocks eventually came into view across the Solent to the north. The brisk wind was now behind him from the east helping to propel him, but it still wasn't fast enough. He didn't often wish for a motorboat or a more powerful engine but this was one occasion when he would willingly have exchanged what he had for either or both.

Ahead, in the distance, he could see the Wightlink ferries crossing in the middle of the Solent. Cantelli would be on the one heading south for Fishbourne, his mind conjuring up all kinds of possibilities as it did when someone went missing; it was a word that filled every parent with dread and which for him had cast a long shadow over his life, leaving an empty yawning chasm made even more painful because as a child he'd been led to believe his mother had abandoned him for a lover. Even though he now knew that not to be true it didn't ease the constriction in his chest at the memory of his lonely childhood.

He stretched a hand in his pocket and returned his attention to the photograph. Mentally, he ran through what his investigations had unearthed since he'd discovered it on his boat. Fact one, it had been taken during the first student sit-in protest at the London School of Economics on the thirteenth of March, 1967. Fact two, three of the men in the picture were dead: Zachary Benham had died in a fire in a psychiatric hospital in Surrey in 1968; James Royston of a drug overdose in a bedsit in London in 1969 and Timothy Wilson, Lord Eames' friend by his own recent admission, had been killed in a motorcycle accident on the A345 from Salisbury to Marlborough the same year. Fact three: Professor Thurstan Madeley, an expert on crime, and a consultant to various UK police forces including Horton's own in Hampshire, had compiled an archive file on the student sit-in protest but hadn't included this picture because it had been in a private collection. He claimed to know nothing about the men in the photograph but he'd given Horton a name, Dr Quentin Amos.

Horton recalled the skeletal, sharp-brained man in the dingy urine-smelling flat in Woking. Amos had been easy to find. He had several criminal convictions not only for assault during violent protests throughout the years but also for importuning in a public place and having sex with under-age males. Amos had told him that Jennifer had worked as a secretary at the London School of Economics in 1967 and that she'd also helped to organize the Radical Student Alliance, which all these men with the exception of Lord Eames had belonged to. She wasn't in the photograph but Amos had said her connection with the Alliance had got her the sack. So what had happened to her after that? Amos had intimated that one of these men might know. With three of them dead and the fourth, Lord Eames, a peer of the realm who was clearly going to continue denying any knowledge of Jennifer that left Horton with two to trace: Antony Dormand and Rory Mortimer.

Clearly, Amos had more to tell him, and he had no reason to lie – he was a dying embittered man. But Horton had caught the smell of fear about him and the sense that although Amos might not have lied, he'd said what he'd been told to say. So what did the intelligence services have over him that would make him obey their instructions by giving Horton only the information they wanted him to have? Or was he just being paranoid? Perhaps. Because he also believed that Professor Thurstan Madeley, who had pulled together the archive project on the student sit-in protest, was in league with Lord Eames.

The Solent was now getting busier. He'd need all his concentration to get through the hundreds of boats. Stuffing the photograph back in his pocket he pushed thoughts of his own personal investigation aside and turned his mind to Johnnie. Perhaps their fears would be unfounded and by the time he and Cantelli reached Cowes Johnnie would have shown up with an apologetic grin on his dark features wondering what all the fuss was about. God, he hoped so.

He caught sight of the police launch heading towards him, weaving its way gently through the yachts and motor cruisers. Then suddenly out of nowhere a RIB appeared and shot across its bows causing Ripley to veer off course. Horton eyed the idiot hanging off the side of the RIB with a camera pressed to her face. The helmsman spun the RIB round and headed out into the Solent. Horton turned the yacht towards the pontoons and a few minutes later he was tying up as Ripley came alongside him.

'Who was the fool in the RIB?' he asked Elkins, climbing back on-board his yacht.

'Sarah Conway, one of the official photographers,' Elkins replied, handing Horton a line. 'Mad as a hatter. I warned her yesterday about being reckless. She said, "What are going to book us for, sergeant – dangerous driving or being drunk in charge of a boat? Not guilty on both counts."' A brief smile crossed Elkins' malleable face; Horton could see he had a soft spot for Sarah. Then Elkins' expression fell as he recalled why Horton was here. He instructed Ripley to stay with the police launch and contact him by mobile phone if they were needed on the water, and together they headed towards the promenade. Elkins continued: 'Scott Masefield's currently racing. He's expected in at about three thirty.'

Horton consulted his watch. He hadn't realized it was that late. No wonder his stomach was making peculiar noises. He hadn't eaten since the very early hours of the morning, and then only sketchily. But he pushed thoughts of food aside. According to Elkins' reckoning that left them with an hour to kick their heels but there were things they could do before then.

'He'll come into Shepards Wharf,' Elkins added.

Horton knew it. The marina was situated at the further end of the small town close to the chain ferry that clanked and rattled its regular way across the River Medina between West and East Cowes.

'What do you know about Masefield?' he asked as they stepped on to the crowded promenade.

'Not much, only that the yacht is called *Naiyah*, and is sponsored by Xander Andreadis, who isn't here.'

'Why not?'

'No idea. Perhaps he had more important things to attend to.'

'Does he usually race at Cowes?'

Elkins shrugged. 'Perhaps Masefield is here in his place.'

Perhaps, thought Horton, catching sight of Cantelli weaving his way through the crowds and the many side shows on the promenade. With concern he noted that Cantelli's usual leisurely gait had been replaced by agitated strides and a worried frown graced his lean, olive-skinned face instead of his normal easy, laconic smile. Horton's heart went out to him. But emotion was no use, only action was.

'I've tried Johnnie's mobile phone again but the line's still dead,' Cantelli said the moment he drew level, briefly nodding a greeting at Elkins.

Horton didn't like the sound of that but there could be a logical explanation. Perhaps he'd broken it or lost it, or perhaps the battery had run down. But why not borrow someone else's phone or use a pay phone to contact his boss and his mother? He was sure Cantelli had run through the same scenario. They sidestepped some dawdling holidaymakers and began to thread their way through the crowded winding streets towards Shepards Wharf.

'When was the last time Isabella saw Johnnie?' Horton asked.

'In January when he came home for my dad's funeral.'

And that had been when Horton had last seen him too. 'How did he seem then?'

'Upset over his grandad's death.'

Which was to be expected. 'Has he been in touch with any of his cousins since then?'

'I've rung round all the family, and asked my kids, but no one's heard from him for ages.'

'Is that usual for him?'

'Ellen says so.'

Ellen was Cantelli's eldest daughter and the nearest in age to Johnnie at seventeen.

'What about any of the social networks? Could Johnnie have posted something on one of them?'

Cantelli looked annoyed. 'I should have thought of that. And I call myself a detective.'

'You're worried.'

'Yeah, and that won't achieve anything.'

'Call Ellen now and ask her to check.'

By the time Cantelli came off the phone they had reached the police station. 'She'll call me back.'

'Let's get a copy of the report.'

It hardly told them anything except that Masefield had telephoned to report a member of his crew missing. He'd given the name and said he'd come along to the station after racing to give further details.

'And you were satisfied with that!' Cantelli declared in disgust, eyeing the young uniformed officer malevolently. Horton had seldom seen Cantelli lose his temper but he thought he was about to now and he didn't blame him. He quickly interjected by addressing Cantelli.

'Have you got a photograph of Johnnie?'

Cantelli took a deep breath. 'Only an old one on my mobile phone.'

'Email it to this officer.' But Horton wondered if it was worth them circulating it here in Cowes because as yet they didn't know where Johnnie had gone missing. Again to Cantelli he said, 'Have you checked the local hospitals?' Horton could tell by Cantelli's expression he hadn't and that he was cursing himself for not doing so. Horton asked Elkins to do it and to let him know the outcome. Then he made his way with Cantelli towards the bustling marina where music and laughter seemed to mock their solemn mood.

Horton asked in the marina office for the location of Masefield's berth. It was at the far end of the marina. They headed towards it but still had half an hour or more to wait until the boat came in so he suggested they grabbed something to eat. Cantelli refused saying he wouldn't be able to swallow a mouthful. But Horton insisted. 'Starving yourself isn't going to make Johnnie appear.'

Reluctantly, Cantelli acquiesced. Horton ordered two baguettes and a large cup of tea for Cantelli and a black coffee for himself and managed to get a table outside with a good view of the pontoon where Masefield would moor up. His phone rang. It was Elkins with the news that no one fitting Johnnie's description had been admitted to the hospital on either the Isle of Wight or in Portsmouth. Horton relayed the information to Cantelli but it wasn't much comfort to him. And Ellen's call to say that Johnnie hadn't used the most popular social networking sites for at least six months didn't raise his spirits.

'This isn't looking good,' Cantelli said, anguished. He'd hardly touched his food.

'Let's get some facts first. If we can find out exactly where he was last seen that would help.' And Horton looked up to see two large sleek yachts approaching, one of which by Elkin's description was Scott Masefield's. But it was the one behind it that drew Horton's attention. Or rather the slender attractive woman in her mid thirties at the bow who caught his interest and sent his pulse rate up. Only a few hours ago he'd brushed past her in a fury after his meeting with her father, Lord Eames. Did Harriet Eames know that her father worked for British Intelligence? Had he told her about Jennifer's disappearance? Did it matter if he had? No, because he could forget any chance of a relationship with her; Agent Harriet Eames would return to her job at Europol in The Hague, and he would get on with his. And the sooner the better, he thought, rising.

'Masefield's yacht.'

As they made their way towards it, Horton's mind went back to his first meeting with Harriet Eames in June when she'd been seconded to an investigation he'd been working on. Cantelli had been on holiday. From the beginning Horton had felt attracted to her. He'd got the impression the feeling was mutual but that was about as far as any relationship between them, apart from a professional one, had got and was ever going to get. Their backgrounds were poles apart, but even if he ignored that, her father's involvement with Jennifer made it impossible for him to consider developing a relationship with her. He knew it wasn't her fault who her father was. His argument wasn't with her. But he could never get close to someone he thought might relay confidences to a man he believed was partly to blame for ruining his childhood – a childhood that had taught him to trust no one and suspect everyone.

He saw her raise her arm in a greeting, and her fair face lit up with a broad smile, and for one brief heart-stopping moment he thought it was directed at him, before a broad-shouldered man, in his early forties, with short-cropped dark hair, stepped forward, took the line as she jumped off the yacht and threw his arms around her. She didn't look as though she was protesting. She laughed and gently pushed him away, and as she did her eyes caught his. Another smile formed on her lips and faded as quickly as it had appeared. He didn't return it. He glanced at her coolly, aware that his expression conveyed none of his mixed-up feelings for her but perhaps hinted at hostility. He had enough problems without getting involved with Harriet Eames, so the less encouragement he gave her, and the more he steeled himself against feeling anything for her, the better. He turned his thoughts to the more important and pressing matter of Johnnie Oslow. Addressing the lean man who leapt off Masefield's yacht, he said, 'Mr Masefield?'

'He's at the helm.'

TWO

'We had instructions to pick him up from Oyster Quays in Portsmouth on Wednesday at four thirty. He didn't show.' Masefield, an athletically built man in his late thirties, studied Horton with keen, intelligent brown eyes. They were sitting in the main cabin. Horton could hear the four crew members moving about on deck.

'Didn't you think that strange?' Cantelli asked, his voice unusually sharp as he looked up from his notebook. The fact that he had made no protest about going on-board or that he didn't look the least bit conscious of being on the water was testimony to his anxiety. They'd agreed not to mention that Johnnie was related to Cantelli in case it made Masefield or one of the others more reticent or skew the facts. Horton hoped that Cantelli's feelings weren't going to betray him. He couldn't blame him if they did, but Cantelli was a professional and hopefully his training would help him to keep a lid on his emotions.

Masefield said, 'I thought he'd missed the flight or the train from London, and that he'd make his own way over to the Island.'

'You didn't try calling him then?' Horton quickly asked before Cantelli could, throwing him a swift glance which he knew the sergeant would correctly interpret as *take it easy*. He caught a slight flicker of acknowledgement in Cantelli's dark and troubled eyes.

'No. Why should I? It was nothing to do with me.'

'He was a crew member,' Horton said incredulously.

'Yes, but not one of the crew.'

Horton looked puzzled, as did Cantelli.

Masefield explained, 'Xander Andreadis owns the yacht. He decided to send Johnnie Oslow over to make the team up to six, although we were and are quite capable of racing with five.' There was no mistaking the bitterness in Masefield voice. This was confirmed when he added, 'Maybe Andreadis thought a bunch of damaged ex-servicemen would run amok on it.'

'Damaged?' Horton hadn't seen any physical signs of that. On the contrary, he'd seen five very fit suntanned men aged between mid-thirties and early forties on-board.

Wearily, Masefield said, 'Not all damaged servicemen and women are those who lose limbs or who are physically scarred by their experiences.'

Horton got the point. 'You mean mentally damaged.'

'Traumatized, yes.'

'And you?'

'Yep. Me too. Royal Navy, and that's all you're going to get out of me and the others about our service backgrounds. I don't know theirs and they don't know mine. It's part of the deal. We don't talk about it. We accept each other as we are from the moment we meet, we don't know about each other's past, and we don't ask questions.'

'So the sailing is therapy.'

'Yes. I got sick of the system of counselling, of going over and over things, again and again; dredging it up only seemed to make it worse. Sailing, and particularly yacht racing, helped me to put the past behind me, and I thought it would help others. In racing you need to be focused and fit, able to work in a team and respect each other.'

'A bit like being in the services then.'

'Yes,' Masefield answered, evidently surprised that Horton had understood. 'It's also dangerous and daring, so you get that adrenalin kick.'

Horton knew that, having raced himself. 'How did you get on today?'

A shadow of annoyance crossed Masefield's face. 'Came second. Crawford's yacht won.'

And that had been the yacht Harriet Eames had been aboard. No wonder she had looked radiant. Horton had met Rupert Crawford on a couple of occasions. The fact that he was an investment banker was one reason why Horton hadn't taken to the blonde, aloof and arrogant bastard; the other had been that he had believed he was Harriet Eames' boyfriend. But perhaps Crawford had been given the elbow in favour of the man she'd greeted so warmly on the pontoon. Horton got the impression that he knew him from some-where, but he couldn't place where. He wasn't about to waste time trying to remember either.

'So how did you get Andreadis to sponsor you?'

'I approached him two years ago with the idea, and he liked it.'

Cantelli interjected, 'How do you know him?'

'I met him on the sailing circuit.'

And clearly, judging by his expression, that was all Masefield was prepared to tell them.

Cantelli said, 'Then you know Johnnie?'

But Masefield was shaking his head. 'No. I've never met him. Andreadis told me last Monday that Oslow was coming over. He said he was an experienced sailor and that he not only crewed for him on his Superyacht but also raced on one of his yachts.'

'But you still resented it,' put in Horton provokingly.

Masefield eyed him steadily and with a slightly patronizing exasperated air. 'I didn't resent it. I just didn't see that it was necessary.'

'And did Andreadis say why he was sending Oslow?'

'Said the experience would be good for him.'

And perhaps he'd said more than that, but again Masefield wasn't going to divulge what that was. Maybe he didn't think it worth mentioning, or perhaps he thought it reflected badly on his abilities.

'So you didn't phone Johnnie Oslow *or* Xander Andreadis when Johnnie didn't show up?'

'I didn't have Oslow's mobile number, and I didn't see any reason to bother Andreadis about it. We sailed back here, went out sailing on Thursday and didn't get in until late. I had no idea Oslow was missing until Andreadis phoned this morning to wish us luck. He asked how Oslow was getting on and I said he hadn't arrived.'

'And Andreadis's reaction?' asked Horton before Cantelli could.

'He was surprised, said he'd make some calls and get back to me. He did about an hour or so later to confirm that Oslow had definitely left Sardinia on Wednesday morning and that Nat Boulton, Andreadis's skipper on his personal yacht *Calista*, had telephoned Oslow's family, who said they hadn't heard from him. Andreadis told me to report it to the police and to keep him informed. But as we were just about to race I telephoned the local police, gave them the gist of it and said I'd call in afterwards. Guess I don't need to do that now you're taking the details. Andreadis has obviously called in the big guns. Still, he can do that. No point in having wealth if you can't use it.'

Again Horton thought he detected a hint of bitterness, but perhaps that was just Masefield's manner, because the man should certainly be grateful to Andreadis for distributing some of that wealth in his direction by coughing up at least a quarter of a million pounds for this yacht.

Masefield didn't seem at all concerned about Johnnie's disappearance, but then as he'd never met him he probably didn't see any need to worry. In fact, thought Horton, Masefield might even be glad that he hadn't shown up and that he and his crew didn't have to worry about a new boy fitting in and disturbing their rhythm.

Horton said, 'Why didn't you contact the Portsmouth police? It's where you had arranged to meet Johnnie Oslow.'

'I didn't have their number, and it hardly warranted dialling nine nine nine. The number of the local station is in the marina office. Oslow probably just wanted a free trip home on Andreadis and has either had enough of working for him or is shacked up with a girl.'

'Is there a reason why he should have had enough of working for Andreadis?' asked Horton.

Masefield shrugged. 'He's young, perhaps he wanted a change. I've no idea. I've never met him.'

'So you said.' Horton held Masefield's steely gaze and thought he saw a hint of amusement in it. He hoped Cantelli hadn't seen it, but by his glowering expression and white knuckles gripping the pencil hovering over his notebook he guessed he had. And Horton had the impression that Masefield had registered the reaction and was mildly interested but not enough to comment on it. But he was right about the big guns. No one of Horton's rank or even Cantelli's would be allowed to investigate this unless Johnnie was vulnerable, underage, had done something criminal or posed a danger to himself or others.

Horton's mind flicked back to the disappearance of his mother: she'd only got a PC, and one who he now believed had been bribed into conducting only the skimpiest of investigations. PC Adrian Stanley was dead so Horton couldn't prove that, but the fact that Stanley had tried to tell him something as he lay dying in hospital recently about a brooch worn by Mrs Stanley, his dead wife, which had since gone missing along with all photographs of it, was suspicious enough for Horton to believe that Stanley had either stolen it from Jennifer's flat, or been given it as payment for keeping his investigations low key and his mouth shut. Horton doubted the intelligence services would have bribed Stanley with money or jewellery – their methods were bullying and threats – so it was likely that someone else had urged Stanley to keep quiet . . . and that someone could have been connected with a master criminal code-named Zeus, who DCS Sawyer of the Intelligence Directorate had told Horton he was after, and who Sawyer believed Jennifer had run off with. That theory looked a lot less likely to Horton, however, now he knew about Lord Eames' involvement.

He said, 'Where is Andreadis now?'

'Porto Cervo.'

Cantelli explained, 'Northern Sardinia on the Costa Smeralda. It's where all the celebrities and millionaires hang out.'

'Andreadis is on-board his Superyacht,' Masefield added.

'We'll need his number.'

As Masefield relayed it, Cantelli jotted it down. Horton didn't think there was much more that Masefield could tell him for now. He asked if they could talk to the rest of the crew.

'Be my guest.'

As Cantelli went through the same questions they'd asked Masefield, Horton studied the crew. They'd introduced themselves and Horton found himself wondering what acts of war had trauma-tized each of them. All looked extremely fit and healthy but behind the dark eyes of Craig Weatherby, a muscular man in his early-thirties; Martin Leighton, mid-thirties, sturdily built, brown-eyed with an open face; Declan Saunders, lean, shaven-headed, wide mouth, late-thirties; and Eddie Creed, broad-shouldered, fair-haired and grey-eyed were horrors that Horton could only guess at and barely imagine. He doubted if the sea could completely banish them.

The crew members confirmed what Masefield had told them and denied knowing Johnnie or ever having met him. Their attitude to him joining the crew was indifference. Apart from being curious about their backgrounds, Horton didn't think there was any point in questioning them further, but as they left he wondered how Johnnie would have fitted in with such an experience-hardened crew, all of whom were at least twelve to fifteen years older than him. He thought Johnnie a strange choice for Andreadis to send to check out his investment – if indeed that had been the reason, and they only had Masefield's slightly embittered view on that.

They met up with Elkins at the entrance to the marina.

Horton said, 'We need to find out if Johnnie ever reached Portsmouth.'

Cantelli quickly caught on. 'You mean he could have gone missing in Sardinia?'

'Masefield says he left there, but how does he know? How does this Nat Boulton know? Just because he didn't show up at Oyster Quays doesn't mean he ever got there. He could have gone missing in London or on the way to Portsmouth. He could have stopped off somewhere to visit someone.'

'But he wouldn't miss the sailing, and he wouldn't risk losing his job by going AWOL,' Cantelli insisted.

It was out of character, but then Horton hadn't been close to Johnnie for years. Gently, he said, 'How do we know that, Barney? He might have been sick of sailing. He might have got tired of working for Andreadis, as Masefield suggested. Or they had a row. He might have been offered another job.'

'But he would have told his mother,' Cantelli again insisted.

'Perhaps he was meaning to and wanted to tell her face to face and is plucking up the courage to do so. I'm just saying we have to explore every option.'

'Yeah, and one of them could be he's had an accident,' Cantelli replied despondently.

'If he went missing before he reached Portsmouth then we need to check out the hospitals in London, assuming he would have flown into Heathrow or Gatwick and caught the train from London to Portsmouth. Ring through to the station and get someone working on that.'

Cantelli moved away, reaching for his mobile. When he was out of earshot, Elkins, with a worried frown, said, 'He could have been mugged and his wallet and phone stolen.'

And if he had been, then three days was a long time to be lying somewhere injured. Horton didn't like to think it was a possible scenario but he knew it was. 'I'll get the details of his credit or debit cards and put a stop on them. If someone has used any of them, or tries to use them, then we might be able to pinpoint where an attack could have taken place.'

Elkins' radio crackled. It was Ripley. 'Do you need me, Andy, only—'

'No, you go.'

'Let me know if there's anything else I can do.'

Horton heard Elkins ask Ripley to pick him up at Shepards Wharf.

Cantelli came off the phone. 'PC Allen's working on it.'

'Good.' They headed out into the street. Horton broached the subject about Johnnie's credit or debit cards.

'I'll need to ask Isabella.'

'Before you call her, I'll speak to Andreadis. Someone who works for him will be able to give us Johnnie's bank account details and more information on his travel arrangements. That way we might not have to make Isabella any more worried than she is already. I'll call him from the station.' Horton knew that the Greek tycoon would need to call back to check he was who he claimed to be.

Ten minutes later Horton, with Cantelli beside him, was seated at a desk in a small back room of the police station. He punched in the number Masefield had given him and was surprised when the line was answered almost immediately and by Andreadis himself, who announced himself promptly. Horton had envisaged having difficulty contacting him, and Andreadis couldn't have recognized the telephone number although the UK code might have given him a hint of who was calling.

Andreadis quickly explained, however. 'Scott called me to say that you were investigating Johnnie's disappearance, Inspector, and that he'd given you my number. I'll help all I can.' He spoke with only a slight trace of accent.

Quickly, Horton flicked the phone on to speaker so that Cantelli could hear. Andreadis declined the invitation to call back to check he was who he claimed to be, so Horton began by asking him to confirm that Johnnie had been due to come to Cowes.

'Yes. A crew member took him ashore from *Calista* in the tender, early on Wednesday morning. A taxi was waiting to take him to the airport.'

'And have you or any of your staff heard from him since?'

'No. My skipper, Nat, made inquiries.'

'How did Johnnie seem?'

'Fine, as far as I know.'

But would Andreadis know? 'He wasn't worried or excited about coming to Cowes?'

'He seemed pleased to be going home to see his family.'

'Was it your idea for Johnnie to come to Cowes?'

'I agreed it would be good for him to spend some time racing with a different crew.'

'So he suggested it?'

'No.'

'You ordered him to come?'

'I don't order anyone,' Andreadis replied with surprise. But

Horton thought he caught a hint of hardness in the voice. And he couldn't see Andreadis making and holding on to his millions without giving orders. He didn't know much about him, but that could easily be remedied. Andreadis was saying, 'It came up in conversation. I can't remember how exactly, but as I wasn't racing at Cowes this year, and as Scott was representing me, I thought Johnnie would not only be close to his family, but also that Scott would benefit by having an extra team member. Johnnie was very keen to go.'

'So you didn't trust Scott Masefield and his crew.' Horton used the word 'trust' deliberately to provoke a reaction, and he got one.

'Of course I trust them,' Andreadis said curtly with a touch of acidity.

'But why put a young man with such an experienced crew? Surely introducing a new crew member so late would unbalance the team.'

There was a moment's pause as Andreadis considered the best way to answer this. Horton guessed he was reassessing his original view of him. Andreadis must now know he was talking to someone who knew about sailing.

'OK, so I admit I was curious to see how Scott and the others handled that. In yacht racing, Inspector, crew members can get injured and pulled out at short notice. The skipper and crew need to be flexible, and Johnnie needed experience of being pitched into a team at the last moment.'

'He isn't a very good team member then?'

'On the contrary, he is excellent, but he's been sailing with the same team and working with me and the same staff for the last five years. I thought it was time he started to broaden his skills, and as I said he wanted to spend some time with his family.'

Horton picked up on this. 'When was he due back?'

'He had a week off after Cowes Week.'

Horton threw Cantelli a glance. He shook his head to indicate it was the first he'd heard of it. Not that there was anything suspicious in that. Johnnie might have intended to surprise his mother, or perhaps he had arranged to stay with someone else. Who though? A friend? And was he now with that same friend?

'Was there anything troubling him?'

'Not that I'm aware of.'

'Has he ever disappeared like this before?'

'Never. He's very reliable and an excellent sailor. He has a lot of talent and a passion for it.'

'There's never been any illness?'

'No. He's a very fit young man.'

'How did he travel to the UK?'

'My secretary booked his flight.'

'From where?'

'Here, Sardinia.'

'I'd like the details please.'

'She's away with her family until Monday.'

Horton saw Cantelli open his mouth to protest but stilled him with an upraised hand. He knew that Cantelli was thinking someone else could look up the information, or Andreadis himself could obtain it, it could only be a matter of accessing a computer, but obviously that was beyond the scope of a millionaire.

'It is very urgent, sir,' pressed Horton. 'Johnnie could have had an accident, and we need to trace his movements to find out where it could have occurred.'

Again there was a moment's silence before Andreadis answered. 'I'll call her now.'

'We'd also like details of Johnnie's bank account in case he's been attacked and his debit and credit cards stolen.'

'That information might take longer to obtain. My finance director is not contactable until Monday. I'll get Sophia to call you, though. What number shall I give her?'

Horton relayed his mobile number. 'I was wondering if you have a recent photograph of him we could circulate.' Cantelli's was OK but rather out of date.

'There are many taken during racing. I understand you are at Cowes, Inspector. Why don't you ask Sarah Conway? She's a professional photographer who's taken many pictures of my team, Johnnie amongst them. I'm sure she'll let you have copies. I'll also call her and ask her to give you every cooperation.'

'Thank you.' Into Horton's mind flashed the image of the woman he'd seen hanging off the edge of the RIB which had cut across his path earlier. Horton hung up.

Cantelli threw himself back in his seat and said, 'He's lying.'

'He's not comfortable about something, that's clear, but that might be annoyance because he's been personally inconvenienced. This is a man who has everything done for him; he doesn't normally have to bother himself with small matters like staff problems.'

'The more I hear the less I like it.'

Horton couldn't help agreeing but he wasn't going to tell Cantelli that.

'And it doesn't get us much further.'

'It does,' Horton contradicted. 'I'll get a photograph from Sarah Conway and get it circulated. There's nothing more you can do here, Barney, so get back to Portsmouth and liaise with PC Allen. Also find out if Johnnie said anything to Isabella or anyone else in the family about staying on here that extra week. Ask Isabella if there was any change in his manner or if he'd ever mentioned being fed up with his job.'

Mournfully, Cantelli said, 'I've ruined your sailing.'

'No, you haven't,' Horton firmly replied, thinking that by now he might have been well on his way to France but he was damn glad he wasn't. And he was glad that Cantelli had summoned him back, though not for the reason he had. He watched a forlorn Cantelli leave and went in search of the photographer.

THREE

He found Sarah Conway in a corner of the marina office hunched over a laptop, drinking coffee and tearing hungrily into a Danish pastry. She looked up distractedly as he addressed her. Her expression quickly cleared as he explained who he was and showed his warrant card.

'Xander said you'd find me.' She waved him into the seat beside her, quickly removing from it her sailing jacket and camera paraphernalia.

The Greek millionaire had been hot off the mark; not that Horton was complaining about that – speed was vital if they were going to find Johnnie, and there had been a decided lack of it so far. The seriousness of his tone must have made an impact on Andreadis; at least he hoped so.

Horton eyed Sarah with interest. Despite the fact he'd glimpsed her hanging over the side of the high speed RIB, nothing had prepared him for her youth and natural beauty. She was much younger than he'd anticipated, about mid twenties, with the most unusual eyes he'd ever seen: pale blue with a darker blue surrounding the iris. She was wearing crumpled white shorts and a light blue T-shirt that had seen better days, no make up and her fair skin was only slightly tanned. Her boyish manner and very short hair reminded him of the pathologist Dr Gaye Clayton, only she was auburn whereas Sarah Conway was blonde.

'Xander told me you'd like some photos of his crew.' She pushed the rest of her pastry into her mouth as though she hadn't eaten for hours, managing to make it a sensual gesture rather than a greedy one. Horton suspected she'd sacrificed food throughout the day in order to get some good shots and, judging by what he could see on the computer screen in front of him, they were superb.

'Of Johnnie Oslow,' he corrected.

'He's missing, is that right?'

'Yes. Do you know him?' She had a small piece of pastry left in the corner of her wide mouth but far from being off-putting he found it rather attractive and was suddenly filled with an impulse to reach out and brush it gently from her lips, but he quickly pulled himself up. His business here was serious.

She shook her head. 'I've spoken to him a few times but I wouldn't say I know him.'

'Impressions? Thoughts?'

'Seems a nice boy.'

He suppressed a smile. She could only be a couple of years older than Johnnie.

'Always seemed very cheerful,' she added.

'And Xander Andreadis? How well do you know him?'

'He's a client, and a very good one,' she replied earnestly with a broad grin.

I bet, and one who pays handsomely. 'And you must be a very good photographer for him to commission you, and I can see that you are.' Horton jerked his head at the pictures on the laptop.

'They're not bad, are they?' She ran the back of her hand over her mouth, brushing away the remains of the Danish pastry.

'That looks like Scott Masefield and his crew.' Horton pointed to one of several images on the screen.

'It is. Xander wants a selection of shots from each of their races. They did well today but not well enough for Scott. He's very competitive, but then show me someone in yacht racing who isn't! Competitive and mad. Do you sail?' she asked, eyeing him in a way that he found rather intoxicating. She was a tease and fully aware of her sexual charm. Even if he hadn't witnessed her in action on that RIB her sense of adventure would have communicated itself to him. She'd be fun to be with, and he hadn't had fun for a very long time. Neither did he have time now with Johnnie missing. But he found himself saying, 'Yes. I sail.'

'Thought so, you look the type.'

'You mean laid back and relaxed?' he suggested, tongue in cheek.

'No.' She laughed. It was full throated and infectious. Despite himself he found his body responding to it. 'The complete opposite, I'd say.'

'Mad and competitive.'

'You bet.'

Once, maybe. But who was he kidding? He still was competitive and maybe mad too, he had to be to pursue his mother's disappearance. But Sarah Conway's enthusiasm suddenly filled him with a desire to return to competitive sailing; with whom though? He could enter single-handed races, he supposed . . . and suddenly he recalled the identity of the man Harriet Eames had greeted so warmly. It was Roland Stevington, one of the most successful single-handed sailors of all time, having won the gruelling Around Alone, and then the Velux 5 Oceans round the world yacht race, and who, he'd read, was gearing up to try for a hat trick. Horton thought *he'd* prefer to have company though. Harriet Eames? But she was off limits. Dr Gaye Clayton sailed, perhaps he'd ask her. And Sarah Conway? Did she sail? He'd only seen her on the RIB, but he knew she must sail.

'Can you find me a couple of shots of Johnnie Oslow?' he asked, pushing the thoughts aside.

'Yes, hang on.' She scrolled through her pictures. He noted there were no rings on her fingers. In fact she wore no jewellery at all. He guessed it would only have got in the way of her job. 'There he is,' she cried triumphantly, calling up one picture from a gallery.

Horton studied the photograph of a confident, bronzed Johnnie Oslow, a white visor shading his eyes. He was wearing navy shorts and a white polo shirt, the same as the rest of the crew, who were all hanging off the side of a white hulled yacht with white sails, racing through a choppy sea that was so blue it almost hurt his eyes. Behind them were about a dozen yachts. Johnnie's team were in the lead. He was much more strongly featured than Horton recalled from the boy he had taken out sailing seven years ago and who he had placed in the sailing charity, Go About. Although he'd seen Johnnie in January when he'd returned to Portsmouth for his grand-father's funeral, Horton had only caught a glimpse of him in one of the funeral cars. Horton hadn't gone to the committal or the wake. But this was clearly Johnnie's natural habitat, and it showed in his enraptured expression.

'I took these at the St Maarten Heineken Regatta in the Caribbean in March,' Sarah explained. 'There were lots of different types of boats racing. I used a long telephoto lens to compress the fleet and slightly blur the background to make the lead boat stand out using a Nikon D200 three hundred millimetre lens . . . I'm losing you, aren't I?' She laughed, then seemed to remember why he wanted the picture. 'Sorry, I get carried away.'

'Please, don't apologize. Could you email those to me?' He could get the station to print them off. 'And perhaps you could send one to my mobile phone.'

'Of course.'

He handed her his card.

'I'll crop into Johnnie on one of them and enhance it; that'll give you a good close-up shot of him.'

He watched as she did so, seeing Johnnie's young suntanned face fill the screen and become more defined. He'd matured a lot in the last seven years. Horton could see, by the set of his jaw, that Johnnie had blossomed under Xander Andreadis's patronage. He was far more confident, and determination was etched on his dark, good-looking features.

Sarah emailed the picture to the address on his card and sent it to his mobile phone where it appeared a couple of seconds later. He studied it. It was a very clear image. He'd got what he'd come for and should leave but he found himself lingering.

'What made you take up yacht-racing photography?'

'How long have you got, Inspector?'

He felt like saying *as long as you like* but he smiled and replied, 'Not that long.'

'Then perhaps I'll get the chance to tell you some other time when you're not so busy. We could go for a sail.'

'I'd like that, but only if you promise not to take any photographs of me.'

'Shame. But the shortened version of my life history is that I sailed competitively as a child before I could walk; my parents used to take me on their boat and strap me on deck in a small cage. They'd probably be done for cruelty now but I survived and grew up loving the sea. They're sailing somewhere in the Caribbean at the moment. I graduated from that to competitive solo sailing and then with several teams competing in all major races including the Fastnet. I've always taken photographs, and it sort of developed from there into a business.'

'Do you still race?'

'Occasionally, but I prefer racing around taking photographs. I cover all the major races and as many others as I can get to.'

And Horton knew that involved a considerable amount of travelling around the world. So no personal commitments then, unless the man piloting the RIB was her partner or boyfriend. He didn't ask.

'Have you any idea why Johnnie is missing?' she said.

'I was going to ask you that.'

She shrugged. 'Like I said, I don't really know him.'

He left her to her photographs, wondering how long she'd work that evening. The idea of asking her for a drink played at the edges of his mind – it would have been a good way to unwind after a long and emotionally draining day which had come hot on the heels of a physically and mentally exhausting night. But he'd be poor company, probably too tired to make decent conversation and certainly too tired for anything other than that. Besides, she was probably due at the yacht club to take pictures of the race winners – and he had other things to do connected with Johnnie's disappearance, and that took precedence over everything.

He'd barely gone two steps from the marina though when he was arrested by a cry of, 'Daddy!' He spun round to see Emma bolting toward him with a broad smile on her elfin face, and within an instant he'd swept his daughter up in his arms and was spinning her round in the air. Her laughter, and the smell and feel of her small body, made his heart ache, and out of nowhere a memory assailed him. He was on a pontoon, he'd run into his mother's arms, she'd crouched down and hugged him, she was laughing. His stomach felt cold with the pain of the memory. Where had they been? Which marina? There was a large boat. A man on the boat. Was it London or here on the South Coast? Was it somewhere else in England? How old had he been? About Emma's age? Eight. No, younger.

Suddenly, he was conscious that Emma was wriggling. He set her down, running his hand over her hair and enjoying the feel of it.

'Are you having fun, sweetheart?' he asked, *and without me*, he thought with anguish, recalling all the years he had been part of this and now no longer was. He so wanted her to say that she missed him or that it wasn't the same without him, but he knew she wouldn't remember much of what they had shared at previous Cowes Weeks, just as that memory of him with his mother evaded him. He didn't want his daughter to be miserable and lonely without him, but part of him couldn't help wishing that she felt at least a little sorry he wasn't there.

'We've been out on the boat every day,' she chattered away enthusiastically. 'Grandad's teaching me to sail.'

Sod Grandad. It should be him! Not stiff and pompous Toby Kempton who hated Horton with a vengeance. Struggling to keep a tight rein on his bitterness, he said, 'And you can show me how good you are when we go out again on my boat.' He'd only managed to take her out once since he and Catherine had split up.

'When can we go, Daddy? Before the end of school holidays?'

'Definitely.'

'Goody.'

'Emma.'

Horton looked up to see Catherine heading towards them wearing a short printed summer dress that showed off one of her best assets to perfection: her legs. Her face was made-up, and she was wearing what looked to him to be expensive silver or white gold jewellery, her blonde highlighted shoulder-length hair was expertly cut.

Emma broke into an excited chatter as her mother drew level. 'Daddy's going to take me out on his boat before I go back to school and I can show him what Grandad's taught me.'

Catherine's blue eyes darted up at Horton, full of spite. He bristled. Why the hell shouldn't he be with his daughter? What right had Catherine to prevent him?

'There might not be time,' she said sternly.

'Of course there'll be time,' Horton said with an effort at sounding relaxed – he certainly didn't feel it, but he didn't want to upset Emma, or give Catherine the satisfaction of seeing he was piqued by her attitude. 'School doesn't start until the beginning of September.'

'There are things to do, uniforms to buy, and don't forget we're going to Auntie Geraldine's for a week,' Catherine said to Emma, whose bottom lip pouted. Emma reached out and took Horton's hand. He felt like saying bugger Aunt Geraldine, but Emma said it for him in her own way.

'I don't like Aunt Geraldine. She smells. I want to go sailing with Daddy.'

'And you will, darling,' he said.

'Promise.'

'Promise.'

'You shouldn't make promises you can't keep,' Catherine said stiffly, eyeing him like he was something that had just crawled out from under a stone.

'I don't, Catherine,' he evenly replied, holding her stare and feeling a minor victory when she glanced away. Then addressing Emma he said, 'We'll go sailing, just the two of us.'

'You can come with us tomorrow, can't he?' Emma looked pleadingly up at her mother.

If only he could, but that would never happen. He saved Catherine from answering. 'No sweetheart, I can't. I'm working.'

Her face crumpled.

Quickly, he said, 'But I'll make up for it when we go sailing together. You look very pretty in your dress,' he added, anything to delay her leaving him, and she did look gorgeous in the pink and blue patterned summer dress.

'It's new. We're going to have dinner with Peter and Grandma and Grandad.'

'Peter?' He flashed a glance at Catherine.

'Come on, Emma, we'll be late.' Catherine reached out her hand.

'He's Mummy's friend. He's quite nice, but I wish you were with us instead.'

Yes, victory at last. Clearly, this Peter was Catherine's new boyfriend. The last one had been a slob with a penchant for hardcore porn and sadomasochistic tendencies. He'd soon made sure to kick him out of his daughter's life. He hoped Catherine had chosen a more suitable bed companion this time. 'Peter who?' he asked, but Catherine had sussed out his motives.

'That's enough, Emma,' she snapped. 'Our taxi's arrived.'

Horton watched as it drew up at the marina entrance where Toby and Iris Kempton appeared. Their horror-stricken expressions as their eyes fell on him clearly showed he was not welcome.

Emma refused to budge though. She said, 'Peter's got a big motorboat. We've been on it a few times.'

I bet you have. And again, in his memory, he was back on that pontoon with his mother and the man on the boat. It too had been huge, or perhaps it hadn't been that big but had only appeared that way to a child. He couldn't remember going out to sea on it, but he did remember playing with the wheel at the helm while his mother and this man talked. Was it Edward Ballard? It could have been.

'Come along, Emma. We'll be late for dinner, and Daddy's got to work.'

Catherine made it sound as though work was something only idiots and the lower classes did, even though she worked herself as Sales and Marketing Director for her father's marine engineering company. But Horton knew what she was implying – that she was moving in much more elevated circles than those of the lower and middle ranks of the police force. She had been ambitious for him once, but that had been before his suspension had scuppered his promotion chances.

Brightly, although he felt anything but bright, he addressed his daughter. 'Have a lovely time, poppet, and enjoy your sailing.' He hugged and kissed her then swiftly turned and didn't look back.

His fury was churning inside him as he made for the police station but it slowly turned to bitterness and then regret. Feeling the dark cloud of depression threatening to settle on him he took a breath and with an effort pushed thoughts of Emma behind him. He knew that thinking about what he'd lost would poison him and the only person to suffer would be him. He had a job to do, and that was to help his closest friend find his nephew. Bewailing his past certainly wasn't going to achieve that.

FOUR

Horton settled himself at a spare desk and computer in the small police station and was soon engrossed in his work. An hour later he had the information he needed, which he'd gleaned not only from interrogating the Internet for flights from Sardinia to England but from Sophia, who had called him on Xander Andreadis's instructions ten minutes after he'd arrived at the station. She had apologized for not having all the details at her fingertips because she was away from her office, however her memory was excellent. He relayed what she'd told him and his findings to Cantelli over the phone.

'Johnnie flew from Alghero to Rome, economy class, leaving Alghero at seven a.m. last Wednesday. I checked online, and the flight was scheduled to arrive in Rome at five minutes past eight. He then caught the onward flight from Rome to London Heathrow which got in at eleven thirty a.m. I put a call into the Border Agency who rang back and confirmed he was on that plane and was checked through.'

Cantelli said, 'He didn't tell anyone in the family that he was staying over. His line's still dead. I tried it before you rang. I'd like to apply for access to his mobile phone records.'

Bliss wouldn't sanction it because Johnnie's disappearance was ranked low priority, but sod that. He'd get that changed. He agreed. Cantelli wouldn't be able to apply for the phone records until Monday though, and if they were able to gain access to them it would still take some time first for them to come through and then to be analysed.

He said, 'Sophia says she booked him on the London Waterloo to Portsmouth train, to arrive at Portsmouth Hard at seven minutes past four. Scott Masefield said they were due to pick him up at Oyster Quays at four thirty, so that time fits.'

'I'll get down to the railway station now; someone might have seen him alight.'

Horton understood Cantelli's need for action and his sense of urgency. He was just as keen himself, but it was eight thirty and he didn't think it would do much good because the staff who would have been on duty during the weekday might not be there now. He said as much, but Cantelli replied, 'I still think it's worth a try.' He didn't need to add *and I have to do something* because Horton knew that was what Cantelli was thinking.

He told him about the photograph Sarah Conway had given him and said he'd send it to Cantelli's phone. Cantelli said he would also check if the railway station had the footage from the security cameras for last Wednesday and find out who the guard on Johnnie's train had been. 'He might remember seeing him as he walked through the carriages checking the tickets.'

Horton doubted it but he wasn't going to discourage Cantelli. He said he would sail back to Portsmouth in the morning. 'I'll call in at the marina office at Oyster Quays to check if Johnnie showed up early or late and missed Masefield. There'll be no one there now,' he added, pre-empting Cantelli volunteering to do so after he'd been to the railway station. 'I'll see if the control room has a copy of the CCTV coverage for the boardwalk for Wednesday afternoon.'

'I can do that tonight.'

Horton relented. 'OK.' He knew that if they had it then Cantelli would spend the night scouring the video for signs of Johnnie. But then he'd have done the same if it had been his nephew.

Cantelli added, 'I'll also check with the city office to see if they still have the recordings for along the Hard.'

Horton didn't think they would unless there had been a fight or theft there that day or night. He told Cantelli to check the log, but he knew that nothing had been reported to CID because he'd have remembered, even though he and Cantelli had been embroiled in a murder investigation last Wednesday.

Cantelli said, 'PC Allen can't find any record of Johnnie having been admitted to any of the hospitals in and around London.'

Horton knew that wasn't necessarily a comfort. Quite the reverse. He said, 'Call me after you've been to the railway station or if anything occurs to you; it doesn't matter what time it is.'

Cantelli said he would and rang off. Horton sat back with a worried frown. Perhaps Johnnie had never got on that train in London. And if that was the case then God help them because people could vanish without trace in the vast overcrowded city. Just as his mother had vanished in a much smaller city, Portsmouth. But

Portsmouth bordered on the Solent and that could hide the dead for years, sometimes forever.

He rose and stretched his back, turning to stare out of the window at the bustling street that led down to the sea. It had grown dark. His mind travelled back to the council tower block he'd lived in with his mother. According to a neighbour Jennifer had left the flat at midday dressed up, wearing make-up and had been happy. It had been too early for her to go to work at the casino. After coming home from school and grabbing something to eat he'd sat in front of the telly and played with some toys until he was tired and it was time to go to bed. He did it often because his mother worked until the early hours of the morning, but when he awoke the next day she wasn't there.

His stomach lurched and his fists involuntarily clenched as he recalled that night and the many others following it which he'd tried so very hard to obliterate from his memory, with some success. He didn't want to remember because he didn't want to feel the hurt and the emptiness of despair. Perhaps that's what Scott Masefield meant when he said they never discussed the past. It only brought pain.

No one had thought to question why she hadn't shown up for work that night or the nights after that. The casino owner was dead now and the business closed. Those who had worked there had scattered far and wide and would be highly unlikely to remember her. It would involve too much time tracing them, and for what? Nothing.

He sat down and retrieved the black and white photograph from the pocket of his trousers, recalling Quentin Amos's words: *The second from the right with a beard is Antony Dormand; next to him again with a beard is Rory Mortimer . . . I don't know what happened to them or where they are now but you'll probably be able to find out.*

Horton had checked the Police National Computer but neither man had a criminal record. He hadn't had time to run them through the other databases to establish where they worked or even if they were still alive, but he needed to make time. He sat back frowning in thought. Something was niggling at him. What, though? Was it connected to what Amos had said about the two men or a comment that Lord Eames had made? *She was friendly with one of the men. James Royston, I think his name was.* But Amos had said none of them had been Jennifer's lovers. Amos had believed there was someone else. Who did Horton believe? Perhaps neither of them.

He fetched a coffee from the machine in the deserted staff room and returned to his desk. He was thankful that the station was quiet and that no one was the slightest bit interested in him, probably because they were all too busy with the crowds outside. That suited him fine.

Drinking his coffee he called up the Internet and soon was reading about the devastating fire that had swept through the second storey wing of the Victorian built Goldsworth Psychiatric Hospital in Surrey in 1968 which had killed Zachary Benham and twenty-three other men. Had Benham been a patient, or had he been working there after he had left or had been expelled from the London School of Economics?

Horton read on. The fire had started in a locked secure ward, housing mainly elderly bedridden men. Zachary Benham must only have been about twenty-three. There was no indication that this was an institution for the criminally insane, and neither had Horton any intelligence that Benham had committed a crime for which he'd been judged insane and locked up – but then, he silently admitted, he had very little intelligence about him or the others. His question was only partly answered when he went on to read that it was normal practice in the 1960s to lock patients in their wards. The poor buggers didn't stand a chance, he thought, swallowing his coffee.

Had someone had Zachary Benham committed, or had he committed himself? Had he been taking drugs, and had the drugs scrambled his brain? Perhaps the same drugs that Royston had taken and died from a year later? He'd have to do more research, and that would have to wait. It was late. He was exhausted. He shut down the computer and headed through the teeming streets towards his yacht, the happy crowds irritating him and clashing with his sombre mood. He was about to descend into the cabin when a voice on the pontoon hailed him.

'I wondered if I could have a word, sir.'

He turned to find himself facing Agent Harriet Eames. What else could he say except, 'OK.'

'Scott Masefield told me you're looking for one of his crew who's gone missing,' she said, climbing on-board. Her blue eyes looked troubled, and her fair face was creased with concern. He thought it genuine, but that didn't erase his suspicions that her father might have sent her here to find out what he knew about Jennifer's disappearance, or rather about her father's involvement in it.

She was wearing tailored navy blue trousers, deck shoes and a tight fitting blue and white T-shirt, all of which showed off her figure to perfection . . . and it was a nice figure. He caught the soft smell of her perfume as she descended into the cabin, and he thought of Sarah Conway. Not because she had worn perfume or smelt as soft as Harriet Eames, but both women heightened the ache of his loneliness. He'd been too long on his own. His marriage was over. Catherine was never going to be his again, and he didn't want her, but he wanted something, someone. He'd thought that he had found that person not long after the breakdown of his marriage, in January. But Thea Carlsson, a woman he'd got close to during an investigation into her brother's death, had returned to Sweden, her home country. She hadn't been ready for a commitment, and neither had he, but he missed her and she'd made it difficult to find her. He hadn't tried.

Harriet Eames was standing so close to him that he had only to reach out and touch her. He had the feeling she wouldn't resist. But it was a boundary he couldn't cross, not with her. Her father had made any relationship with his daughter impossible.

'Is it true that the missing man is Sergeant Cantelli's nephew?'

'How do you know that?' They hadn't given Masefield that information, and Harriet Eames hadn't met Cantelli. He saw a flicker of surprise in her blue eyes at the sharpness of his tone.

'Scott told me why you were at the marina, and then I ran into Sarah. She said a good-looking detective had wanted a photograph of Johnnie Oslow. I called the police station and got the details. I thought you and Sergeant Cantelli had left the Island, but the Commodore of the yacht club told me that he'd given the police berth to a Detective Inspector Horton.'

And why did he tell you that? How had his name come up in conversation? And if Agent Harriet Eames knew he was here then her rich daddy certainly knew too.

She said, 'I've come to see if I can help.'

Did he believe her? He recalled the scene in the yacht club earlier that morning when she'd stumbled on him and her father in a heated exchange. Maybe she did want to help in the search for Cantelli's nephew, but he also knew there was another reason why she was here.

He said, 'And you're curious to know what my argument with your father was about.'

She eyed him coolly. 'Yes, but I don't expect you'll tell me any more than he did when I asked him, so I'm not even going to waste my breath. I'd like to help you find Johnnie Oslow.'

'Why? You don't even know Cantelli,' he said with a touch of scorn. He was cross with her for making him so hostile.

'That doesn't stop me caring or being a police officer,' she sharply rejoined. 'And don't say that because I'm at Europol I'm just pen pusher. I'm not, and you know it. So, do you want my help or not?'

'What about Rupert?' Horton sneered.

'What about him?'

Horton held her angry eyes. Did she mean it? Could he trust her? God, he wanted to, and badly. But trust was something he found so very hard to give. The small voice inside him warned caution. She could be here under daddy's instructions to wheedle her way into his affections (which wouldn't be difficult) in order to discover what he would do next in his search for his mother. But would Lord Eames use his daughter in that way? The answer came back almost immediately: you bet he would. Whether Harriet Eames would allow herself to be used though was another matter. He didn't know the intricacies of her relationship with her father, only that he remembered her telling him the first time they'd met in June that her family hadn't approved of her choice of career. With that thought came the memory of a fleeting expression of sadness crossing her face when they'd been on-board the ferry together, sailing to the Island from Portsmouth while on duty, and she'd told him her father owned a house there. But whatever his feelings for her and her father, they were nothing compared to his concern for Cantelli and his family over Johnnie's disappearance. That took priority. He needed all the help he could get, whatever form it came in. And the form couldn't get better than Harriet Eames.

His phone rang. 'It's Cantelli,' he said, quickly answering it.

'There's no one on duty who was working on Wednesday,' Cantelli said dejectedly. 'The guard on that train from London Waterloo will be on duty tomorrow. I got his home address and telephone number but there's no answer. I'm outside his house now in Portsmouth. He's not in. I'll try tomorrow.'

And tomorrow meant another night of not knowing, just like the many nights Horton had experienced throughout the years of not knowing, maybe never knowing. No, he didn't even want to consider Cantelli and his family experiencing that.

Cantelli continued: 'The security manager said that they'd be able to tell if Johnnie's ticket had gone through the automatic barriers on leaving the station because of the bar code on it. If we can get hold of the ticket booking reference number then it would speed things up, otherwise they can conduct a computer search if the ticket was booked in his name or if we give the name of the person booking it.'

'Sophia can tell us that.'

'Yeah, and probably not until tomorrow or Monday,' Cantelli said, somewhat exasperated.

'Even if she had it now, Barney, I can't see any IT department working on this overnight or on a Sunday.'

'I guess you're right,' Cantelli reluctantly agreed. 'The security officer is looking out the CCTV footage for me and so are the Oyster Quays security team. I might get them tonight, but it's more likely to be tomorrow.'

'You'll have fresh eyes on it then, Barney.'

'I know. I just wish there was something more I could do.'

There was nothing, except to issue Johnnie's photograph to the London police, which Cantelli said he would see to, and Horton knew that would have about as much effect as dropping a grain of sand in a sandcastle. He rang off without telling Cantelli about his guest. There was no need.

'Drink?' he asked her.

She held his eyes. 'Tea would be nice.'

Horton flicked the switch on the kettle and gestured her on to the bench seat the other side of the galley table. She slid on to it, and while he waited for the kettle to boil he relayed what they'd discovered, which didn't take him long, ending with the fact they didn't know where Johnnie had gone missing except that it had been in England.

'Would he have gone missing deliberately?' she asked.

He turned away to pour hot water on her tea bag and on the instant coffee in his mug. 'Cantelli swears not. Even if he was in trouble I can't see him causing his mother so much anguish.' But as he spoke he thought back to the arson. Johnnie hadn't given a thought to his mother's feelings then, although there had been extenuating circumstances.

As he handed her the mug of tea her fingers brushed lightly against his causing a slight hiatus in his pulse. Taking his coffee he sat opposite her, his knees almost touching hers. If he moved an inch he'd connect with her. The music and laughter from outside carried on the night air to them. He said, 'Johnnie does have a criminal record.' He told her about Johnnie's conviction for arson. 'It was following the sudden death of his father. He got in with the wrong crowd.'

She looked thoughtful. 'He was easily led astray once, he could have been again.'

'But the circumstances now are completely different from then. He has a good job, one which he loves—'

'He might have grown sick of it.'

'Xander Andreadis told me that he was keen to expand Johnnie's experience, which was why he was here to race with Masefield, but perhaps Johnnie thought Andreadis was trying to push him out.'

'And Johnnie decided to jump ship rather than wait until he was pushed.'

'But why not tell his family?'

'Perhaps he's too scared, knowing that everyone will think him foolish for throwing in a good job. Maybe he thought he'd wait until after Cowes Week to tell them.'

'But that doesn't explain why his mobile phone is dead.'

'Perhaps he dropped it and it's broken.'

She was voicing many of the thoughts he'd had. 'He must have known that sooner or later during the week someone would start to ask questions about why he wasn't here for the racing. But Masefield didn't seem bothered, and if it hadn't been for Andreadis calling him to wish him luck and asking after Johnnie no one would have known now.'

'Perhaps Johnnie was counting on that.'

Horton considered this. Was it usual for Andreadis to call up his teams before a race and wish them luck? He didn't know but he'd like to. He eyed her keenly. Perhaps Harriet Eames could tell him that and more. 'So, tell me about Xander Andreadis.'

'What makes you think I know him?' she asked, eyeing him steadily.

He began to count off on his fingers. 'One, you're a Europol Agent and Andreadis is Greek; two, you move in the same exalted sailing circuits where Andreadis is known; and three, why else are you here if, as you say, it's to volunteer your help? You didn't expect to carry a torch and search the streets and marinas for Johnnie, so it must be because you have information.'

There was a moment's pause. He wondered if she was considering how much to tell him. She nodded and smiled. It was a nice smile if a little reserved, but he didn't blame her for that. He wasn't exactly being friendly towards her.

'OK, official Europol background first. Xander Andreadis, as you are already aware, is a very wealthy man. Aged thirty-seven, he is the oldest son of Christos, now in his early sixties, and brother to Giorgos, who is thirty-three. Mother died when he was eighteen. The family are worth just over six billion dollars.'

Horton emitted a low soft whistle. 'No wonder Xander Andreadis can experiment by buying yachts for the likes of Scott Masefield without batting an eyelid. How did the family make their money?'

'We're not quite sure of the origins but—'

'Dodgy?'

'Not necessarily, but it's true to say that Christos started with nothing. He worked on the Greek-owned Chandris fleet as a deck-hand, sailing on the *Patris*, the Australian migrant ship, taking migrants from Italy and Greece to Australia during the 1960s until 1975. Christos left it while it was moored in Darwin for nine months providing emergency accommodation for those made homeless by Cyclone Tracy on Christmas Day in 1974. He took a passage working his way to Singapore then came to England where he arrived in 1977, returning to Greece in 1979 where he began to build his empire. In various articles written about him Christos claims he made a couple of shrewd investments using money he had saved while working in England. Records certainly show he worked in the Savoy as a barman and at other top-class establishments in London prior to leaving the UK, which would hardly have given him a fortune.'

'You've investigated him?' Horton asked, interested.

She shook her head. 'No. There's never been anything suspect about his dealings.'

'As far as you know.'

She shrugged. 'Perhaps he was lucky in roulette or won on the horses. Anyway, he returned to Greece in 1979 with money to invest, firstly in a couple of bars, and then he bought up a number of hotels. The golden touch, or so the articles claim. He certainly seems to have had that. The Andreadis family now own several businesses – not only hotels and clubs, but shipping, petroleum, telecommunications, computer software and hardware companies, and they seem to be thriving despite the dire economic climate and austerity cuts in Greece, which have hardly dented their fortune. And so far there's not even a hint of corruption or tax evasion.'

'You suspect some?'

She shrugged again.

'But you've checked?'

'Both sons entered the business, but Xander Andreadis, the more academic of the two, came to England in 1995 and gained a PhD in Economics at the London School of Economics.'

Horton paused with his coffee cup halfway to his lips.

'Is there something wrong?' she asked, studying him.

It was a coincidence, that was all, because the timing was years away for any connection to the men in that black and white photograph from 1967. He swallowed a mouthful of coffee. 'Go on.' He noted she had avoided answering his question about the Andreadis family being investigated.

'On his return to Greece, Xander took a major role in the business, eventually taking over from his father, making it even more successful, and diversifying into the custom-built luxury mega-yacht market – both the motorized and sail type – and into private jet hire. He also indulges his passion for yacht racing, as you know.'

'And his brother, Giorgos?'

'He also works in the business, but the rumour has it that he's not so keen and that Xander tolerates him. Giorgos' passions are fine art, property, cars and women, not necessarily in that order. Divorced twice, and about to be for the third time, while Xander is still married to number one, Diona, and has two daughters, aged fifteen and thirteen.'

'Do they sail?'

'Of course.'

It wasn't relevant. They were too young to be of interest to Johnnie, because the idea had flitted through Horton's mind that Xander might have wanted Johnnie out of the way if one of his daughters had become rather too keen on him. 'And Giorgos, does he have children?' Horton asked.

'A son, Yannis, aged fifteen from his first marriage, another son, Zoi, aged ten from his second marriage and a girl, Theodora, from the third, aged four.'

So that ruled out that theory.

She continued: 'Christos Andreadis is not in the best of health, having suffered two heart attacks, and he no longer takes an active part in the business, but he's still a very strong influence and is fully aware of what is going on.'

'And is that anything illegal?'

'Not that we have discovered.'

Evasive. 'But you're still checking.' He thought he detected a hint of hesitation before she answered.

'Xander Andreadis races yachts around the world. He goes in and out of ports, but we have no reason to suspect him of any illegal activity, or his brother, who doesn't sail.'

No *reason* perhaps, but *suspicion* maybe. And was that why she was here and interested in Johnnie's disappearance? Did she suspect that Johnnie had discovered something about Xander Andreadis's sailing exploits that had prompted his disappearance? If that was the case then it didn't bode well for Johnnie, he thought with trepidation. And it meant she must have called in to her bosses as soon as she got the missing persons report from the local cop shop. It crossed his mind that her arrival at Cowes might not be purely for the racing or to be reunited with her family. Perhaps she was working. But if so, then had she and her bosses expected Xander Andreadis to show up? Or had they been waiting for Johnnie? If the latter, though, surely she would have discovered he'd gone missing before now and alerted the police. Perhaps she had – but not the local force, clearly.

A prickling sensation between his shoulder blades made him wonder if she'd alerted Europol and Interpol. And now that Johnnie's absence had been brought to the attention of the local police she'd been ordered in to help find him. Perhaps she and her bosses hadn't known that Johnnie was the nephew of a local copper. ·

'So on to your second point,' she said, placing her mug carefully on the table in front of her and holding his gaze. 'You're correct, I have moved in the same exalted sailing circuits as Andreadis, not only because of competing in races but also because my father is a personal friend of Christos.'

He might have known. 'And that means you know Xander Andreadis.'

She nodded. And knowing what he did about her father that made her appearance at Cowes Week even more suspect, along with his growing conviction that she must know her father worked for British Intelligence.

She said, 'Xander was here in July.'

'That recent!'

'For the Cowes to St Malo race. One of his yachts, *Medussa*, was entered. He was here from the tenth of July to the seventeenth.' Before he could ask, she added, 'You're wondering if Johnnie was with him.'

He nodded and drank his coffee.

'He wasn't on *Medussa* with Xander, but he might have been on-board Xander's personal Superyacht, *Calista*. It was moored off the Island. You might remember seeing it – a 1930s retro design fore-and-aft rigged yacht, with three closed decks. Two hundred and sixty feet long, with an owner's suite on the lower deck and four guest cabins.'

A classic beauty, and he had seen it, but he'd had no idea who it had belonged to. The fact that Cantelli had said none of the family had seen Johnnie since January should have meant he wasn't on-board . . . but Horton had an uncomfortable feeling that he might have been, and this reluctance to contact his family concerned him deeply.

She said, 'I'll ask Xander if Johnnie was here.'

But Horton wondered if she already knew the answer. And if she did, then why not tell him? Perhaps she needed authority to divulge that information. But why, for heaven's sake? Eyeing her closely, he said, 'Has Europol got anything on Johnnie Oslow?'

'Not that I'm aware of,' she answered steadily, but he knew she was lying and her eyes said *don't ask me again because I can't tell you*. Not yet, maybe, but she would. He'd make sure of that.

She slipped out of the seat. 'I'll find out about Johnnie's movements in July and contact you. Will you still be here?'

'No. I'm heading back to Portsmouth early tomorrow morning.'

'OK. I'll call you.'

He watched her leave with mixed feelings. His heart wanted to trust her, but his head and his gut told him he couldn't. She halted on the promenade, and her head turned to the right as if someone had hailed her. Following the direction of her gaze he saw Stevington join her. He kissed her – not passionately, but with enough vigour to cause Horton a twinge of jealousy, especially as she didn't put up any kind of protest. They broke apart as another couple joined them. It was Sarah Conway and the skipper of her RIB. Stevington said something. They all laughed. Horton turned away, feeling sore.

But why shouldn't they laugh? Johnnie meant nothing to them and he meant nothing to Harriet Eames.

He stood in the cabin, trying to ignore the smell of her perfume and his confused feelings for her. It was late, but he knew sleep would elude him, and there was only one way to banish that perfume. He made the yacht ready to sail.

FIVE

Sunday

Horton swung the Harley into a side road close to Oyster Quays on the Portsmouth waterfront. It was just before nine. He felt refreshed after a good night's sailing and six solid blissful hours of dreamless sleep, which surprised him given there was so much to occupy his thoughts. He hadn't heard from Cantelli which meant there was still no news of Johnnie, and as he made his way through the busy Wightlink car ferry terminal and past the modern apartments that fronted on to the narrow strip of Portsmouth Harbour he didn't even want to think they might never find him, or discover the truth behind his disappearance, because he knew how that could destroy a family.

There had been no chance of Jennifer's disappearance haunting her parents though because he'd discovered through the Register of Births, Deaths and Marriages that her father had died when she was seven and her mother shortly before Jennifer had taken herself off to London aged sixteen. As far as he was aware she'd had no brothers or sisters. He'd also checked to see if there was a record of her death, but there wasn't – not in that name, and certainly not in the UK. He'd never looked further into her family background, and the social services files on him had conveniently gone missing, but the fact that no relative had come to claim him made him believe there wasn't anyone, or if there were then the last thing they had wanted was to be saddled with a child. And if that was how they had felt, then the last thing he wanted was anything to do with them.

He located the marina manager and asked him what time Masefield's yacht, *Naiyah*, had moored up there last Wednesday. The manager, a bulky man with a shock of light grey hair and a wide friendly grin, consulted his records and confirmed that it had been three forty-five p.m. 'It left just after five,' he added, pointing to the log on the narrow counter in front of them.

Half an hour after Johnnie was supposed to have met them. Masefield hadn't hung around for very long.

'Did you see anyone join them?' Horton could see from the log that Johnnie hadn't signed into the marina, but there would have been no need if he'd been leaving almost immediately by boat.

The marina manager shook his head.

Horton showed him the photograph of Johnnie that Sarah Conway had sent to his mobile phone, but the manager didn't recognize him and neither did the other two members of staff who had also been on duty on Wednesday. It seemed likely then that Johnnie had never arrived, and perhaps the railway station security cameras and IT department would confirm that he'd never alighted from that train from London.

Heading for the station, Horton again wondered why Masefield hadn't been given Johnnie's mobile phone number to liaise with him in case of a problem with travel arrangements, which given the change of flights and the rail journey would have been highly likely. Was Masefield telling him the truth? Or did he simply not want to get sucked into the investigation when clearly he hadn't been too keen on having Johnnie along in the first place? He'd ask Sophia and Andreadis if either of them had relayed the number to Masefield – something he should already have checked, he thought, annoyed with himself for not doing so. But then he couldn't see Masefield being caught out in so simple a lie.

There was no sign of Cantelli's car in the car park which meant he might be interviewing the guard. Horton hoped it would be with a positive result. There was also no sign of DCI Bliss's sports car or any other senior officers', but that was to be expected. Good. He could not only pursue his personal research but also that of Johnnie's disappearance without the wicked witch of the north poking her beaky nose into both.

The smell of disinfectant from the cells followed him through the rear entrance to the canteen, almost putting him off any break-fast. But at least that was better than the stench of puke and piss, he thought, ordering a bacon sandwich and a coffee. He took them to a table by the window where he'd spotted PCs Kate Somerfield and Dennis Seaton. Both were keen to get into CID but with government cutbacks that seemed unlikely for a while. They showed no surprise at his appearance which, he thought, was a sad reflec-tion on his private life rather than his dedication to duty. Swiftly, he gave them an outline of what had happened. They both looked concerned. He sent a picture of Johnnie to both their mobile phones and asked Seaton to print off copies.

'Show them around at the Hard; ask the taxi drivers if any of them remember seeing Johnnie or picking him up as a fare.' He didn't expect a positive outcome because he was growing more convinced that Johnnie had never reached Portsmouth, but it was worth a try.

With his bacon sandwich and black coffee he headed for CID, where he made his way through the deserted room to his office beyond. Balancing his breakfast on a pile of files and paperwork he opened the window to let in some of the hot sultry August air and to let out the smell of food, and then fired up his computer.

He called Xander Andreadis, but his phone was on voicemail. It was what he should have expected. Andreadis might be deliberately blocking his calls, or perhaps he was sailing. Horton left a message and asked him to call back. He hoped that Harriet Eames might have more luck. He wondered how long she and Stevington had stayed drinking in the yacht club last night. It was none of his business if they had partied all night, he thought irritably, calling Sophia, but with the same result – no answer. He left another message requesting information about Johnnie's train ticket and asked her to call him back. Then, biting into his sandwich, he was about to begin his inquiries into Antony Dormand and Rory Mortimer when his fingers froze over the keyboard.

He put down his sandwich and sat back. Picking up his pen he began to twirl it idly, his thoughts returning to Harriet Eames' visit to his boat last night and before that the niggle he'd experienced in Cowes Police Station. The niggle began to take shape. Finally, it crystallized into a question. What was Lord Eames expecting him to do?

The answer was precisely what he had been about to do: try and trace the other two men in the photograph from 1967; request the coroner's reports and investigation details into the deaths of Zachary Benham, James Royston and Timothy Wilson; re-interview Dr Quentin Amos; and continue with his search for Edward Ballard and the truth behind Jennifer's disappearance. But if Eames and his colleagues in intelligence had fed him Professor Thurstan Madeley and Dr Quentin Amos then they had a reason for doing so, and that reason was that they wanted him to find either Ballard, Dormand or Mortimer, or the person who had taken the picture. And if all the resources at the disposal of the intelligence services couldn't locate whoever it was they wanted flushing out, then how the devil could he?

So what if he did nothing? He threw down the pen and sprang up. Turning, he stared out of the window into the almost deserted car park. If he took no action, what would happen next? What would Eames or one of his cronies or even Eames' daughter throw at him? Perhaps they'd toss him another piece of the past for him to try and fit into the puzzle. And what would that be? To date, he'd been given a reference to Jennifer by a criminal she'd associated with who was now dead; a brooch that had gone missing, as had all pictures of it; Ballard's photograph from 1967; and Thurstan, Amos and the names of the men in the picture. So what next?

He resumed his seat. No doubt he'd find out, and soon. Abandoning his personal research he called up the details of the arson attack committed by Johnnie and his mates seven years ago. He remembered most of the facts, but he wanted to be sure. He hadn't investigated it because he'd been seconded to Basingstoke at the time and Cantelli had been working at Gosport. But before he could begin reading, a noise in CID caught his attention and he looked up to see Cantelli enter.

Horton called out to him, and a few moments later Cantelli flopped dejectedly into the seat across from Horton's desk.

'The guard can't remember him. The train was packed, and he didn't get through all the carriages.'

That wasn't really surprising. London Waterloo to Portsmouth was a very busy commute. 'There's still the fact we can track the ticket, and there's the security camera footage to view both from the Oyster Quays and the railway station.'

Cantelli hauled himself up. 'I'll start running through them now.'

'Get yourself something to eat and drink first.'

'I—'

'You're no good to anyone if you keel over.'

Cantelli gave a tired smile. 'Yeah, OK.'

Horton watched him trudge out before returning his attention to his computer screen. The four youths with Johnnie who had been convicted of arson on the Locks Lake Sailing Club were Ryan Spencer, Tyler Godfray, Kyle Proctor and Stuart Jayston; all had been aged sixteen at the time. The sailing club was at the end of a long road that contained mainly residential properties, but on the

north side, not far from the end of the road which led down to
Langstone Harbour, were the grounds and main entrance to the
psychiatric hospital. Locks Lake gave on to Langstone Harbour, to
the south of which was Southsea Marina, where Horton lived on
his boat. Fortunately, no one had been in the club, which had been
in the process of being refurbished, but it had gone up like the
clappers because of the paint and other inflammable materials inside,
and the fire had spread to the dinghy park outside. It had caused
several thousand pounds worth of damage, and it had been a miracle
the boys hadn't been injured or killed. Eye witnesses from the nearby
houses had seen youths running away at approximately eleven twenty
p.m. They had been arrested as they'd run out of the grounds of the
psychiatric hospital by a patrol car on its way to the scene.

Johnnie had instantly confessed. Horton could still see Cantelli's
horrified and stricken countenance at discovering the news that his
nephew was an arsonist, and he could see Johnnie's terrified expression when he realized what serious trouble he was in. Tyler Godfray
and Stuart Jayston had very quickly owned up, but Ryan Spencer,
with previous convictions for theft and being drunk and disorderly,
and Kyle Proctor, with convictions for vandalism, theft and assault,
were harder to crack . . . although not that hard.

In the Magistrates' Court Horton had watched Johnnie trying
valiantly to hold back the tears, torn between wanting to look at his
mother for comfort and reassurance and avoiding her glance for
fear it might cause him to break down completely. Isabella, stiff
and upright, had sat immobile, as though lack of movement might
anaesthetize her to the pain she was feeling for her only child.

Although neither Stuart, Tyler nor Johnnie had criminal records,
Horton, like Cantelli, suspected that each had committed petty
criminal offences before; they'd just not been caught. They were
given community sentences and ordered to work on the community
payback scheme, while Ryan was given a detention and training
order of one year, spending six months in the secure centre for
young offenders and six months serving in the community, and
Kyle, with his more serious previous convictions, was given a
custodial sentence and sent to a secure centre for young offenders
for eighteen months.

Horton looked up to see Cantelli return from the canteen with a
sandwich and large paper cup of tea. Johnnie's community payback
had been to clean graffiti off the underpasses in Portsmouth, a

soul-destroying task made shameful by the fluorescent vest he and others had to wear, advertising to the world their criminal background. The lad had been ashamed and humiliated, his confidence shattered, his grief at his father's death deepened. He had let everyone down, his family, his dead father, himself and his mother. He had become withdrawn, he'd stopped eating and Isabella, clearly distraught at her son's descent into depression, had gone to her brother at her wits' end. Cantelli had tried talking to Johnnie, but nothing had any effect. Horton had thought back to his own long days of misery before his foster parents, Bernard and Eileen Litchfield, had given him love, stability and trust. But Bernard had also given him the idea of becoming a police officer like him, and it was in the police force that Horton had his first taste of sailing. It had transformed his life. He'd thought it might do the same for Johnnie.

Go About, a sailing charity run by Don Winscome, had changed Johnnie's life completely and, despite what Harriet Eames had said about Johnnie possibly being led astray again, Horton just couldn't see him returning to crime after that bitter and shattering early experience. But the others? He couldn't recall coming across them recently, so perhaps they'd stayed clean.

He keyed the names into the Police National Computer and discovered that Kyle Proctor had been killed in a car accident on the M27 on Fareham Hill, along with one other person, a man, who had been standing beside his broken down vehicle on the hard shoulder awaiting assistance. The autopsy on Proctor had shown he had been well over the drink legal limit for driving and witnesses claimed he'd been texting on his mobile phone immediately before the incident. A fact that was borne out from the telephone records. What a bloody fool, and what a waste of two lives.

Tyler Godfray and Stuart Jayston had no further convictions. Ryan Spencer, however, had two more petty offences to his name. The last one committed a year ago for which he'd escaped with a community sentence. According to their records Spencer was living in Paulsgrove, a large council estate to the north of Portsmouth, while Godfray lived in Gosport, across the harbour from Oyster Quays, and Jayston at Havant, a town to the east of Portsmouth. Maybe they should check if Johnnie had been in touch with any of them.

His mobile rang. It was Harriet Eames.

'Johnnie Oslow was here in July,' she announced without preamble. 'He was working on-board *Calista*.'

'You've spoken to Andreadis?' Horton asked surprised.

'Yes.'

Then why hadn't he returned Horton's call? Because *he* wasn't a personal friend. And perhaps he didn't think he needed to now.

Eames continued: 'Xander returned to Sardinia on *Calista* on the eighteenth of July with Johnnie on-board. He had business to get back to and couldn't make Cowes Week. The *Medussa* and its team, minus Xander, aren't at Cowes either now. After the Cowes to St Malo race they left for St Tropez. They're competing in Les Voiles de St Tropez in September and Xander is joining them there.'

That didn't surprise Horton. St Tropez, on the French Riviera, was famous for its millionaires.

'Why didn't Johnnie race on the *Medussa*?'

'He's not used to racing on that class of yacht.'

But Horton recalled what Andreadis had said about it being time to broaden Johnnie's experience. Then why not let him crew on the *Medussa*?

'So sending him back to Cowes just three weeks after he'd left was a last-minute decision.'

'Not necessarily,' she answered – slightly cagily, he thought.

But it sounded as though Andreadis had had some doubts about Masefield. Again he considered whether a young man of twenty-three was the right person to send to check that out, and again he doubted it.

He said, 'Find out if Johnnie went ashore while on *Calista* and if so where he went and with whom.' Clearly, it hadn't been to see his mother. 'Unless you're too busy racing. I was forgetting you're meant to be on holiday.' He knew she would hear the scepticism in his voice and wondered how she would react.

'I said I wanted to help,' she answered lightly enough, but he thought he detected tension.

'Good. Then as you have access to Andreadis, and probably his skipper, see if you can find out if Johnnie ever confided in anyone. Was he close to anyone in particular? Did he have any girlfriends? What was his mood like recently?'

'Right.'

The crispness of her response made him wonder if she was gritting her teeth, biting back the response that she knew how to do her job. Before she could ring off he quickly added, 'Did Andreadis give Masefield Johnnie's mobile number?'

'No.'

'You asked?' he said, surprised.

'No, Xander said you had left a message asking him that.'

'Why didn't he give Masefield the number?'

'He probably didn't think of it. And I'm not sure that Nat, Xander's skipper, or Sophia, his secretary, know Scott Masefield. I'll check,' she hastily added before he could instruct her to do so.

She rang off. He tried ringing Andreadis's number but again got his voicemail. So how come Eames had got through when he couldn't? Had her timing just been luck? Or perhaps she had access to another number for the tycoon – one that was very private, only used by close friends and family.

He joined Cantelli in CID. 'Anything?'

Cantelli shook his head.

Horton took the seat at the opposite desk. 'Did you know that Johnnie was here in July?' Clearly not, judging by the sergeant's expression. Horton relayed what he'd just learnt.

Frowning as he considered this, Cantelli said, 'I don't think he contacted Isabella but I can ask her. He certainly didn't visit her, otherwise she would have told me.'

'Leave it for now. We don't want to add to her worries. Johnnie might simply have been too busy to see his mother. He was working.'

But Horton was getting the distinct impression that Johnnie had been avoiding making contact with his family. Why?

His office phone was ringing. He hesitated about answering it in case the desk clerk had spotted his Harley in the car park and was now summoning him to investigate a new crime. DC Walters was duty CID. Not that he was in the station, but they'd have his number to call him. Andreadis had his mobile number so it couldn't be him, but it could be someone from Cowes police station with news about Johnnie. He returned to his office and lifted the receiver.

It was PC Seaton. 'We've got a sighting, sir,' he said excitedly. 'One of the taxi drivers at the Hard remembers Johnnie.'

Horton's pulse skipped several beats. This was a breakthrough. He looked at Cantelli in the CID office; he didn't want to raise his hopes only to have them dashed. 'He's sure?'

'Positive.'

'Where did he take him?'

'He didn't. He just says he remembers seeing him and speaking to him.'

'Is he still there?'

'Yes.'

'Then tell him to stay put; we're on our way.'

SIX

'I've missed three fares because of you. Hope you're going to compensate me for that,' the taxi driver grumbled as he drew heavily on his cigarette. 'I've got a living to make, and hanging about to please you lot costs me time and money.'

Judging by Cantelli's cold stare Horton thought the type of compensation he had in mind was to book the obese taxi driver for having bad breath and dandruff. Thrusting Johnnie's photograph at the big beer-bellied man, Cantelli said sharply, 'Are you sure you saw this man on Wednesday afternoon at approximately four o'clock?'

'How many more times do I have to say it? Yes, that's him,' the taxi driver shouted exasperated and flicked his fag end into the gutter where it sat smouldering like Cantelli's fury.

'How are you so sure?' Cantelli snapped.

'Because I've been in this business more years than a tart can shake her tits at a punter. You build a memory for faces and names and a nose for the toerags who want to puke in your cab and avoid paying the fare. You know when someone's bullshitting you – you can smell it a mile away, even on an outgoing tide.'

'And that's what he was doing?' Cantelli stabbed at the picture of Johnnie, his heavy, dark eyebrows knitting in puzzlement.

'He asked the cost of the fare to Hayling Island, said thank you and pissed off.'

'Maybe he didn't like the look of your vehicle,' Cantelli sniped, running an experienced and suspicious eye over the scratched and battered Vauxhall.

'There's nothing wrong with it. You can check my insurance and MOT,' the taxi driver said hotly, but Horton reckoned Cantelli would put in a call to traffic anyway.

Horton interjected: 'Whereabouts on Hayling?'

'Don't know. He didn't say, and I'm not a mind reader. What's he done? Can't have robbed a bank because he wasn't flush enough to take a taxi. He walked off, and he didn't ask any of the other drivers like I thought he would, to try and beat us down on price.'

Cantelli was looking increasingly perplexed. Horton didn't blame him, he was too. Hayling Island could be reached in two ways: one by a small passenger ferry from the far eastern edge of the city at the end of the road where he lived at the marina, or alternatively by road: north on the M275 out of Portsmouth, then east along the M27 and finally south, crossing a bridge on to the small semi-rural island. But whichever way you got to it, Hayling Island was not Oyster Quays, where Johnnie was supposed to have met Masefield, and neither was it anywhere near Cowes. It confirmed that Johnnie had arrived in Portsmouth, and that was one step forward. But why Hayling? And why ask and then not go?

'What did he do after that?' asked Cantelli eagerly.

'No idea.' The taxi driver shrugged and took a packet of cigarettes from the top pocket of a crumpled, open-necked checked shirt.

Horton noted the sweaty armpits. 'In which direction did he walk?'

'That way.' He jerked his head in the direction of Oyster Quays.

'Can you describe what he was wearing?'

Cantelli quickly retrieved his notebook from his jacket pocket and the short stubby pencil from behind his ear.

'Light coloured trousers, beige, casual, a pale-blue polo shirt.'

'Any logos on it?' Horton interjected.

'Don't know, didn't take any notice.' The taxi driver lit his cigarette and blew out some smoke before continuing. 'He was carrying a large dark-blue and yellow bag though, like you see the posh yachtie crowd carting when they get off the boats at Horsea Marina. I've had enough fares from there to know. He was tanned, dark-haired, young, about twenty-three, didn't look like your average yobbo, but he must have done something to have you lot sniffing around. I asked the uniformed plod why the interest but he wouldn't say.'

And neither would Horton, because as far as they knew Johnnie hadn't done anything. And even if he had he wasn't going to tell this man. He was thankful that Seaton and Somerfield, who had left to attend a domestic, hadn't said anything either, but then both were experienced enough to know when to keep silent, and they didn't have all the facts of the case anyway. Horton said, 'Thanks for your help.'

'That's it?'

'For now. But we'll need your details in case we need to come back to you for a statement.'

'Well, make it when I'm not bloody working.' Grudgingly, he relayed his full name, address and home telephone number to Cantelli.

'Not the most public-spirited of citizens,' Horton said as they watched him waddle back to his cab where a fare was waiting. Horton saw him open the door and take the woman's suitcase to the boot of the car.

'No.' Cantelli turned away, eyeing the busy road in the direction the taxi driver had indicated. 'Johnnie must have been making for Masefield's yacht.'

And had never reached there. Or had he, nagged the little voice in the back of Horton's mind. The marina manager said not; perhaps he was mistaken. He said, 'Let's take a walk.'

They set off in the same direction. Cantelli voiced the thought that had already run through Horton's mind. 'Why ask for the fare to Hayling Island if he was going to Cowes? If he'd wanted to go to Hayling, why not break up his journey from London and get off the train at Havant? He could have got a cab from there on to the Island. It's only three miles.'

'Perhaps he intended going there after Cowes Week. According to Sophia he had a week's holiday after the racing. Maybe he had arranged to meet or visit someone on Hayling after Masefield dropped him back to Oyster Quays following the racing. He was just finding out in advance how much a taxi would cost instead of catching the train from here to Havant and then taking a cab from there. Does he know anyone on Hayling?'

'Not that I'm aware of.'

But one name had sprung into Horton's mind. Stuart Jayston. OK, so he didn't actually live at Hayling, but he did live at nearby Havant.

Cantelli said, 'All he had to do was ask me, my brother Tony or Isabella, and we'd have taken him there.'

Horton threw Cantelli a glance.

Cantelli sighed. 'OK, no need to spell it out. He didn't want us to know. Why?'

'Because you might disapprove,' answered Horton.

'You mean a girl?'

'Not necessarily.'

Cantelli eyed him astounded. 'You don't mean Johnnie's gay?'
Horton shrugged.

Cantelli was adamant that Johnnie wouldn't have put his mother
through so much worry if he had run off with a girl – or a man,
come to that. But Horton wasn't so sure; people did strange things
when they were infatuated. He'd seen it happen before, and so too
had Cantelli. There were women who men would leave their wives
and kids for: they'd throw in good jobs, sacrifice their standing in
the community and risk their reputation for them. They'd even kill
for them. They breathed danger. Had someone like that got her
claws into Johnnie? Sex was a powerful driver.

'Let's concentrate on what we've got,' Horton said, sidestepping
a gaggle of Japanese tourists and halting outside a café which was
next to a tattoo parlour. 'I'll take the tattoo parlour and you ask in
the café; someone might remember seeing him.'

It was a very long shot. Cantelli didn't look hopeful, and Horton
didn't feel optimistic himself. The answer was as he expected:
negative. They walked on; Horton hoped it would spark some ideas.
Soon they came to the entrance of the Oyster Quays shopping
complex, where Johnnie would have turned into in order to reach
the marina. Ahead and on the opposite side of the road were the
grounds of HMS *Temeraire*, home to the Royal Navy School of
Physical Training, a satellite of the Maritime Warfare School, which
was responsible for training members of the Royal Navy to become
Physical Training Instructors. It made him think of Masefield and
his crew. Masefield had said he was ex Royal Navy, but Horton had
no idea what he'd done in the navy and he didn't know in which
services the crew had served. It didn't matter anyway. That could
hardly have any bearing on Johnnie's disappearance.

He glanced up at the modern apartments behind a high brick wall
on his right. Could Johnnie be staying with someone who lived
here? But why not call his mother to tell her or his boss to say he
wouldn't be joining Masefield's yacht in Cowes? Had he simply
walked out on the job, so besotted with a woman that he didn't care
about anyone else including his family? And why wasn't his mobile
phone working? Did this girl (or man, as he'd suggested to Cantelli)
have such a pull over Johnnie that she'd persuaded him to break
off contact with everyone he knew and start again?

Horton stared at the busy road ahead. If Johnnie had continued
walking straight on he would have passed one of the many university

buildings in the city, the grammar school and Portsmouth Museum. But if he had taken the road on their right, he would have reached the Isle of Wight car ferry terminal. There was another entrance from there into Oyster Quays. It was a roundabout way for him to have arrived at the marina when it was much simpler to access it via the pedestrian underpass, but a thought suddenly struck Horton, which he voiced to Cantelli.

'Perhaps Johnnie didn't know or had forgotten that Masefield was picking him up in the yacht. Masefield claims not to have Johnnie's mobile number, so Johnnie might not have had his either. He could have thought he had to make his own way to Cowes.'

'You mean he took the ferry,' Cantelli said, quickly catching on.

'Yes.' But Horton saw the flaw in that theory as they turned into Gunwharf Road and headed for the terminal, and it didn't take long for Cantelli to spot it either.

'Why didn't he take the Fast Cat to the Island? All he had to do was step off the train and it's right there.'

But Horton had an answer. 'Perhaps he thought someone was collecting him by car.' The Fast Cat only took foot passengers.

Cantelli looked far from reassured by his answer. Horton didn't blame him, because if Johnnie had travelled to the Isle of Wight either via the car ferry as a passenger in a vehicle or as a foot passenger on the Fast Cat service it didn't explain why he hadn't shown up in Cowes.

They turned into the busy car park and several minutes later Horton, seated in a small and paper strewn office, was explaining the situation to Jean Spendlove, the ticket office supervisor – a middle-aged woman with short white blonde hair, who had a no-nonsense expression on her stern-featured face.

After flicking up the computer screen she said, 'Eight people travelled by foot on the two sailings you mention, the four thirty and the five o'clock. Two paid by credit card and the names don't match; the other six paid cash, and they were all day returns.'

So that seemed to rule out Johnnie: he would have purchased either a single or a period return. But Horton gave her a photograph of Johnnie and requested that it be circulated to the ticket office staff in case Johnnie had decided it wasn't very much more expensive to buy a day return as a single. And there was still the chance that he had travelled as a passenger in a vehicle. Perhaps one of the marshalling staff or crew would remember seeing him.

Jean Spendlove looked up the rotas. 'The relevant staff members won't be on duty until midday tomorrow.'

Horton said he'd send someone over to interview them. He requested a print out of the vehicles booked on both sailings and a few minutes later left with a list of the vehicle registrations, the length of the vehicles, and the names of those who had made the bookings. There were rather a lot of them.

'We can rule out the lorries and commercial vehicles,' he said to Cantelli as they headed back to the car, but that still left about fifty vehicles to run through the database on each sailing. And Horton wasn't sure what they were looking for. From a quick glimpse down the list none of the names matched those of Johnnie's former partners in crime, but he hadn't thought they would. He told Cantelli to contact the Isle of Wight police to find out if any taxi drivers had picked up Johnnie from the ferry terminal at Fishbourne. Tomorrow he'd send DC Walters to interview the marshalling staff and crew. And tomorrow he'd request the investigation be upgraded. They needed to make a public appeal.

At the station he left Cantelli to his calls and headed for his office. He'd barely stepped inside it when his mobile rang. It was Agent Eames.

'Johnnie went ashore on the thirteenth and the sixteenth of July,' she said.

'Alone?'

'Only on the sixteenth. On the thirteenth he went with a crew member to stock up on supplies from the local Waitrose supermarket. On the sixteenth, his day off, the tender from *Calista* took him into Cowes at eight thirty in the morning and collected him from Ryde at ten o'clock that night. No one knows where he went. The skipper, Nat Boulton, has asked the crew, but it seems Johnnie didn't tell anyone. They assumed he went across to Portsmouth to visit his family.'

'He didn't. Any feedback on his mood?'

'A couple of the crew thought he seemed excited, and there was talk that he might have got himself a girlfriend. That might just be hindsight though because they know he's missing.'

'Is it so unusual that he might have a girlfriend?' Horton asked with sharp interest.

'He's very focused on his sailing. The general opinion seems to be that he didn't have a lot of time for girls, and no one can remember seeing him with one. According to the skipper, Johnnie's not one for wearing his heart on his sleeve or for gossiping or gadding about. He's quiet, self-contained, gets on with his job and is discreet.'

Horton wished he could interview the crew, but he didn't think Bliss would sanction a flight to Northern Sardinia – and that wasn't where Johnnie was, anyway.

Eames said, 'The skipper has checked his cabin. Johnnie's clothes are still there.'

'All of them?' Horton asked, knowing Eames would have asked the question. He guessed the answer, but she confirmed when she replied.

'He couldn't say. But the photograph of his mother which he keeps in a drawer beside his bed is still there.'

Which indicated he planned to return . . . but then he could have taken other photographs of her with him and left that one to make them think he was returning, ditto the clothes. And he knew that if *he* was thinking that, Harriet Eames would also be considering it. She said, 'Boulton says he's met Scott Masefield a few times when he's been with Xander but doesn't really have anything to do with him. I can't get hold of Sophia to ask her if she knows Masefield but I left a message on her voicemail.'

That made two of them. Horton relayed what the taxi driver had told them and added, 'I'd like to know where Johnnie went on the sixteenth of July.' It might have nothing to do with his disappearance, but an entire day out, which he hadn't spent visiting his family, suggested either he'd spent it with a woman, visited old friends or perhaps he'd gone for a job interview. Horton hoped it was nothing more sinister, like meeting someone connected with an illegal activity. 'Ask at the Cowes Red Jet and Red Funnel ferry terminals to see if he travelled to Southampton from there?'

'I'll also make enquiries at the Wightlink Fast Cat terminal and at Hover Travel in Ryde. He might have returned to the Island via that route, seeing as he was picked up by the tender from *Calista* at Ryde.'

'I'm only assuming he was picked up at Ryde Marina.' Horton reached into his pocket for his tide timetable. July the sixteenth . . . yes, it had been high tide at twenty-two forty-two so Ryde would have been accessible by boat. The tide went out a long way, leaving vast stretches of sandy beach, but at ten p.m. the tender – a small motorboat or RIB – could have moored up at the small marina. It would have been dark, and perhaps no one would have noticed a young man hopping on-board the boat, but he would ask the local police to show Johnnie's photograph to the boat owners. He said as much to Eames, adding that he'd also circulate Johnnie's picture to the taxi firms and bus companies in case anyone remembered seeing him on the sixteenth of July. Just because he was picked up from Ryde didn't mean that he had left the Island. But Horton knew the chances of anyone remembering him so far back were pretty remote.

He joined Cantelli in CID where he relayed what Eames had discovered. Cantelli confirmed that none of the family had seen or spoken to Johnnie on the sixteenth of July.

'I can't see any sign of him on the CCTV from the railway station but the station is very busy so he could easily have slipped through. And there's no sign of him either on the Oyster Quays cameras.'

Horton told him to start running the vehicles that had been booked on to the Wightlink ferry sailings through the database to see if any threw up connections with Johnnie. Again, Horton didn't think they'd have any success because they didn't really know what they were looking for. Cantelli probably thought the same, but doing something, anything, was better than doing nothing.

Horton returned to his office, but he couldn't settle. His thoughts returned to the taxi driver's evidence. If Johnnie had turned into Gunwharf Road but hadn't entered the ferry terminal then where else could he have gone? A left turn at the ferry terminal would have taken him through Lombard Street to the Cathedral, and eventually from there he could have walked to the funfair and seafront where the hovercraft terminal was based. He could have travelled to the island via that route, and if he had, then he had disappeared on the Island. Harriet Eames was checking if Johnnie had travelled by hovercraft on the sixteenth of July but not last Wednesday. He called PC Seaton and asked him to do that as soon as he got the chance.

He let his thoughts return to Johnnie's journey. If he hadn't gone in that direction he could have walked straight ahead to the ancient fortifications of Old Portsmouth and the harbour, where he could have met someone. But there was another possibility, and the more he considered it the more likely it seemed. He should have thought of it earlier, but he'd been distracted by the idea of Johnnie catching the ferry.

Grabbing his jacket and his helmet he crossed to Cantelli in CID. 'Johnnie could have met someone on a boat at the Camber.'

'But if he did then where is he now?'

Horton didn't know, but it didn't bode well.

'Could it have been Masefield?' Cantelli asked anxiously.

'You mean he changed the rendezvous point?'

Cantelli nodded.

'If he did then it means he and his crew are implicated in Johnnie's disappearance.'

Cantelli grew paler as thoughts chased themselves through his mind. 'Could Johnnie have had an accident on-board and they're covering it up?' He didn't need to spell out the consequences of that.

Or maybe, thought Horton, they'd got rid of him for some reason, and that also meant he had to be dead. 'I'm heading down there,' he said.

Cantelli looked as though he was about to ask if he could join him but there was still the list of vehicles to check.

Within ten minutes Horton was standing on the Camber quayside by the fish market. Across the small marina the Bridge Tavern was doing a roaring late-afternoon trade. The quayside opposite was packed with people drinking and eating, their voices and laughter carrying across to him on the warm breeze, which also brought with it the smell of fish and diesel, the latter from the Wightlink ferry he could see getting up steam to leave its berth.

The Camber manager wasn't in his office but he'd be there tomorrow morning, Horton was told. He would have access to a list of vessels that had stayed overnight and those permanently moored there, but Horton couldn't see how that was of any use. If Johnnie had met someone on-board a boat here then it could have been one that had slipped in and out of the marina within minutes, and there would be no record of that.

He found a handful of people on their yachts and motor cruisers but all of them shook their heads when he showed them Johnnie's photograph, and none of them claimed to have been in the Camber last Wednesday. There were only three fishermen on-board one of the blue and white fishing boats, sorting out their nets and equipment. They had been out fishing on Wednesday at the time. It had been high tide. Horton decided he'd get a couple of officers out here tomorrow when the fish market was open and someone would be in the offices. He also considered conducting a house-to-house in the dwellings that overlooked the Camber, but for that he needed the inquiry upgraded to high priority.

Disappointment was fast becoming a regular feature in their search for Johnnie, although he reminded himself they'd had one break today, the taxi driver. He called Sarah Conway, thinking she wouldn't answer because she'd be out photographing the racing, so he was pleasantly surprised when she did.

'That finished three hours ago,' she said, when he expressed this.

Was it that late already? He saw that it was after six. He asked her if she could email him a photograph of Scott Masefield's yacht and the crew. He'd get the officers to show that around here tomorrow.

'Of course. I'll do it later tonight. I'm just off to photograph the presentations to today's race winners.'

'How did Masefield get on?'

'Came in first.'

'And Crawford?'

'Third.'

'I don't expect that pleased him.' But it did Horton.

'They're obviously missing Hattie,' Sarah said. 'Roland Stevington told me she was helping you try to find Johnnie Oslow. He raced in her place. Probably a case of two many skippers and not enough skivvies. Rupert likes being in charge, and Roland is used to being his own boss. Any progress on finding Oslow?'

'Some. Not much though.'

She didn't ask why he wanted a photograph of Masefield's yacht and his crew, and for that he was grateful . . . and a little bit curious. But then Sarah Conway was only interested in one thing, and that was her photography.

Horton returned to the station where he updated Cantelli on his lack of progress. He asked Cantelli how he'd got on checking the Wightlink vehicles.

'The majority come from outside Hampshire. There's some from Yorkshire, Kent, Devon, several from Surrey, Berkshire and London.'

That was to be expected. The Island was a popular holiday destination.

Cantelli added, 'Some of the owners have convictions for petty crimes and speeding offences, but nothing major and nothing that on the surface of it connects with Johnnie. I don't recognize any names.'

And short of interviewing them all, which was impossible without the assistance of many other police forces across the country, Horton didn't think this was going to get them far.

Seaton phoned to say there was no record of Johnnie Oslow having travelled on the hovercraft last Wednesday, but he'd left his photograph and asked that Horton be contacted if anyone remembered seeing him. And Harriet Eames rang to say the same of the sixteenth of July. No record of Johnnie having travelled from Cowes or Ryde that day on any of the ferries.

'What are you going to do now?' she asked.

'Get the investigation upgraded and continue with our inquiries.'

'Let me know if there's anything else I can do,' she added before ringing off.

Rupert Crawford would be pleased to have her back on the team tomorrow.

It seemed they'd come to a dead end. Reluctantly, Horton had to call it a day.

Cantelli went home to spend another night worrying and speculating and Horton returned to his boat, troubled and with a terrible feeling in his gut that this was going to end badly. Tomorrow they would have Johnnie's bank details and be able to put a trace on his credit and debit cards, and tomorrow the railway company might be able to confirm that Johnnie's ticket had been surrendered at the Hard, which would back up the taxi driver's evidence. And, as he'd told Harriet Eames, he'd request that the investigation be upgraded, and if it wasn't then he'd simply go over Bliss's head and enlist the full cooperation of Sergeant Warren's uniformed officers. He'd also contact Leanne Payne, the crime reporter at the local newspaper, and give her the story and Johnnie's photograph. That should get things moving. But still the gloom refused to budge.

He took his coffee up on deck, and as he watched the sun slowly set and the twilight give way to darkness he ran through what they had – which was precious little, except that according to one man's evidence Johnnie had arrived in Portsmouth as planned.

Harriet Eames' words again returned to torment him – *he was easily led astray once, he could have been again* – and this time Horton considered them in the context of Johnnie's former partners in crime. He didn't want to believe that Johnnie had resumed contact with any of them (in fact, there was no reason why he should have done) but perhaps he'd accidentally run into one of them. Sardinia was, after all, a popular holiday destination. Could Johnnie have come across one of them there? Perhaps not the exclusive Costa Smerelda, but at Stintino or Olbia. Johnnie could have been coerced into becoming involved in something that he hadn't realized would turn out to be illegal and potentially dangerous. Or perhaps he'd willingly got involved. Jesus, he hoped it wasn't acting as a mule, carrying in drugs. And although he told himself it was unlikely the idea refused to budge. It had to be checked and hopefully eliminated, and there was only one way to do that. Tomorrow he and Cantelli would interview the other lads who had committed that arson attack with Johnnie, and they'd start with the man who had the highest number of criminal convictions: Ryan Spencer.

SEVEN

Monday

Cantelli pulled up outside the shabby terraced council house. Horton eyed it with weary resignation. He knew what to expect. He'd been to many such properties in his police career. He couldn't see how Johnnie could once again have become involved with Ryan Spencer, and the thought that they were wasting their time crossed his mind as they stepped around an assortment of abandoned broken toys in the small front garden that wouldn't have known a blade of grass if it had had the gall to poke up from between the rusting child's bicycle, dirty pushchair, old rotting sofa and split bags of litter that the urban foxes and magpies had pecked at. He felt sorry for the neighbours, whose gardens were neat and well tended and whose windows gleamed and sported crisp clean curtains and blinds.

He had called Cantelli and had asked him to get in early. He knew that wouldn't be a problem for the sergeant, who had probably spent a very restless night. The heavy circles under his dark worried eyes bore testimony to that. Horton hadn't exactly had a blissful night's sleep either. His mind had refused to stop whirling for some time after he had stretched out on his bunk, and when he did sleep his dreams had been a mixed-up mash of Johnnie and Jennifer leaving him to wake with a dull headache of the sort he used to experience when he'd drunk too much booze.

He'd stopped in his office long enough to email DC Walters the photographs that Sarah Conway had sent to him late last night. There were some good close-up shots of Masefield and his crew and two of the yacht, one from the side looking up at it and the other front on. She might have shot them on a long lens, but however she had taken them Horton knew it would have involved the risk of being thrown overboard from that RIB. On their way to Paulsgrove Horton had called Walters and brought him up to speed with events.

'Wondered why it was like the haunted house in here,' Walters had said. 'That's a bit of a bummer the sarge's nephew missing.'

Horton had given him instructions to get down to the Wightlink ferry terminal at midday to interview the marshalling staff. 'You'll have to go on-board the twelve thirty and one o'clock sailings and ask the load master, crew and the catering staff if they remember seeing Johnnie, but for goodness' sake try not to get caught on-board when the bloody ship sails. Is Bliss in?'

'Hang on, I'll check.'

Horton had heard him put down the phone and clatter across to the window.

'She's just pulled in to the car park.'

Horton had instructed him to liaise with Sergeant Warren and get some officers down to the Camber to show the pictures of Masefield's yacht and those of Johnnie. He'd then called Bliss on her office number. Swiftly, he'd told her that he and Cantelli were following up a couple of leads on a missing person's inquiry and relayed the details.

'Does it need both of you?' she'd demanded curtly.

He told her that the person in question was Cantelli's nephew.

'Then I would have thought it best to send another officer. One who wouldn't be emotionally compromised.'

'They wouldn't have the background knowledge that I and Sergeant Cantelli have,' he had answered, without saying anything about Johnnie and his mates' convictions for arson, adding, 'and there wasn't time to brief anyone this morning.'

He heard her sniff derisively. 'I want to see you the moment you return, Inspector, and I mean immediately.' The line went dead.

An expression of empathy might not have gone amiss, he thought as Cantelli rapped loudly on the battered and scratched door of Ryan Spencer's house, but that was just wishful thinking. He had about as much chance of getting empathy from the ice maiden as he did of being knighted by the Queen.

'What the bloody hell do you want?' an obese woman in her early twenties, with straggly dyed black hair hanging around a sullen pale spotty face, demanded as she wrenched open the door and eyed them with open hostility. In her fat tattooed arms she held a child of about a year wearing only a soiled nappy with a snotty nose and a chocolate stained mouth.

'Ryan Spencer?' Cantelli answered, raising his voice above the noise of a television blaring out.

'Yeah, and who the fuck are you?'

Tight-lipped, Cantelli showed his warrant card.

'Might have guessed.' She turned and screeched up the stairs, 'It's the pigs for you,' before turning into a room on her left.

Cantelli flashed Horton a pained look as they stepped inside. Horton knew his thoughts. How could Johnnie ever have associated with people like this? He closed the door behind him and eyed the dirty narrow hallway with filthy clothes and toys littering the thread-bare carpet. The smell of urine, dirt and fried food was cloying.

Ryan Spencer appeared at the top of the stairs in low-slung jogging pants and a baggy, dirty, grey T-shirt over his skinny frame. He shuffled down the stairs, eyeing them with alarm. 'I ain't done nothing,' he whined.

'We'd just like a word,' Cantelli answered, having to raise his voice above the sound of the television. 'Shall we go in here?' He indicated the scuffed and yellowing door on his left.

Cantelli stepped inside while Horton followed the skinny anaemic-looking Ryan into the dirty room that stank of nicotine and soiled nappies. Horton caught sight of one poking out behind the sagging old settee and quickly turned his attention from it to the widescreen gigantic plasma television set that dominated the room, almost blocking out what little light managed to break through the grime on the window behind it. In front of it, sitting cross-legged on the floor, was a boy of about four. Horton feared for his eyesight, not to mention his hearing. Horton asked the mound of tattooed flesh to turn down the volume. She looked as though she was about to tell him to sod off or worse, but holding her gaze she must have seen something in his expression that made her obey, albeit grudg-ingly. The instant the sound decreased minimally the boy looked up, startled, and began to cry, and the baby decided to join in.

'Now look what you've done,' the mountain of flesh declared, glaring at Horton with real hatred. She grabbed the boy by the arm, violently wrenching him up from the floor so that he wailed even louder. Cantelli looked as though he was going to scream. Horton addressed Ryan Spencer, who seemed oblivious to the commotion.

'Outside,' he curtly commanded.

Ryan Spencer sniffed, grabbed a packet of cigarettes from the mantelpiece and shuffled out. They followed him.

'When did you last see Johnnie Oslow?' Horton commanded sharply as soon as they were standing in the littered front garden.

The quicker they got this over with the better. He registered a flicker of surprise in Ryan Spencer's shifty eyes.

'Not for years.' Ryan lit his cigarette, adding, 'Why, what's he done? Set fire to something again?'

Horton felt Cantelli tense. He wasn't a violent man, but extenuating circumstances might provoke him, and this looked like being one of them. Horton quickly interjected: 'Has he been in touch by phone, text or email?'

'No.'

'Never?'

'No.'

'Where were you last week?'

'Eh?' Ryan eyed Horton as though he'd just asked him to explain Newton's theory of relativity.

'Your life that exciting that you don't remember?' Horton said facetiously.

Ryan wiped a hand across his nose and drew on his cigarette. Horton could hear the children crying inside the house and Ms Tattoo shouting at them to shut the fuck up. Poor little blighters didn't stand a chance.

'OK, then let me be more precise,' Horton continued. 'What were you were doing on Wednesday?'

'Signing on.'

The answer came so promptly that Horton knew it must be the highlight of his week. 'All day?' he sneered.

'Nah, course not.'

'So after signing on . . .' This was like pulling teeth.

'I went down the town, hung around the shops a bit, then went for a drink.'

'Where?'

Ryan flinched at the sharpness of Horton's tone. 'The White Swan. Guildhall Walk.'

That wasn't far from the town centre, but it was a fair distance from the harbour. 'How long were you there?' Horton asked as Cantelli took notes.

'Dunno. A few hours.'

'When, exactly?' Horton felt like shaking him.

'Didn't look at the clock.'

'What time did you get there?'

'Look, what is this? The third degree?'

Horton leaned forward and fixed his cold stare on the little weasel. 'Yes. And if you don't feel like answering my questions here then perhaps you'll feel more like it at the station.'

'All right, keep your hair on. I had something to eat and was in there all afternoon.'

'Anyone vouch for that?'

'A few of me mates and the barman.'

They could check, but Horton was beginning to think there was no need. But to make sure he said, 'Ever been abroad on holiday?'

Ryan looked so shocked at the question that Horton knew the answer before he spoke, and that it was genuine.

'No.'

'Do you own a car or a motorbike or scooter?'

'No.'

Johnnie hadn't met Ryan Spencer.

'Is there anything else, 'cos I'm cold, hanging around out here.'

'In August!'

'Yeah. Why? You going to arrest me for that?'

If only . . . Horton held his lairy, hostile glance. He was sick of Ryan Spencer, and by Cantelli's expression he was too. Abruptly, Horton turned, giving a nod to Cantelli.

When they reached the car Horton turned back, but Ryan Spencer had already slunk into his shabby house.

Cantelli exhaled and let down the car window as though wanting to get the stench of Ryan and his wasted life out of his nostrils. Horton didn't blame him.

'Thank God Johnnie got away from that,' he said, starting the engine but not moving off. 'And I've got you to thank for that, Andy.'

'The sailing did it, not me. Come on, let's hope that Tyler Godfray is a little more intelligent and pleasant.'

He might have been if he'd been at home.

'He's at work,' announced his mother, a lean, neat and tidy brunette in her mid forties. Karen Godfray stood in the narrow, spotlessly clean hall in one of the terraced houses not far from the waterfront of Gosport. Horton recalled her from the Magistrates' Court. She'd sat upright and tight-lipped as she'd listened to the charges against her son and the punishment meted out to him. He remembered Tyler Godfray as being dark-haired and dark-eyed, and that he had avoided looking at his mother.

'He's not in trouble, is he?' she asked sternly rather than anxiously. Horton wondered why she had leapt to that conclusion instead of being alarmed that he might have been involved in an accident, which was the usual assumption of many people when police officers appeared on their doorstep.

He said, 'We just want to talk to him.'

'I told Tyler that if he got into trouble with the police again he'd be out on his ear. Not having a dad to discipline him, I've had to be strict. It's not easy bringing up a kid on your own,' she added defiantly, and a little defensively, thought Horton.

'What happened to his father?' he asked out of curiosity, wondering if Tyler had also rebelled following the trauma of his father's death.

'He died in an accident on the building site when Tyler was three,' Karen Godfray answered. 'A wall fell in on him. Of course I didn't want Tyler to end up on the sites, but what can you do?'

'He works in the construction industry?'

'He's a painter, went to college after that bit of trouble with Johnnie Oslow, a bad influence, and that useless, worthless article Ryan Spencer. God knows where they are now – prison more than like. And I don't want to know, and neither does Tyler.'

This wasn't turning out to be a good morning for them, and particularly not for Cantelli. 'Can you tell us where to find Tyler, Mrs Godfray?'

She drew herself up and eyed him squarely. 'I don't want him bothered at work. His boss might get the wrong idea.'

'Where is he working, Mrs Godfray?'

She hesitated. Horton waited. After a moment she said grudgingly, 'Portsmouth, on a house redecoration.'

'Where exactly?'

'Old Portsmouth. I don't know the number. It's in White Hart Road, not far from the Isle of Wight ferry terminal.'

Horton's ears pricked up at that, and he sensed Cantelli's heightened interest. 'Have you and Tyler ever been abroad on holiday?'

'Yes. Why? What's that got to do with anything?' she asked, surprised.

But Horton wasn't going to answer that question. He'd leave that for Tyler Godfray. He said, 'Was Tyler at home on Wednesday night?'

She narrowed her eyes at him. 'Of course he was.'

'All night?'

'Yes.'

'What time did he arrive home from work?'

'Look, what is this?'

'The time, please, Mrs Godfray.'

In a clipped voice she said, 'Just before six. Satisfied?' she added.

Not really, thought Horton, but they might be when they spoke to Tyler.

Cantelli didn't need telling where to go next. On the way Horton's mobile rang. It was Sophia, who apologized for not returning his call yesterday. She hadn't been able to get a signal. Horton didn't think that was the truth; she just hadn't wanted her Sunday disturbed. She confirmed that she hadn't give Scott Masefield or any of his crew Johnnie's mobile telephone number.

'Isn't that a little odd?' he asked.

'I didn't make the arrangements for him to meet Mr Masefield,' she answered politely. 'I only booked his travel as Mr Andreadis requested.'

He asked if she had phoned Harriet Eames with that information.

'No. I called you first.'

Horton said he would ring Harriet to tell her. He did so. Her mobile was on voicemail. He glanced at the clock on the dashboard. It was just after ten. Perhaps she was racing. He left a message relaying what Sophia had said.

The house that Tyler was working at was easy to spot because of the white van outside and the front door being wide open. From inside came noises of a drill, and just as Cantelli was about to call out a man in his mid-fifties, wearing dusty and grimy jeans and a white T-shirt, emerged.

'Can I help you, guv?' he said pleasantly.

Cantelli asked if Tyler Godfray was there. Horton thought he caught a brief flash of irritation in the man's hazel eyes, but was that at being disturbed in his work or because they wanted to talk to Godfray?

'He's on the top floor. I'll fetch him for you. Can I say who wants him?'

Cantelli showed his warrant card and got a slow nod but no comment.

A couple of minutes later a surly young man in his early twenties with thick gelled dark hair, sullen eyes, wearing paint-spattered white overalls joined them.

'What do you want?' he demanded sulkily. 'I'm working.'

Horton wondered if his mother had called or sent him a text to say they were asking questions. 'I'm very pleased to see that you are, Mr Godfray,' he began overly polite. 'Shall we step outside.'

It wasn't a question. Tyler swaggered out, but he scanned the road nervously and seemed very reluctant to focus on them. He thrust his hands into the pockets of his overalls and shuffled his feet.

'When did you last see Johnnie Oslow?'

His head came up. 'Why do you want to know that?' He eyed Horton warily.

'I think you'd get back to work a lot quicker if you just answer the question.'

'Haven't seen him for years. Not since he dropped us in it.' The false bravado was back.

'He dropped you in it!' Cantelli couldn't help exclaiming.

Tyler eyed him cockily. 'Yeah, he went squealing to the police. He got scared. Went running out of that mental hospital like a lunatic.'

'Yeah, and you all followed him like headless chickens,' hissed Cantelli.

Tyler's mouth turned down further, and his eyes narrowed at Cantelli's tone.

Horton said, 'Were you working here last Wednesday afternoon?'

'Course I was.'

'Did you see Johnnie when he walked past? Maybe you were looking out of the window or were out here having a fag.'

'I don't smoke, and I wasn't looking out of any window. Didn't know he walked past.'

Truth or a lie? Tyler didn't look surprised at the question or concerned that he might have been caught out, just moody. 'It was about four o'clock,' Horton pressed.

'I didn't see him. Like I said, I haven't seen him for years. Now I've got to get back to work.'

But Horton hadn't finished yet. 'Been abroad on holiday recently?'

'No.' Tyler answered promptly and without surprise at the question, which was a sure-fire sign that mummy had called him and relayed their conversation to her son.

'That's not what your mum said.'

'Yeah, well, you said *recently*,' Tyler sneered cockily. 'It was two years ago.'

'Where?'

'What's it to you?'

Horton felt like slapping him. He said nothing, just stared at him. Tyler shuffled, twitched his shoulders and said, in as lairy a manner as he dared, 'Some place in Sardinia.'

'Where?' rapped Horton.

Tyler flinched. 'Can't remember.'

Horton put his face very close to Tyler's, forcing him to jerk his head back. 'Try,' he said menacingly.

'Badesi. Didn't like it much, too hot, and the food was crap.'

'Meet up with Johnnie there?'

'No.'

Horton thought his answer genuine. Besides, the timescale was too long ago to have any relevance to Johnnie's recent disappearance.

Tyler added, 'Like I said I—'

'Haven't seen him for years,' Horton finished wearily. He nodded as if to say he could go. Tyler looked relieved and turned towards the house, but he'd only gone a couple of steps before Horton called him back. 'Just one more thing, Mr Godfray. How do you get to work?'

'Eh?' Tyler turned back.

'By car?'

'No. Failed me test.'

'A motorbike or scooter then?'

'I catch the ferry from Gosport and someone picks me up this side.'

'Must be awkward when you have a job further afield.'

'Someone always collects me from the ferry.' He made to turn away, but Horton said:

'When did you last see Ryan Spencer?'

'Bloody years ago.

'And Stuart Jayston?'

'Are you kidding?'

'No,' Horton said, perplexed.

'I work for his dad, Jaystons Building and Decorating.'

'And does Stuart also work for his father?'

'No, he thinks he's the bloody boss.'

They let him return to his work.

Horton said, 'I think both Ryan and Tyler are telling the truth. They haven't seen Johnnie. Tyler's holiday in Sardinia is too long ago to connect with Johnnie's disappearance, and I can't see that their paths could have crossed there.'

'I'm glad about that.' Cantelli zapped open the car. 'That just leaves Stuart Jayston.'

And Horton thought they'd get the same result.

EIGHT

B ut there was no one at the address Horton had for Stuart Jayston. They located the company's office on an industrial estate on the northern outskirts of Havant, where they were told Gordon Jayston and his wife, Jean, were away until tomorrow and Stuart had gone to a property in the New Forest to take details of a potential new job. No one knew when he'd be back. Horton got the impression from the woman they spoke to that she didn't much care either. They obtained his mobile phone number, but Horton wanted to interview him face to face. He didn't leave a message for Stuart to get in touch with them. There was still the possibility that Johnnie could have met up with Stuart or been in contact with him, but that avenue was looking less likely. And Horton would be only too pleased if that was so. He knew Cantelli would be too.

They returned to the station, where Horton reported to Bliss while Cantelli headed for CID to see if anything fresh had come in on Johnnie's disappearance and if any other crimes had occurred that needed their attention. Horton suspected there would be a few new ones to add to the already outstanding amount that Bliss was bound to remind him about.

Tight-lipped, wearing her customary crisp white shirt, and black skirt, with her light-brown hair scraped back in a ponytail off her narrow unmade face, she jerked her head at the seat across her desk. 'I've reviewed the missing persons file,' she said crisply. 'There's no evidence that Johnnie Oslow is in danger or a danger to the public, he's not vulnerable, and he's an adult. Being Sergeant Cantelli's nephew is not enough to allocate scarce resources to the investigation, especially when we have other priorities.'

'Such as?' he answered tightly. Technically speaking she was right, but he didn't give a toss about technicalities.

'The other cases that are littering your desk, and the fact that you haven't written up your report from the last investigation! Detective Superintendent Uckfield has requested it by tonight.'

'I'd like to put out a public appeal.'

'It's too early.'

'I disagree.'

'Whether you agree or not is immaterial. If Sergeant Cantelli is too emotionally comprised to do his job then I suggest he take some leave.'

And I suggest you take a flying leap off a long pier. He made to speak, but she cut him short. 'That's all, Inspector.'

Horton marched out, wondering what on earth he'd done to deserve her. He fetched a sandwich and Diet Coke from the canteen and returned to CID where Cantelli shook his head. There was no sign of Walters, which meant he must be at the Wightlink ferry terminal. Horton relayed what Bliss had said, including her refusal to go with a public appeal.

'So we do nothing,' Cantelli declared hotly.

'No. We do everything, but we do it without telling Bliss. I've been considering the matter of a public appeal. Although it might throw up some sightings of Johnnie it will also bring out all the loonies and expose you and your family to the media.' Horton held up his hand to stem Cantelli's predictable reply. 'I know you don't give a damn about that but I was thinking of Isabella, because if we do leak it to the press they're going to dredge up Johnnie's previous criminal conviction and all the dirt on that arson attack. I'm not sure they'll paint him in a glowing light, especially if they put that with the fact he's left the employ of a millionaire.'

Cantelli winced. He got the picture. 'They'll say he's stolen from Andreadis.'

'Or something like it. If the press talk to Karen Godfray or, God forbid, Tyler or Ryan, then you can imagine what they'll come up with.'

Cantelli's face paled. 'Ryan would probably say anything if they bunged him a few quid.'

'And Tyler will probably make himself out to be whiter than the first flakes of snow just to stop his mum from scolding him.'

'You're right, Andy. I hadn't though of that.'

Neither had he until a moment ago. He left Cantelli to write up the interviews they'd conducted that morning and to pull together everything they had on the investigation. When Walters returned and the officers reported back from the Camber, Cantelli would analyse that and add it to the case file. He just hoped that something new would come in that could take them a step forward to finding Johnnie.

Horton rang Andreadis, because he still didn't have Johnnie's bank details. Again he got his voicemail. Annoyed at the delay and lack of communication he left a terse message and did the same on Harriet Eames' voicemail, asking in a slightly facetious tone if she'd mind contacting her friend Xander and chivvying him up. Then he turned his attention to the paper on his desk, where he found a message bearing Walter's scrawl, which he'd taken at eleven fifteen. A Clive Teckstone had called and asked to be contacted as soon as possible. Horton didn't know or recognize the name or the telephone number, but the district code told him the call had come from Woking, and that was where Dr Quentin Amos lived. Of course, Amos wasn't the sole inhabitant of Woking, but Horton couldn't think of any case he was handling that linked with Woking, fifty miles to the north and out of their territory.

With curiosity and a sense of eagerness he rang it and found that he was speaking to a firm of solicitors. Mr Teckstone was out of the office and wouldn't be back until late afternoon. Was there a message?

Horton asked if anyone else could help him, but Teckstone's secretary claimed not to have any knowledge of her boss's telephone call to him. He asked what area of law Mr Teckstone specialized in and was told he was a general practitioner, which Horton thought covered a multitude of sins. 'Criminal law?' he inquired of the secretary. No, he was informed, which meant that Teckstone's call couldn't be about an investigation. He said he'd ring back. He'd been tempted to ask if Amos was one of their clients but he curbed his impatience and threw himself into his work. He'd just finished writing up his report from the previous investigation when he heard Walters return. Glancing up at the clock, he was surprised to see it was almost four. Walters had taken his time, which meant that despite his warning Walters had managed to get stuck on the ferry, a fact he confirmed when Horton joined him and Cantelli in CID.

'I couldn't interview the crew while they were loading up,' Walters quickly explained before Horton could complain. 'So I travelled across on the twelve thirty, talked to them all and then hung around at Fishbourne and caught the two o'clock sailing back from there and interviewed that lot on the way back to Portsmouth. No one remembers seeing Johnnie.'

Cantelli also despondently reported that the officers making inquiries at the Camber had drawn a blank with Johnnie's photograph and no one they had interviewed remembered seeing Masefield's yacht. The phone records still hadn't arrived. And neither did they have Johnnie's bank details. He was about to try Andreadis again when Harriet Eames called on him on his mobile. He hoped with the information they wanted.

'I called Xander as soon as I picked up your message. He gave me the finance director's number and I rang him immediately. I have the details of Johnnie's bank account.'

Oh, the power of personal contact. She relayed it. Horton jotted it down and handed the scrap of paper to Cantelli, who immediately picked up his phone. It was a local branch of a national bank. 'How did you get on today?' Horton asked Harriet Eames.

'Came first.'

He heard the triumph and pride in her voice and imagined her fair, lovely face flushed with exhilaration. It filled him with a longing to have been with her on-board that yacht, minus Rupert Crawford and Roland Stevington – *if* the latter had been there, because with Harriet Eames on the team Stevington would probably have been surplus to requirements. The whole ruddy crew would have been surplus as far he was concerned if he had been with her, he thought, despite his resolve not to get emotionally involved. Masefield would be pissed off at not gaining top place and that rather pleased him. He passed on his congratulations, rang off and waited for Cantelli to come off the phone.

'I've got an appointment with the manageress in fifteen minutes,' he said eagerly, gathering up his jacket.

Although she might not let them have full details of the account without an official request, they knew her well enough to obtain the date, time and location of the last transaction and to put a stop on the account. It was now just before five, and Horton rang Teckstone's. This time he was in luck.

'I'm afraid I have some bad news for you,' Clive Teckstone announced solemnly after Horton had introduced himself. 'I regret to tell you that Dr Quentin Amos died on Sunday evening.'

Horton started with surprise. He had known that Amos was terminally ill, but he hadn't expected his death to be so imminent.

He thought he'd have time to speak to him again. His tactic of doing nothing had backfired on him. Controlling his disappointment, he said, 'His death seems rather sudden.'

'He suffered a heart attack.'

Brought on by natural causes or induced, wondered Horton, his suspicions in overdrive. Could Lord Eames and his cronies have engineered this to prevent him from speaking to Amos again? But why was Teckstone telling him this?

'Before he died Dr Amos left explicit instructions for me to contact you as soon as possible after his death.'

So the trail wasn't dead. Dare he hope?

'Dr Amos deposited a document with us, which is to be given to you personally, on receipt of formal identification.'

'What kind of document?' My God, was he finally going to learn the truth? Did Eames and the intelligence services know about this document?

'I have it in the safe. How soon can you collect it?'

'What time do you close?'

'In five minutes, I'm afraid, and I'm due at a meeting so I can't stay on.'

Horton silently cursed.

'Could you collect the document first thing in the morning? We open at nine.'

Then he would be there at two minutes to nine. He got the address and rang off, his mind racing with thoughts. He'd waited so long for the truth and faced disappointment so many times that he didn't dare to hope. But the thought that this might be one of Lord Eames' tricks tormented him. He had decided to do nothing, to see what the intelligence services would do next. Hastening Amos's death seemed a bit extreme, but doing so – and making sure there was some kind of document for Horton to collect – seemed even more outrageous, because Amos must have deposited this document some time ago. Or had he done so after Horton's visit to him last week? Damn, he hadn't asked Teckstone that. He was tempted to call him back but didn't. He'd find out soon . . . but not soon enough.

Cantelli called him. 'The last time Johnnie used the account was in London last Wednesday. He bought something to eat and drink from an outlet at Waterloo station. Nothing since. The account has been stopped. I thought I'd try Stuart Jayston again.'

Horton was about to say go easy but didn't. He dealt with some more paperwork, read through Walters' report, and the reports of the officers who had questioned the boat owners and staff at the Camber, in case something new occurred to him. It didn't. Then he called it a day after making sure that Uckfield got *his* report. He managed to avoid Bliss, who was in one of her interminable meetings, and headed for his yacht.

On arrival he saw he had a message from Cantelli to say that Stuart Jayston wasn't at home. He'd waited for a while but didn't think it worth hanging on for longer. 'He could be out all night,' Cantelli had added. 'I'll try him first thing in the morning.'

Horton went for a run, showered and made himself something to eat, but he'd only managed to take one mouthful when his mobile rang. It was the station. It was five minutes past ten. A call at this hour could only mean one thing: trouble. And was that connected with Johnnie, he thought with consternation, answering it.

'There's been a fire at the Hilsea Lines, the old bastions, sir.'

That wasn't usually his province unless it was arson, and even then uniform would deal with it and report it to the fire investigation officer. But he knew why he was being informed, and he felt a cold shiver run down his spine. They had a body. This was confirmed by the officer's next words.

'Any ID?' Horton asked anxiously, unable to stop himself thinking about Johnnie.

'I don't know, sir. They didn't say.'

'I'm on my way.'

Hastily, he locked up. As he made for the north of the city he mentally ran through what he knew of the bastions that formed Hilsea Lines. There were several of them, originally built to protect the north of the island from attack in 1544. Since then they had been rebuilt, some time in the 1700s, he thought, and again, he seemed to recall, in 1871 with the renewed threat of a French invasion, which had never happened. They had belonged to the army, providing barracks, ammunition stores and a series of tunnels beneath the earth mounds, before becoming derelict and overgrown with grass, shrubs and trees. But some years ago (he forgot when), the Hilsea Lines had been designated a conservation area with a series of nature trails around the moat and the creek which made Portsmouth an island; or rather it would have done, but for the two road bridges over it and the motorway on the western shores.

Was it Johnnie, he thought fearfully. But it couldn't be, because the bastions were about four miles from where Johnnie had last been seen at the southern end of Portsmouth. But despite telling himself that several times as he made his way through the dark, humid night, he couldn't shake off the terrible feeling that he was about to look upon the charred remains of Cantelli's nephew.

NINE

'The fire was just inside one of the tunnels on the top of a bastion to the east. It's where the body is,' the fire service watch manager reported to Horton as he joined him and DC Maitland, the fire investigation officer, in the small gravel car park at one of the entrances to the Hilsea Lines. The area was bathed in lights from the two fire engines and the police vehicle. Horton had steered the Harley through the outer cordon where a small crowd, mainly residents from the nearby houses and flats, were being kept at bay by PC Benton. To the south were a number of small industrial units, while a footbridge to the north led over the motorway to more houses, shops and offices. The air was heavy with the smell of smoke.

'Man or woman?' asked Horton.

'Can't tell.'

'That bad?'

'Well, there's not much left of whoever it was.'

Horton suppressed a shiver.

The watch manager continued: 'We've put up a temporary light at the scene. We're still beating down around the area, but the fire's out and it's safe enough for you to view the body.'

'We'll need these, Andy.' Maitland opened the rear of his grey van and indicated the protective clothing.

Decked out in a thick scene-suit, stout boots, fire resistant gloves, a hard hat, and carrying a torch, Horton followed the lean figure of Maitland up a short track lined with trees and shrubs, at the top of which they turned right. Soon they were walking along the top of the bastions, which were burrowed beneath them in the grass and earth. Mentally, Horton began to prepare himself for what lay ahead. Perhaps it was a tramp who had come to shelter in one of the bastions for the night. He'd lit a fire or a cigarette, had fallen asleep and set fire to the place. He'd had no time to get out. But as Horton weaved his way along the narrow footpath, he still couldn't rid his mind of the thought that it might be Johnnie. If it was his body though, why now? Why not soon after he'd disappeared, and where had he been since Wednesday? Why come here? No, it couldn't be him.

He heard the drone of the traffic on the motorway to the north and occasionally caught a glimpse, through a gap in the foliage, of headlights flashing past. The smell of burnt earth grew stronger, and thoughts of another fire sprang to mind: in that psychiatric hospital in 1968, where the body of Zachary Benham had been discovered. Had anyone grieved for him? And who would grieve for Dr Amos, Horton wondered. Did he have any relatives or friends? Perhaps tomorrow when he visited Teckstone's he'd find out, along with what Amos had bequeathed him in an envelope.

'Who reported the fire?' Horton addressed Maitland.

'Anonymous,' Maitland tossed over his shoulder. 'The call came from a mobile phone, but I'm betting it's a pay as you go one which we won't be able to trace and which is now either at the bottom of the moat or in the creek.'

Horton didn't like the sound of this. 'You think it's murder?'

'The timing of the call to the fire brigade is wrong for it to be a dog walker or someone who just happened to see the smoke and wanted to remain anonymous. It was timed at twenty-one fifteen; the first appliance was here at twenty-one nineteen and the fire had only just started.'

Horton didn't need Maitland to spell out what that meant. 'The fire setter called the emergency services before setting the fire.'

'Looks that way.'

Which had given the perpetrator only four minutes to get away, maybe eight maximum, allowing for the firefighters to reach the fire. It wasn't long, but in the dark, and with the dense cover of the summer foliage, not to mention the number of tracks that sprang off this place, it would have been fairly easy for the fire setter to do so without being noticed. Horton wasn't certain how far into the nature trail they were, but tomorrow in daylight he would check. And by the sounds of what Maitland was saying it probably ruled out the body being that of a tramp. If this was murder, which was looking highly likely, then it would take precedence over the investigation into Johnnie's disappearance. *Unless it was him.*

Maitland halted. Horton could see some firefighters beating the bracken to their left, making sure the last of the embers were out, while others were reeling in a hose. They'd obviously drawn some water from the moat. The ground was muddy, and the lights of the cars on the motorway were visible through the blackened and twisted remains of the trees.

'Ready?' asked Maitland.

As ready as I'll ever be. He nodded and followed Maitland a few paces down a track to their right, where Maitland paused. In front of them was a step that led down to a brick archway, now blackened by the fire, as was the vegetation around and above it. The air was heavy with a smell of burnt flesh that reminded Horton too much of roast pork.

The archway was about three feet wide and five feet high. There were four steps down to it and then another step into the entrance. Horton ducked his head and followed Maitland inside the narrow tunnel, which came to a halt after about three yards. To Horton's right, about two feet inside the entrance was a small brick chamber, and there Maitland shone his torch. In the far right-hand corner Horton saw what was left of a human being. His stomach heaved. The watch manager had been right. There was no way of knowing from the blackened remains whether this was male or female; only Dr Clayton would be able to tell them that, and hopefully more. Making an effort to keep his stomach under some control he steeled himself to study the body more closely, without moving towards it. He didn't want to disturb the scene for Maitland and SOCO. There were no clothes left on it, and there didn't seem to be any remains of personal belongings lying around the area or anything to say this person had been sleeping rough.

Maitland said, 'Seen enough?'

Horton nodded. He silently recalled his own harrowing experiences of being trapped in a fire more than once, and he shivered as he stepped outside the tunnel into the warm, still night. He wished he could shut out the image of that charred, shrunken body, its facial features distorted by blackening and skin contraction, grotesquely resembling a creature out of the grimmest horror movie imaginable, but he knew the sight and smell of it would linger with him a long time.

He returned to the car park where he called in and requested the Scene of Crime Officers and the forensic photographer, Jim Clarke. Then he asked for officers to be sent to the eastern end of Hilsea Lines and all the other entrances to the area and to make sure they were all cordoned off. He didn't think anyone would arrive to walk their dog at this time of night in the dark, but the press might use them to gain access to the scene. Two from the local newspaper were already here. He wasn't surprised to see Leanne Payne the crime reporter and Cliff Wesley the photographer. Someone in the watching crowd must have alerted them. Ignoring Leanne's calls for a comment and Wesley's flashing camera, Horton divested himself of his protective clothing and, turning his back on them, rang Detective Superintendent Uckfield, head of the Major Crime Team, on his mobile number.

'What?' Uckfield barked down the line. Horton could hear laughter and chatter in the background. He'd joined the force with Steve Uckfield and had been best man at his wedding to the former Chief Constable's daughter, Alison. They'd remained friends, but that friendship had been tested when he'd been suspended on false rape allegations and when Uckfield had appointed that big hulking oaf DI Dennings to his team instead of Horton as promised.

Horton told him what they had without mentioning anything about Johnnie being missing, or the fact that it had crossed his mind this might be him. No point in jumping to conclusions before they had some facts.

'I'm in Cowes,' Uckfield said.

Horton hadn't known Uckfield was on holiday and said so. He assumed that Uckfield was on his motorboat over there. It meant he'd have to call Dennings and he would only cock things up.

But Uckfield said, 'I'm back in tomorrow, deal with it until then. Brief me in the morning, eight o'clock.' He rang off.

At least he was spared Dennings, but the briefing would put back the time of his visit to Teckstone's, which was irritating but unavoidable. Hopefully, Clive Teckstone would be in his office until later tomorrow, and the envelope would certainly still be there.

He saw Maitland approaching and headed towards him.

'There appear to be two seats of fire,' Maitland reported. 'One inside the chamber where the body is, and the other on the bank leading down to the moat. The one in the chamber was lit first, and the second as the arsonist was leaving the scene. I haven't examined either in detail yet. I don't want to disturb the scene before we've mapped, photographed and videoed it.'

Had the fire been set to cover up a death, or had it been used as the murder weapon? Whichever way he looked at it though Horton knew that someone had wanted this body found. But for the fire it could have lain inside that chamber for ages without being discovered.

Maitland continued: 'It's too early to say how the fire was ignited. A flammable liquid most probably; petrol or diesel. I need to make a more thorough investigation to determine that.' He glanced towards a white van pulling in and behind it photographer Jim Clarke's estate car.

Maitland moved off to liaise with SOCO while Horton gave a brief statement to reporter Leanne Payne, if only to get rid of her. She pressed him for more information than 'a body has been discovered by firefighters and we're currently treating the death as suspicious', but there was nothing more he could say at this stage, and even if there were he wouldn't. Wesley took several photographs while he was speaking; Horton hoped the newspaper would use a picture of the fire engines, the fire investigation vehicle or the SOCO team, rather than him.

Questions ran through his mind. How had the victim and the killer got here? There was no car in the small car park or down the lane. The fire setter would have cut it fine returning here to a car after calling the emergency services. But there was nothing to prevent him from parking at one of the other access points to the area, and perhaps after calling the fire brigade he'd returned to it and driven away. Could the victim have come here with the killer, either willingly or under duress? That seemed likely, because Horton thought it a very long way to carry a dead weight. Perhaps this had been a lovers' meeting place. They'd rowed; the killer had hit out, then seeing the victim unconscious or even dead, had tried to cover up his tracks. But why call the fire service? And why so quickly? All these were questions that would need answering, and nothing much could be done on that front until tomorrow when they had more information from Dr Clayton and could view the scene in the daylight.

He stayed until SOCO had finished and Clarke had taken all his photographs and videos. Taylor, the head of the Scene of Crime team, could add nothing to what Maitland had already told him except that no camping equipment or bedding had been found inside the bunker, which confirmed what Horton had already seen. There was no sign of an accelerant. That didn't mean that one hadn't been used, just that no container or evidence had been discovered near the seats of the fire. He'd organize a search of the area for tomorrow.

Maitland said he'd return in the morning to re-examine the scene, and Horton agreed to meet him at nine. That visit to Teckstone's was being put further and further back. But he couldn't do anything about it.

By the time he left the scene it was the early hours of the morning and the crowd had dispersed along with Leanne Payne and the newspaper photographer. He made sure the scene was tightly sealed and the area access points policed for the night then he headed for his boat trying to blot out thoughts of that twisted contorted body, but he knew he wouldn't be able to. The horrifying vision stayed with him, mingling with images of another fire where twenty-three men had lost their lives including Zachary Benham. He tried to shake them off along with the smell of burnt flesh that stung his nostrils and filled his mouth with bile but he couldn't. As the minutes slowly ticked by, the sound and rhythm of the sea reached into the small space of his yacht. For once he found no comfort in it or his isolation. He willed the dawn to hurry, and he vowed that as soon as it did he would call Dr Clayton and beg her to give him something, anything that would rule out the possibility that what he had seen in that dark tunnel buried beneath the blackened earth were the remains of Johnnie Oslow.

TEN

G aye Clayton was in the mortuary already gowned and booted when he arrived at seven thirty. He'd waited an hour after dawn to call her, and on hearing his concerns she'd hurried there as he knew she would. Before heading to the mortuary he'd called Uckfield and given him a quick update, again without mentioning anything about Johnnie. There was no need yet. Not until he at least had the gender, and he prayed Dr Clayton would be able to give him that. Uckfield agreed to postpone his briefing until Horton had spoken to Dr Clayton. In the meantime he said Sergeant Trueman would prepare the crime board and get Clarke's photographs and the SOCOs' initial report. Horton didn't call Bliss. He didn't want her blurting out something that could alert Cantelli. But he'd remembered with relief that Cantelli was going to speak to Stuart Jayston this morning and wouldn't be in the station until later. That gave him some breathing space.

Tom, the brawny auburn-haired mortuary assistant, handed Horton a gown with a look of concern on his big careworn face. He had a penchant for whistling tunes from Rodgers and Hammerstein musicals while he worked, but not this morning.

Horton's stomach churned at the smell of the mortuary and at the blackened human remains on the slab, which didn't look any better than it had last night. In fact it looked even worse in the glare of the mortuary lights. He willed his mind to be objective, told himself he was being fanciful, that it could have no connection with Johnnie's disappearance, but the thought refused to budge. It took all his mental control to blot out the vision of the young handsome eager face, with its determined expression, he'd seen in Sarah Conway's photographs.

'All right?' Gaye asked, concerned.

He gave a curt nod.

She ran her practised eye over the contracted remains. After a moment she began. 'As you can see the body has assumed a pugilistic posture with the limbs flexed as is usual in the circumstances; tissue desiccation and fractures produce body shortening.' She peered more closely. 'There are fractures in the front of the skull, but they could have been caused by the fire.' She pointed to what had once been a forehead.

Horton forced himself to look. 'I need to know if it's a man or woman,' he said anxiously. 'Can you tell me that now?'

She eyed him steadily, her freckled face solemn and her green eyes full of concern. 'Apart from male bones being heavier than female bones there are other indications that provide the gender. A male's skull will generally have a more rounded supraorbital margin, or brow ridge, and a bony glabella, the portion of bone between the eyebrows and nose.' She indicated the area with her gloved fingers. 'The mastoid process, behind the ear, is larger, the mandible more squared, and the forehead slightly backwards-slanting. The nasal cavity of a male will be longer and narrower. I'll take measurements to confirm it, but these are the remains of a man, Andy.'

Horton's heart sank. But it didn't mean it was Johnnie. Surely it couldn't be him. 'Can you give me height or age?' he asked with a hint of desperation.

She eyed him sympathetically, 'Sorry, not yet.' She glanced at the clock on the wall. 'I'll have more for you in about four hours, possibly less. I'll call you as soon as I have anything.'

And he'd have to be content with that, he thought, stepping outside and taking a few deep breaths as he gazed down on the city laid out before him below the hill. Beyond it the Solent looked sluggish and grey, under a heavy sultry sky. He couldn't keep the fact they had a suspicious death from Cantelli, or that it was male, and he knew that Cantelli would leap to the same conclusion as him – *it could be Johnnie* – just as every parent whose child goes missing thinks it's *their* child when a body is recovered from the sea or found in an isolated spot. He looked over to the motorway running from east to west and, beyond it, the patches of woods the other side of the creek where the body had been discovered. It was about two hours to high tide, and he could see the grey water snaking in from Langstone Harbour to the east and Portsmouth Harbour and Tipner Lake to the west, running adjacent and below the motorway. In four hours' time they might have the answer; meanwhile there were things to be done.

He rang Walters who, as usual, answered the phone in CID with his mouth full. Horton told him what had occurred.

'Heard about that on the radio this morning coming into work,' Walters said.

Horton hoped Cantelli hadn't. If he had though he'd have been on the phone to him. 'What did they say?' he asked anxiously.

'Not much. Gave it about two seconds. Sounded like it might be some dosser. Is it?'

'Check to see if any males were reported missing last night.'

Then he called Uckfield and told him what Dr Clayton had said, adding that it could be Cantelli's nephew. He gave him the gist of their investigation so far. Uckfield grunted and huffed but made no comment except to say he'd call up the report. Horton said he would ring in after speaking to Maitland at the scene. He'd be early and Maitland might not be there, but Horton could fill in the time by taking a good look around the area in daylight. He hoped that Bliss would be stuck in a meeting, which would give him another hour's grace before she started bellyaching down the phone at him.

He made for Hilsea Lines where a handful of people were behind the cordon. PC Seaton said he'd had a few complaints from dog walkers who didn't see why a death should prevent them from walking their pooch there but otherwise all was quiet. Horton was pleased to see that Maitland was already there. His van was parked in the small car park but there was no sign of him, which meant he must be where the body had been found.

Horton headed up the track to the top of the bastions and turned on to the footpath eastwards. The view to the motorway on his left was obscured by the dense summer foliage and the sound of the traffic slightly muffled by it. He brushed away the flies and an occasional wasp thinking again that it was a damn long way to carry a body. The bracken either side of him didn't look broken or trampled on, so the victim must have been alive and had either arrived with the killer or had agreed to meet him here. And if the victim was Johnnie then why would he have come here? And where had he been since Wednesday? Horton again wondered if he'd been with a woman.

A blackbird squawked noisily and in panic as he disturbed it, and a robin watched his progress from the branch of a tree unperturbed. Above, the seagulls screeched as they came in on the tide. If the body wasn't Johnnie, then who could it be? Again Horton considered a lover's tiff that had gone wrong, but fire setting was usually committed by men, a woman would probably have just fled the scene, although there was nothing to say the lovers couldn't have been two men. But why call the fire in so early? Why not wait until it was well alight and cause the maximum amount of damage? As he and Maitland had discussed last night, it smacked of someone wanting this body found and quickly, and that didn't sound like a lovers tiff to him.

The acrid smell of smoke was still strong, and the scene, with its gnarled and blackened trees and grass, looked grim as he approached it. He had just turned right on to the narrow track that led to the step down to the tunnel when Maitland emerged wearing a scene suit, strong boots, a hard hat and a mask, which he removed. He had a liver-coloured Labrador with him on a lead, who barked a welcome at Horton.

Maitland said, 'Duke's picked up the scent of an accelerant.' He patted the dog's head, and it wagged his tail enthusiastically. 'Can't say what it is yet, but you might want to get the area searched in case the arsonist discarded it. My guess, though, is this guy either took it away with him or ditched it in the moat or the creek.'

The creek dried out at low tide so the likelihood was it would be in the moat, and dredging that would cost money and take time. Horton couldn't see ACC Dean authorizing that.

Maitland continued: 'As you can see there is no door or grill across this tunnel, like there is on some of the bastions, and no evidence of there having been one. There would have been plenty of oxygen inside to fuel the fire.'

Horton only hoped that whoever the victim was he'd been dead or unconscious before the fire was lit. He certainly hadn't made any attempt to escape it, but perhaps the poor soul had been restrained. He suppressed a shiver and tried not to think of Johnnie. He followed Maitland's gesture as they stepped up the incline and then down on to the bank to see the second seat of fire. Below Horton was the nature trail that ran alongside the moat and along the other side of the creek. He could see the cars speeding along the raised dual carriageway behind that.

Maitland said, 'Arsonists have been known to return to the scene to watch the fire and the ensuing investigation. This guy called in before he started the second fire which suggests he might have returned last night to see the results of his handiwork or he might return today.'

Horton should have thought of that. He tried to remember who he had seen on the outer cordon. Leanne Payne and Cliff Wesley, certainly. Maybe PC Benton would remember who had been in the crowd. And perhaps Wesley had some photographs of the people who had gathered here. But he wouldn't have been the only one snapping away; everyone took pictures these days with their mobile phones, and those pictures would now be on the Internet.

He thanked Maitland and Duke warmly, but instead of turning back the way he'd come he continued walking along the footpath, heading east. He was clearly travelling along the top of the ramparts and was curious to see where the footpath came out. At a small clearing, though, he called Walters.

'No one reported missing last night, guv.'

Perhaps whoever it was hadn't been missed yet. He said, 'Get on to Traffic, ask if they stopped anyone on the main London Road travelling either off the island northwards or south last night between nine and midnight, and get hold of the CCTV footage.' He didn't think they'd be lucky enough to pick up the arsonist's vehicle on camera or that it might have been stopped speeding away from the scene, but you never knew. 'Also contact the newspaper office. Speak to the picture editor and ask him to email over all the photographs Wesley took. Go through them, in particular those that show the crowd. If you need to get the photographic unit to enhance them then do so. See if you can identify anyone known to us or anyone who is at the scene for the duration, particularly anyone who shows up after the fire is reported. Also do a search on the Internet for any photographs posted from last night; check out the photo sharing websites and You Tube in case anyone videoed it. Get the hi-tech crime unit on to it if you need to.'

'No need, guv, this is right up my street.'

Horton knew as much. As long as Walters didn't have to get off his fat arse then he was happy, and he was good at the techie stuff. Horton also thought it worth asking Leanne Payne who she'd spoken to in the crowd or if she'd noticed anyone in particular hanging around.

He called Sergeant Trueman in the major crime team, relayed what Maitland had said, and told him what Walters was doing. Trueman said he had all the reports on the investigation into Johnnie's disappearance and that Bliss was in with Uckfield. 'Sergeant Winton's on his way with a search team.'

He'd just rung off when Cantelli called.

'Walters has just told me about the fire. Is it possible it could be Johnnie?' he asked anxiously.

'It's male, and that's all Dr Clayton can tell us at the moment,' Horton said sympathetically. 'There was nothing left from the fire to indicate it might be him, no clothes or belongings. And it's some distance from where Johnnie went missing, and that was Wednesday, so the chances are it isn't him.'

'The fire was at the Hilsea Lines though.'

The tone of Cantelli's voice caused Horton consternation.

'My dad's ice cream business was based at Hilsea in the 1960s. It backed on to the Lines. My brother and I used to play there as kids a long time before it became a public footpath and nature trail.'

'Did Johnnie ever go there?'

'No. Dad closed the business before he was born to concentrate on the cafés and restaurants.'

'Then it's not relevant, Barney. Uckfield's team has all the reports on the investigation into his disappearance, and it'll be stepped up now.'

'It might be too damn late.'

'There's no indication it is Johnnie.'

He heard Cantelli take a breath. 'No, I guess not.'

Horton knew he wasn't convinced. 'How did it go with Stuart Jayston?'

'It didn't. He wasn't at home. I called into the office but they don't know where he is either. I didn't try his mobile.'

'Leave him for now. We'll catch up with him later. Give Walters a hand.'

Horton continued along the path. The ground was soft from the rain they'd had recently but not boggy, and there was no chance of getting footprint evidence because too many people had passed this way to lift a definite print. After about half a mile the path came to an end. Ahead there was a wire fence and a sign saying it was unsafe to continue. To his right there were steps leading down, and to his left a track which led down to the moat. A train flashed past on the low railway bridge that spanned both the moat and the creek. Across the creek Horton could see police tape and a uniformed officer on his mobile phone.

Horton turned on to the steps. He came out on to a small car park which he was relieved to see was cordoned off with a uniformed officer stationed at the entrance to it. He spun round surprised to see Horton, who crossed to him and showed his ID. Another of the red-bricked bastions was behind him, boarded up. The road to the small car park ended abruptly with a barrier across the entrance to a factory that Horton could see by the sign was Alanco Aviation. This was the end of the Airport Service Road, so named because once Portsmouth had had an airport. No longer. That had gone in 1973. There was still a small railway station serving the area, which was principally populated by factories, warehouses and small business units and reached via the Eastern Road that led off the island of Portsmouth.

He asked the officer if he'd had any visitors.

'A few dog walkers and some workers from the factory wanting to know what had happened.'

'Is that barrier to this car park closed and locked at night?'

'Yes. I took over from PC Williams this morning and he said someone from the council came and opened it last night when the area was sealed off.'

That didn't mean the killer couldn't have parked in the road outside the car park. The factories and businesses would have been shut, and there were no houses here. It was still a long way to carry a body though, but as he'd considered earlier, the victim might then have been alive.

He headed towards the factory and showed his ID to the security officer, who informed him there were cameras at the barrier to the factory entrance, which Horton had already noted. A few minutes later he was in an office behind reception viewing the footage from the previous night. Not a vehicle in sight from seven o'clock until six the following morning except for the police cars.

On the way back to his Harley he ran into Sergeant Winton, who had arrived with four officers to search the immediate area surrounding the fire. Horton gave instructions for them to bag up everything.

'Even used condoms,' Winton said cynically.

'Especially used condoms.'

Horton didn't think the arsonist had stopped to have sex but who knew for certain and fire did turn some people on. Maybe this killer got his jollies that way, and if that was the case then this had nothing to do with Johnnie.

He phoned Uckfield and relayed what Maitland had told him, the results of his own inquiries and what Walters and Cantelli were working on. 'There's a search of the area under way now, and Dr Clayton should have something for us by lunch time.'

'Briefing at twelve,' Uckfield said before ringing off, and that, Horton thought with relief, gave him time to get to Woking and back.

ELEVEN

Horton stared at the reverse of the long Manila envelope that Teckstone had handed him. It was sealed with red wax, under which were two signatures: one of them Dr Quentin Amos's and the other Clive Teckstone's. There were also two sets of handwritten figures: *01.07.05* and *5.11.09*.

'Do these dates refer to when the document was originally deposited and reopened and resealed?' asked Horton, rapidly trying to think if the dates meant anything to him. They didn't, not on first consideration.

Teckstone, an elongated man in his mid-fifties with a bald domed head and small square gold-rimmed spectacles, furrowed his brow. 'No. Dr Amos gave me that envelope last Friday.'

The day after Horton had called on him. His excitement increased, but he made sure not to show it.

Teckstone continued: 'He telephoned me and asked me to visit him urgently. I thought he wanted to change his will but he gave me that envelope and asked me to put it in our safe and to give it to you immediately after his death. The figures were written on there when I signed on the reverse of it.'

Curious. Horton wondered what they could mean. 'And you've no idea of the contents?' he asked.

'Certainly not!' Teckstone looked offended.

'Did Dr Amos give any indication of why he was depositing this and why I should be contacted?'

'No.'

The solicitor had nothing more to add, except to tell him that Amos had no relatives, so he was arranging his funeral and handling the affairs of his estate, which wasn't considerable, and that everything had been left to Amnesty International. Horton asked to be notified of the funeral date. He was keen to know who would show up for it. Professor Thurstan Madeley perhaps? Or Lord Eames? He doubted it. And would there be anyone from 1967 who might have known Jennifer? Would Dormand and Mortimer, the two men in the photograph he had yet to trace, be there? Horton didn't think he'd be so lucky, but he wouldn't mind betting that someone from the intelligence services would show in some guise or another.

Outside, he hesitated. He so badly wanted to rip open the envelope and read the contents. It might tell him what had happened to Jennifer, but this was hardly the place for him to learn that. No, he needed privacy and space. He needed time. And that was something he didn't have.

He thrust it into his jacket pocket while eagerly scanning the car park and the road. No one had followed him and there didn't appear to be anyone watching him from a car parked nearby, but that didn't mean there wasn't someone. He could have been seen visiting Amos last week, especially if Amos's place had been watched after Professor Madeley had duly delivered Amos's name to Horton. Equally, they could have seen the solicitor arrive and leave and waited to see who showed up here. Amos's phone could have been tapped and the call to his solicitor overheard. Or perhaps Amos had muttered something about the envelope while ill and under the influence of medication. The intelligence services must know that Amos was dead.

Horton headed back to Portsmouth. Who would they report to? Lord Eames? What did those dates on the outside of the envelope mean? Were the contents of the envelope damaging to Lord Eames? If the intelligence services were aware of the envelope, when would they come for it? What lengths would they go to to obtain it? The coldness in his stomach told him they might be extreme.

Teckstone had told him that Amos had died in hospital of a heart attack. There was nothing suspicious about it . . . or was there? Horton checked his mirrors. There didn't appear to be anyone following him. Perhaps his death had been accelerated by a massive dose of morphine, and no post-mortem was going to find that. That Amos's apartment would have been searched, and expertly, was a foregone conclusion. He wondered if anything had been found.

His thoughts took him to the station, where he arrived with more questions than answers and a longing to open the envelope, but he had about a minute to make the briefing on time, and he noted with some consternation that Dr Clayton's red Mini was in the car park. She'd come to deliver the results of the autopsy personally, and he didn't think that was a very good sign.

He made straight for the major incident suite where his trepidation was quickly augmented by surprise. Not only were Bliss, Cantelli and Walters present along with Dr Clayton, but standing beside a glowering, florid-faced Uckfield was the slender, immaculately suited, silver-haired Detective Chief Superintendent Sawyer of the Intelligence Directorate. And beside Sergeant Trueman, sitting at a desk, was Agent Harriet Eames. She threw him a look that he thought contained the hint of an apology, but perhaps he just wanted to think that. His suspicions about the real reason for her presence at Cowes Week and her visit to his yacht at Cowes to volunteer her assistance in the search for Johnnie seemed to have been confirmed. She'd known that Johnnie Oslow was missing, and he didn't think she'd heard it first from Scott Masefield.

With a glance at Uckfield, Horton also saw that he'd known about Johnnie's disappearance long before Horton had told him about it this morning. He was guessing most probably yesterday when he'd been summoned to Cowes to be briefed about it, no doubt by Sawyer and Eames. He felt disturbed by this and angry that neither he nor Cantelli had been taken into their confidence. And how would Cantelli feel about it, he thought, throwing him a glance. The sergeant was pale and restless, too anxious to sit. The strain of the last few days was etched deep on his lean face, and with Sawyer's and Eames' arrival that strain looked about to get a lot worse.

Horton's eyes quickly flicked over the two crime boards that DI Dennings was standing between like a bouncer at a nightclub. On one were details and photographs of the remains of the body found in the fire, and on the other was the smiling handsome face of Johnnie along with details of his disappearance. It was horrific to think the two were connected. This was bad enough for him. It must be torture for Cantelli. Horton's glance at Dr Clayton didn't lift his spirits either; she eyed him solemnly and seriously with sympathy in her green eyes. He prepared himself for the worse possible news, which clearly was what Cantelli was doing.

'Glad you could make it,' Uckfield said sarcastically, before nodding at Dr Clayton to begin.

Crisply, she said, 'I can confirm that the victim is male and white. From studying what I have of the skeletal remains, the size of the prostate gland, the jaw and teeth, he was a young man somewhere between the age of twenty and twenty-five, certainly no older than twenty-six.'

Horton tensed. This didn't sound good at all. Cantelli went whiter, and the room was so quiet Horton could hear the sound of Uckfield's clock in his office, and that was digital!

'The post-mortem height is a little difficult to determine because of the shrinkage of tissues and contractures caused by the fire, but I believe he was approximately five foot ten, five eleven.'

Quietly, Cantelli said, 'Johnnie is five foot eleven.'

Dennings wrote it on both boards. No one spoke as the felt pen scratched the surface. Horton took a breath.

Dr Clayton continued: 'Inhalation of soot particles from fire damages the airways, but I found no evidence of soot in the mouth, nares, trachea, or bronchi of the victim and nothing below the level of the vocal cords. If it's any consolation he was dead before the fire was started.'

It wasn't. 'How long before?' Horton asked.

'Difficult to accurately determine. Could have been hours or minutes.'

Which didn't help them much in establishing if the victim was alive on arrival at the Hilsea Lines.

'I was unable to get any blood or urine samples, but I've taken samples from the skeletal muscle and bile which might tell us if he imbibed alcohol or drugs prior to death. There are no bullet wounds, no knife left in the body or traces of it against the remaining tissue and bones. But there is damage to the thyroid cartilage, the Adam's apple, and to the cricoid cartilage and the hyoid bone just above the Adam's apple. The victim was asphyxiated.'

'Strangled?' asked Eames.

'Yes, but the body is too damaged to ascertain if this was by manual throttling or if a ligature was used. I've sent bone fragments for analysis, and we might pick up traces of a fibre if a ligature was used.'

Horton thought that the victim must have been strangled at the site where his body was found.

'There's no evidence of the victim having had any surgery such as removal of tonsils, appendix, gall bladder, and I can't give you the colour of his eyes or hair, but I looked for tattoos, which can still be visible despite the burned skin because tattoo pigment lies encapsulated deep in the skin and is therefore not easily destroyed. I found very small traces of a tattoo on his right arm.'

'Does Johnnie have one?' Horton swiftly asked Cantelli before anyone else did.

'Not that I'm aware of,' he said hesitantly.

Eagerly, Bliss piped up, 'He could have had one done without your knowledge, and recently.'

I think we could all have worked that out, Horton felt like snapping. Instead he gave her an icy stare, but it made no impression. 'Do you know what it's of?' he asked Gaye Clayton.

'It's not easy to say. It looks as though it was some kind of bird. I'll send over some photographs.'

Harriet Eames said, 'I'll contact Nat Boulton, the skipper of *Calista*, and ask him if he or any of the crew know if Johnnie had a tattoo.'

Gaye added, 'I've taken a sample from the femur and the teeth which will give us DNA, and—'

Uckfield broke in: 'Dental records?'

Gaye answered: 'We've taken post-mortem dental radiographs. The Forensic Odontologist will be able to compare them against any you have.'

Cantelli pulled himself up with an effort. 'I'll get Johnnie's dental records to you, Dr Clayton.'

'Thank you.' She looked as though she wanted to add some words of comfort but, before she could, Uckfield thanked her, making it obvious he wanted her to leave. She did so, throwing a sympathetic glance at Cantelli on her way out and another at Horton, which he interpreted as *keep me posted*.

Horton acknowledged it with a flicker of his eyes before turning his gaze on Uckfield. Tersely, he said, 'I take it that, given Agent Eames' and Detective Chief Superintendent Sawyer's presence, Johnnie's disappearance is now high priority and you believe he has either been killed or is in danger and that this has something to do with Xander Andreadis.'

Uckfield eyed Sawyer grimly, who turned his cool gaze first on Horton and then on Cantelli before saying in his mellifluous voice, 'We have evidence which possibly links Johnnie Oslow to a gang of international jewel thieves.'

Horton started with surprise. Cantelli's dark eyes widened and he looked so shocked that Horton thought he was going to faint or laugh. He stared at Sawyer open-mouthed. Even Walters looked nonplussed. DC Marsden shuffled his feet, Trueman looked his usual stoical self and Bliss was frowning for England, while Dennings folded his arms across his massive chest and Uckfield glared at Horton.

Was it the truth? Horton didn't trust Sawyer one iota, but would he lie about this? He flashed a glance at Eames, whose expression belied nothing except the gravity of the situation. God, if it was true, then Johnnie must be dead and that must be his body. But why kill him here? And why at Hilsea Lines?

'What evidence have you got?' he asked before Cantelli could recover from his shock.

Sawyer shifted his gaze to Horton, where he held it for a moment before nodding at Harriet Eames, who rose and crossed to the front of the room. Horton saw Bliss's narrow mouth tighten. She didn't like being upstaged by anyone but particularly by another female and one of lower rank. She also knew of Agent Eames' pedigree and probably reckoned that would guarantee her favours in the promotion stakes. The fact that Eames was not stationed in the division would make little difference to Bliss. Fiercely competitive, she'd see Eames' involvement as a slight on her ability.

Eames began. 'Over the last several months I've been analysing major international jewel thefts that have taken place across Europe, all believed to be carried out by an international and highly sophisticated gang. It's the investigation which originally brought me to Portsmouth in June.'

But she'd been wrong then, thought Horton, she could be wrong again. The case she and he had worked on in June had had nothing to do with the international robberies. Sawyer had told him in June that he believed the jewellery thefts could be connected with the master criminal, Zeus, who he wanted to apprehend and who he believed Jennifer had known and absconded with. Did Sawyer still believe that, or was he feeding them a line? Sawyer showed no emotion, which was no less than Horton expected, but when their eyes locked Horton wondered if he read something behind them. What, though?

Dennings was scowling. Uckfield sniffed, scratched his crotch and perched his large behind on the edge of a nearby desk. Cantelli looked agitated and white with worry.

Eames continued: 'Four of these robberies, which have occurred over the last thirteen months, form a different pattern to the others, and on closer analysis we believe they were carried out by a different gang. The first was in an exclusive villa situated near Port De Saint-Tropez on the twenty-ninth of September. The next following the same pattern was in an expensive property close to Grand Harbour, Malta on the twenty-eighth of October, with the third, again in a top-market villa, near Simpson Bay Marina, St Marteen on the twenty-sixth of February. The last one we've identified was on the twenty-third of April just outside Falmouth Harbour, Antigua. Until recently each was being treated as a separate incident by the police authorities involved, but because the thefts were of such a high value and from influential individuals they were each notified to Europol and hence Interpol. They have all been at properties close to marinas where Xander Andreadis's Superyacht *Calista* has been moored. Johnnie Oslow is a constant factor in all the thefts.'

'But he's not the only one,' Cantelli declared hotly.

Eames turned her pale gaze on him. Horton liked to think there was some sympathy in it but he wasn't sure. There was an aloofness about her now that he hadn't seen before and a hardness that he found disconcerting.

'He isn't,' she said. 'But all the victims are known to Xander Andreadis, all have been on-board *Calista* at some stage, and Johnnie went ashore with Xander Andreadis to all the victims' properties before they were robbed.'

'And that makes him guilty!' cried Cantelli indignantly.

Sawyer smoothly interjected: 'No, Sergeant, but it makes him a possible suspect.'

Cantelli looked about to protest further but Harriet Eames hastily continued, 'Each robbery was carried out before midnight while the victims were away from the property. On two of these occasions – the one in St Tropez on the twenty-ninth of September and the one on the twenty-third of April in Antigua – the victims were dining on-board *Calista* with Xander Andreadis. On the other two occasions the victims were at a restaurant and casino with Andreadis. The sophisticated alarm systems, all different in each of the properties, were expertly disabled. The thieves knew where the jewels were kept, in safes at each of the properties. Each safe was opened using a small amount of highly sophisticated explosives.'

'Didn't any of these victims have security personnel or staff?' asked Trueman.

'No is the answer to your first question, and yes to the second, but the staff weren't working on the nights in question. All the victims were using their holiday villas so hadn't brought all their staff or valuables with them. However, the haul on each robbery was still considerable, with the amounts totalling two and a half million pounds. There's no DNA or fingerprints, and it's our belief that the thieves wore aluminium gloves to avoid leaving traces of DNA and made off with their haul after carefully cleaning the scene with methylated spirits. It was planned to perfection, the timing is precise and there are no signs of panic. They must have had inside information.'

Stung to interject again Cantelli said, 'Any one of Andreadis's crew could have given them that. Johnnie might even have overheard this person passing on the information, or he suspected someone, and because of it he's been killed.' His eyes spun to the gruesome pictures of the charred body.

'We don't know the body is his.'

'Of course it is. You as good as killed him,' he shouted at Eames.

'Sergeant!' barked Bliss.

Cantelli turned his hurt and angry glare on Bliss and opened his mouth to retort but Horton quickly stepped in. 'Why weren't we informed earlier?' he said, his voice tight with fury. 'He's been missing since Wednesday. We could have got on his trail if we'd known then.'

Sawyer answered. 'We didn't know that he was missing. Agent Eames has been working on the investigation alongside Interpol and the Intelligence Directorate but she didn't know about Oslow's disappearance until you and Sergeant Cantelli showed up on Saturday to question Masefield.'

'And you expect us to believe that!' scoffed Horton.

'You can believe what you like, Inspector,' Sawyer answered coldly. 'Interpol tracked Johnnie Oslow to Heathrow. We knew he had a ticket for Portsmouth and that he was to meet Masefield at Oyster Quays. Masefield showed up as arranged, the Border Agency patrol boat confirmed this, and that he left there just after five p.m. on that Wednesday and sailed back to Cowes. What they couldn't confirm was if Johnnie was on-board. Agent Eames was asked to find out on Thursday, but not to question Masefield or any of his crew. Masefield went out early on Thursday, sailing for the day, when he returned she reported that she hadn't seen Oslow on-board.'

Cantelli said, 'Why not tell us *then*? It would have given us an extra two nights and a day to find him.'

Sawyer held Cantelli's despairing countenance with equanimity. 'Agent Eames was not aware of the relationship between Oslow and you, Sergeant.'

'No, but you must have been,' quipped Horton and got a glare from Bliss, but she could glare and bawl him out all she liked. He didn't care.

Sawyer, showing no signs of being rattled or fuelled with guilt, smoothly continued as though Horton hadn't spoken. 'Just because Agent Eames hadn't seen Oslow it didn't mean that he wasn't on-board. She was ordered to make further inquiries during Friday to see what she could establish but without jeopardizing the operation.'

Stiffly, Horton said, 'You thought Johnnie was there to report to this gang, and you wanted to see who he made contact with.'

'If the gang believed we were on to them and running a full-scale investigation into Johnnie Oslow's disappearance they might panic and go underground.'

Horton felt like saying *bollocks*. Instead, fuming inside, he said, 'So you thought that rather than make it official you'd wait and see what would happen and if the thieves would betray themselves. You played with a young man's life.' He glared at Eames. She didn't flinch at the anger in his expression. Then Horton suddenly got it. 'You've got someone in mind but you can't pin anything on them. It's Masefield and his crew, isn't it?'

Sawyer answered. 'We're not sure who the gang is, Inspector. It could be Masefield and his crew but equally they could be a decoy or innocent.'

'Then Sergeant Cantelli and I showed up and started asking questions so you had to think again. You ordered Agent Eames to find out from me what we'd gathered and to offer her help in the investigation.' Horton's eyes flicked to her. She showed no reaction or emotion.

Dennings piped up: 'This gang might not be at Cowes.'

But Horton answered. 'They are, because Johnnie disappeared here and not on route from Sardinia, or in Sardinia.' Addressing Sawyer he said, 'Has it occurred to you that, like Sergeant Cantelli says, Johnnie could be innocent and was coming here to tell his uncle what he suspected and has been killed as a result?'

Sawyer lifted a slender shoulder as if to say *possibly*, but Horton could see he didn't believe that. Cantelli's body stiffened and his fists clenched.

'You don't seem to have got very far with your investigations,' Horton said with acidity.

'This is a very clever gang.'

If someone had followed Johnnie here with the purpose of killing him then they'd had four days to do so and would have cleared out long before now. 'And what about when Johnnie was here in July?

Do you think he was meeting with a member of this gang to brief them about a possible target?' And he wondered whether that target had been Lord Eames, or someone the Intelligence Directorate had set up in order to trap the gang – only it hadn't come off because the gang had got wind of it and of the fact that Johnnie was a liability. 'You must have had Johnnie watched in July.'

Sawyer answered. 'We did, but he gave us the slip. It wasn't Agent Eames. There's no record of him travelling to Portsmouth on the sixteenth of July by any of the ferry services, so whomever he met was on the Island or picked him up by private boat.'

Cantelli shook his head in sorrow and disbelief.

Horton addressed Eames. Harshly, he said, 'Any robberies in this area in July while *Calista* and Johnnie were here?'

'No.'

'Did you ask Andreadis to phone Masefield to wish him luck, to see what he'd say? Or was that just a fluke and an inconvenient one?'

A fluke, he reckoned. Sawyer gave nothing away though, and Eames remained silent. Horton persisted. 'And Masefield had to say Johnnie wasn't there so he had to go through the motions of reporting him missing. And you still hope to catch them! I doubt they'd be stupid enough to carry out a robbery now,' he scoffed.

'No,' Sawyer said regretfully.

Sharply, Cantelli said, 'Have you considered that Xander Andreadis himself could be behind these robberies? He's the one who sent Johnnie here. Perhaps he did so to get rid of him.'

Bliss said, 'I hardly think Andreadis, a billionaire, needs the money.'

'How do you know?' Cantelli turned on her. 'The dire economic conditions in Greece could have affected him badly. His businesses could be in trouble. And he has a certain standard to maintain. He might be desperate.'

Sawyer interjected, holding up a slender hand to silence Bliss, who snapped her mouth shut quickly, 'We have people looking into his finances. And I mean looking.' He paused before continuing: 'The first robbery occurred on the twenty-ninth of September, which means it was planned sometime before that. Have you, Sergeant Cantelli, or any of your family noticed any change in Johnnie over the last year?'

Cantelli shook his head.

Horton didn't think Cantelli would tell Sawyer if there had been, but Cantelli would tell *him*, and maybe Sawyer knew that. Gently, but with an edge of firmness in his voice, Sawyer said, 'This must be difficult for you, Sergeant. Being emotionally involved in an investigation is never easy. Things can get distorted, coloured by personal feelings, and it's not always easy to see straight or accept that things are not how you thought or would like them to be. We all believe we can keep ourselves detached, that we're professionals, but we're also human.'

Horton wondered whether Sawyer was. As Sawyer had addressed Cantelli, Horton had got the uneasy feeling that he was really talking to him. The room was silent. Tension filled the air. After a moment Cantelli said crisply, 'I can handle it, sir.'

'Good, because we need you to liaise with your family. You could unearth vital information. Talk to them, find out everything you can about what Johnnie said to anyone, who he sent texts or who he emailed over the last year eighteen months, who he sent photographs to, what kind of photographs. What he said or didn't say.'

Cantelli gave a curt nod, his expression serious.

Sawyer continued: 'We've confirmed his ticket was surrendered at the Hard railway station. His mobile phone records will be with us today.'

Horton said, 'If the body is that of Johnnie, why kill him now, why set fire to it, and why there?'

'That's what we intend to establish,' Sawyer said smoothly. He nodded at Uckfield, who hauled himself up. 'DC Marsden, along with the information analyst, will work on the phone records. DCI Bliss will oversee both investigations, working with me.'

Horton didn't think Uckfield would be too pleased about that but guessed the order had come from ACC Dean via Sawyer. 'DI Dennings will follow up the investigations into Oslow's disappearance, collate everything that comes in from it and liaise with Agent Eames – who will also act as liaison between here and the European operation. Sergeant Trueman will oversee all operations in the Major Crime Suite, including that of our victim. Inspector Horton, you will follow up any leads concerning the body at Hilsea Lines; Walters will assist.'

Horton said, 'We need a team conducting a house-to-house in the area. The killer and victim must have arrived by car. Someone might have seen it, or it could still be in the area.'

Trueman nodded. He'd organize that.

Horton added, 'Do we go with a public appeal on Johnnie?'

Sawyer answered: 'Not yet.'

Horton was thankful for that.

Uckfield dismissed the team and returned to his office with Sawyer and Bliss in tow. Harriet Eames turned to address Trueman.

In the corridor outside, Cantelli addressed Horton. Morosely, he said, 'They want me out of the way.'

'Of course they do,' Horton replied as they headed down the stairs, with Walters following them. 'But Sawyer's got a point. You might pick up something from the family, even if it seems insignificant.'

'Do you believe them about Johnnie being involved in these robberies?'

Did he? He recalled what Eames had said to him on his boat on Saturday night about Johnnie having been led astray once and posing the possibility he could have been again. She'd been considering the jewellery thefts and probing him to see if Johnnie might have said or hinted at it to Cantelli. He'd been used by her, and he didn't much care for it.

Cantelli continued, 'I can't believe he'd do such a thing.' Then he added despondently, 'But then I couldn't believe he'd commit arson.'

'There's a lot we don't know, Barney, and this is all just speculation at the moment. They've got no hard evidence he's involved.'

'Maybe they have and they're not telling us everything.'

That was highly likely, but he didn't say. Cantelli hurried off to get details of Johnnie's dentist.

On his return to CID Horton wondered if he might get more out of Sawyer alone. He might even do a trade off. His help on pooling what he had on his mother's disappearance and volunteering to act as bait for Zeus in exchange for Sawyer's full cooperation on Johnnie's disappearance. He wasn't sure it would work though, and the information Amos had given him, in the envelope nestling against his chest, might knock Sawyer's theory of Zeus right out of the window. He hoped so. He was tempted to open it. He knew he should, but he couldn't, not here. He wanted to be alone, and he also knew that part of him was dreading it. He didn't want to know what was inside the envelope for fear that it would change things forever.

Walters had returned to his desk, his computer and his sandwich.

'Anything?' Horton asked, referring to the images on the computer screen that Walters was studying.

'Nothing so far. And no arsonists on the files matching the pattern of this incident, or anyone in the photos, but I'm still wading through them.'

He left Walters to it and headed for his office, his brain whirling with this new information that Sawyer and Eames had tossed into the pot. He was supposed to be investigating the death at the Hilsea Lines, but everything that could be done was being done. And what if it were Johnnie? What if Sawyer and Eames were right and Johnnie was mixed up in the robberies? But if Johnnie had discovered something illegal and was an innocent victim in this then what would he have done? Confided in his uncle? Possibly. As had already been suggested, perhaps he'd been on his way to do that and had been kidnapped and killed. Was there anyone else he was close to who he could have sought help from? Yes, there was, he suddenly realized. A man who Johnnie owed a great deal to. One who had been like a father to him. And, injected with new energy, Horton grabbed his helmet and jacket and hurried out, calling to Walters to contact him if he came up with anything.

TWELVE

'Andy, it's good to see you.' The square-set, grey-haired man beamed as he rose from behind a desk more cluttered with paperwork than Horton's and stretched out a large hand. Horton took the firm grasp and felt flattered by Don Winscom's genuinely warm welcome. He also felt guilty that he'd not been to see him for some months, and neither had he done anything to help the sailing charity he ran except to send along a few wayward boys and a couple of girls. 'Or should I be wary because you're here on business?'

'I am, but it's nothing to do with any of your current crew.'

'I'm glad to hear that. Have you got time for a coffee? We could go to Hardy's and grab one. There's hardly enough room to swing a cat in this beach hut of an office.'

Horton agreed. The café bar and bistro was just a few steps away and despite it doing a brisk trade they found a vacant table overlooking the marina across the road.

'I'd like to talk to you about Johnnie Oslow,' Horton said, taking a sip of his coffee.

'Sergeant Cantelli's nephew?'

'Yes. This mustn't go any further at the moment, but he's gone missing and we're very concerned about him.'

'Good God. I thought he was working for Xander Andreadis.'

'He is, but he arrived in Portsmouth last Wednesday for Cowes Week and hasn't been seen since. When was the last time you heard from him?'

'Must be about a year ago.'

Horton felt the disappointment keenly. He'd been banking on getting a break here, but that now seemed unlikely.

'He came to see me when he was home visiting his mother. He went out for a sail on one of our yachts. Is he in trouble?' Winscom asked, his big malleable face creasing up with concern.

'I don't know. He might be. I was wondering if he'd confided in you.'

Winscom shook his head and drank his tea.

So, dead end. But Horton wasn't going to give up yet. He said, 'When Johnnie was on the sailing courses here and during the time he worked as skipper for you, was he close to anyone? A girlfriend, or someone he went drinking with?'

Winscom considered this. 'I don't remember anyone. He was very popular, but he was also very determined to work hard and put the past behind him. His experience of being convicted and getting a suspended sentence shook him up considerably.'

Horton knew that and was convinced that Johnnie couldn't have willingly returned to crime. 'Did he ever talk about the gang he went around with?'

'No. It was as though he wanted to obliterate them from his mind. In fact he didn't talk about the past at all. He concentrated hard on the sailing and then passing his Competent Crew and Day Skipper exams. I was sorry to see him go, but it was time he moved on.'

'How did he get the job with Andreadis?'

'We entered a couple of teams at Cowes and Johnnie's team won every race he entered by a long head. He was approached by Andreadis himself, who was also there that year, racing. Is he there now?'

'No, but he's got a team entered, the one that Johnnie was due to sail with; Scott Masefield's the skipper.'

'Masefield? Well, that figures.'

'How?' asked Horton, surprised. 'You know him?'

'I should. He spent some time with us.'

Horton didn't bother to disguise his interest, why should he? But he hid his suspicions: yet another link with Masefield. Had Masefield struck up a friendship with Johnnie based on this common background in order to pump Johnnie for inside information on Andreadis's wealthy friends?

'Tell me about Masefield,' he said, sitting forward.

'He was referred to us by the services' community health department.' Winscom put down his mug. 'Over the last two years the charity's remit has expanded to include rehabilitating veterans and serving officers experiencing mental health issues. We get quite a few who find sailing works as a therapy to help them overcome their problems. It doesn't work for everyone, but we've had some successes and Masefield was certainly more successful than even I had anticipated.'

Horton caught a hint of bitterness behind Winscom's words, or was it regret?

'We get a fee,' Winscom continued, 'which is very welcome, but times are difficult, finances are tight. That's why we haven't entered any boats for Cowes this year. We've lost a sizeable proportion of our government funding because of these wretched austerity cuts, which don't seem to be doing much except making everything worse. And like many charities we're fighting for the small amount of money from an ever-dwindling pot because of the recession.'

Horton thought it was about time the station did something to help raise money for them. He made a mental note to act on it.

Winscom continued: 'We're fortunate that we have some very wealthy and generous patrons, individual businessmen who support us, otherwise we would be up the creek without the proverbial paddle. Xander Andreadis *was* one of our supporters until last year when he switched his funds to a new sailing venture. A very worthy one, but . . .'

'Damaged ex-servicemen and Scott Masefield's proposition,' answered Horton. This visit was turning out to be worthwhile after all.

'Yes. I don't begrudge him the money, and I wish him well with his venture. I just wish that Xander Andreadis hadn't decided to switch all of his charitable funds towards it and leave us in the cold. But then Xander is a businessman and Masefield can be very persuasive.'

Horton's interest was deepening. It was sounding much more likely that Masefield was mixed up with Johnnie's disappearance. 'You don't like him,' Horton asked, picking up the vibes.

'I didn't say that.' Then Winscom smiled. 'I forgot I was talking to a policeman, an expert at reading undertones. But the kind of money he's given Masefield for one boat and one crew could have helped a hundred of my people. But, like I said, Andreadis is a businessman, and if Masefield and his crew win races then that's good business for Andreadis.' Winscom eyed Horton over the top of his mug. 'And it's my own fault. I was the one who mentioned Xander Andreadis to Masefield.'

This was proving illuminating. How it helped him find Johnnie though, Horton didn't know, but there were far too many links here for him to ignore. 'So tell me how this referral system works,' he said eagerly.

'Those who get referred to us by the services' community mental health department come from all branches of the services: navy, army, air force, marines. They learn how to sail alongside the young people we get referred by you and other agencies. For those who already have some experience of sailing, like Scott, we put them crewing with a team and then if they show ability make them up as skippers.'

'Do any of them talk about their experiences in the forces?'

'No. That's part of the deal. Just as it is with the young people you refer to us. Their past is irrelevant. It's how they behave and operate here and now that counts. If they talk outside the training then that's entirely up to them. Of course, it doesn't suit everybody, and we've had a few drop out or go off the rails, both from the services and from you.'

'And Scott Masefield took your idea of rehabilitation and sold it to Xander Andreadis.'

'Masefield is a natural sailor, an excellent team leader and skipper. I'm sure he'll be very successful.'

'Do you know any of his crew?' Horton recalled the fit athletic group of men with their wary eyes and reserved manner. 'Eddie Creed, Martin Leighton, Craig Weatherby, Declan Saunders?'

'Only Martin Leighton. He was here, but not at the same time as Scott. He joined six months after Masefield had left.'

'I'd like a list of everyone who was here at the same time as Johnnie.' Horton thought that there might be someone he'd become friendly with or met up with recently and who he might have confided in. And there was still the chance that Sawyer was wrong. Horton wasn't ruling out the possibility that Johnnie had become infatuated with a woman and gone off with her.

'I'll have to go through the database. I'll call you as soon as I have it.'

And there was no harm in checking out Masefield and Leighton. Masefield and his crew had claimed not to know Johnnie, but Horton wasn't so sure they were telling the truth. Even though both Masefield and Leighton had been at the sailing charity at different times to Johnnie it was possible that one of them had discovered that Johnnie worked for Andreadis and had used that information to target him. But none of Masefield's crew could be responsible for the charred body at Hilsea. They'd all been in Cowes last night. *If* they were responsible though and the body *was* Johnnie's then they had to be working with someone.

He asked Winscom who had referred Masefield and Leighton.
'Dr Claire Needham.'

He got the address of the community health department from
Winscom, promised to return for a sail as soon as he could, and
then set off, only to discover that on Tuesdays Dr Needham worked
in her private clinic. Armed with her address, he headed there
and within ten minutes found himself looking up at a large cream-
painted Victorian house in one of the most prestigious parts of
Southsea, not far from the Common.

After announcing himself in the intercom at the double wooden
gates he was permitted entry. Clearly, clinical psychologists did very
well for themselves, he thought, if this house and the very expensive
motor with the personalized number plate standing on the drive was
anything to go by.

He noted with approval the security cameras above the three
stone arches that guarded the front entrance, and there were other
cameras at several strategic points around the two-storey house. He
was being watched. He didn't mind. This property would be a target
for some of the lowlife dregs of humanity that lived in the city.

The door was opened by a stocky dark-haired man in his late
forties with an impressive display of muscles bulging from beneath
the short-sleeved white T-shirt. His deep brown eyes studied Horton
coolly before carefully scrutinizing his ID card. Perhaps clinical
psychologists employed bodyguards, thought Horton, stepping
inside. The man didn't introduce himself, in fact he didn't speak,
but opened a door on Horton's left and nodded him inside. The door
closed quietly behind him. He was alone.

Horton eyed the elegant, tastefully and expensively furnished
pale-yellow lounge. He looked for cameras and couldn't see any
but he got the impression he was being watched. He wondered if
Dr Needham had been threatened by one or more of her unbalanced
patients.

Peering out of the open long sash window into a beautifully
tended and landscaped garden he caught the strong smell of freshly
mown grass and the sight of the man with muscles digging over a
flower bed. As though sensing his gaze, he straightened up and
looked towards Horton for a full four seconds before continuing to
dig with a slow methodical rhythm. Horton wondered who he was
and at the same time whether Dr Needham thought Horton himself
might be a prospective patient. Police officers suffered a high level

of stress not only from having to tolerate low life criminals and witness the appalling things people did to one another but also because of the occupational hazard of having the living daylights kicked out of them and worse.

The door behind him opened, and he turned to find a tall, shapely and long-legged woman in her early forties. Her short blonde hair framed an exquisitely made-up face, and she was studying him with hazel eyes that oozed charm and sexuality. She was dressed in tight black trousers and a small floral patterned silk top that accentuated her breasts and nipped in at her waist before folding gently over her hips. He could see her white bra beneath it. She wore low-heeled sandals and advanced towards him with an outstretched hand; she had long nails, varnished pink. He didn't look to see if the colour matched that on her toes. He knew it would.

'I'm Dr Needham,' she announced in a slightly deeper voice than he'd expected. It added a hint of warmth to the hazel eyes, which otherwise would have been a little too probing and possibly a little too cool. Her handshake was firm. Horton returned the pressure. 'I'm not what you were expecting,' she said with a smile, showing very white, even teeth.

He didn't think he'd shown any reaction but maybe he had. 'I wasn't sure what to expect,' he said truthfully, but now that he'd seen her he wondered what Scott Masefield and Martin Leighton had made of her, and she of them. Had either or both of them fancied her and tried it on? He wouldn't have blamed them if they had.

She gestured him into the room behind her. There was no couch as such but the leather chaise positioned between two long sash windows clearly substituted for one. The room was furnished in a more modern style than the one he'd just vacated; along with the leather chaise there was a modern black ash desk with a laptop computer on it and a matching low coffee table and four easy leather armchairs around it. Dr Needham gestured him into one before taking the seat next to him. The scent of her spicy perfume and her closeness caused him a few moments of unease. He sensed an air of gentle teasing about her that he found both sexually arousing and alarming. Maybe she lured her male patients into a sexual trap and once enslaved they opened up their minds and hearts to her. He steeled himself to guard against her charms, which wasn't that difficult for him; all he had to do was remind himself she was a psychiatrist, a breed he trusted almost as little as some of the crooks he had to deal with, after having been subjected to some members of the species as a troublesome child.

He apologized for disturbing her and showed his ID. 'I'd like your help with a current investigation.'

'You're here officially?'

He wasn't sure if the small frown puckering her smooth forehead was of irritation or surprise because she'd misjudged his visit. 'You can bill us for your time,' he answered, a little more curtly than he had intended.

'I didn't mean that,' she dismissed lightly and pleasantly, but he caught a slight tension in her manner that hadn't been there before. 'It's just not normal procedure.'

'This is not a normal case, if there is such a thing.'

'Not in my experience.'

No, and not in his either. 'Time is critical, and I thought I'd take a chance that you were available and willing to see me, but if you'd rather we request your assistance formerly then—'

'No, not at all. I don't have any patients on a Tuesday. I clear my paperwork.'

He flashed a glance at her desk where there was no evidence of paper of any kind, a bit like DCI Bliss's. 'You seem to have succeeded. Wouldn't like to do mine, would you?'

She laughed lightly, and he found himself comparing it, and her, with Sarah Conway. There was almost twenty years between their ages. Their personalities, mannerisms and occupations were vastly different, and yet he was betting that both women knew the effect they had on men, and both used it to their advantage.

'How can I help, Inspector?' she asked, eyeing him curiously.

He put his full attention on the reason why he was here. 'I understand you assess those who are traumatized by their experiences in the services and refer some patients to Go About, the sailing charity.'

'I do, yes,' she answered, clearly perplexed by his line of questioning.

'Scott Masefield and Martin Leighton being two of those who have been referred by you.'

She sat back, her expression now solemn. 'I can't tell you anything about that. It would be breaching patient confidentiality.'

'Pity, because I was hoping I wouldn't have to request a warrant to see their medical files.'

'Even with one I doubt you'd get access unless the navy give you permission. Why the interest in them?'

'It's my turn to use the confidentiality let-out clause, but they could have something to do with the disappearance of a young man whose life could be in danger and the suspicious death of a man found at Hilsea Lines last night.'

'I heard about that on the news this morning. But I still can't give you the information you need.'

'Not even if it means saving a young man's life?'

'I'd be only too willing to help if I could, but not without the proper authorization.'

'I didn't think you'd be a "more than my job's worth" sort of person,' he retorted, trying to provoke her, but he was wasting his breath.

'You don't know what sort of person I am, Inspector. But I *am* a professional and I *do* respect my patients' confidentiality.'

Horton knew she wouldn't budge. 'OK, then perhaps you can give me some general background. How do service personnel get referred to you?'

She sat back and crossed her legs, studying him for a moment before speaking. 'In 2001 a government review resulted in the treatment of defence mental health patients moving from inpatient care to community-based services in the form of military Departments of Community Mental Health. Since then there has been a number of comprehensive studies and a further review looking into the support given to service personnel and veterans who may suffer from mental health problems because of their experiences in the services. To cut a long story short a number of initiatives resulted from that, including providing early intervention for those suffering from stress, provided by experienced clinicians.'

'Such as yourself.'

'Yes. I work with both veterans and serving members who experience stress and mental health problems. Most mental health problems treated in the military are the same as those for any civilian: a difficulty coping when something happens, such as a relationship ending. This can create anxiety or depression, a dependency on drugs or alcohol.'

Tell me about it, thought Horton, making sure to keep his expression completely neutral. Not that he'd turned to drugs, but he'd certainly turned to drink.

'Service men and women are also more likely to be exposed to violent and traumatic events while serving. But not everyone in the services who has experienced violence is damaged mentally, just as not every police officer or firefighter is damaged mentally by what they see and have to deal with. The services are good for many people. Not everyone suffers from Post Traumatic Stress Disorder.'

'But some do?'

'Yes.'

'Masefield and Leighton?'

'Hospitalization for a mental health problem in a military context is associated with a low rate of retention in service, whereas an outpatient occupational mental health service returns a substantial number of patients to occupational fitness within the armed forces. That is where I and my colleagues come in.'

He noted she hadn't answered his question.

'We offer specialized psychiatric services, including psychiatrists, community psychiatric nurses, clinical psychologists, mental health social workers and occupational therapists. Don Winscom's sailing charity is just one organization which provides occupational therapy for those veterans and serving members of the forces who are likely to respond to it.'

'On your recommendation.'

'Not just mine but the teams who are looking after that individual.'

'And it's worked so well for Masefield that he has enlisted the help of a millionaire to buy him a yacht and aims to set up a charity to help service personnel and veterans by competing in yacht racing as therapy.'

'He does? That's excellent news.'

'You didn't know.'

'He's no longer my patient.'

'How long does someone remain a patient?'

'It depends. Usually a year, possibly longer if they have underlying problems.'

'I won't bother asking you how long Masefield and Leighton were patients because I doubt you'll tell me.'

'No.' She smiled.

He rose. She studied him quizzically for a moment, and he thought how easy it would be to be seduced by her. 'Were Eddie Creed, Craig Weatherby and Declan Saunders your patients?'

She stood up and eyed him steadily. 'You'll need that warrant, Inspector.'

'Then I'd better get back and request it. Thank you for your help.' He stretched out a hand. She took it while studying him evenly and candidly. Oh yes, he thought, it would be very easy to slip into bed with her, and he didn't think she'd complain; on the contrary, he was getting a very strong signal that she'd do anything but. Maybe she'd already been to bed with Mister Bodyguard. He could be her husband or partner. He didn't ask and he didn't need to know, but as he left he saw the man standing at the corner of the house watching him.

His visit to Dr Needham hadn't got him any further forward, but as he headed back to the station he wondered if Sawyer had already accessed that crew's medical records. If Sawyer did suspect Masefield and his crew of those international jewellery raids then Horton was betting he had access to everything, including how much each of them had weighed when born. And he suspected that Sawyer wasn't about to disclose any of it to Uckfield. Then, as though his thoughts had conjured up the big man, he pulled into the car park to see Uckfield marching towards him with a grim look on his craggy face.

'Drink,' he barked.

It wasn't a question but a summons. Horton hid his surprise and resisted the temptation to glance at his watch. It must be about half six by now. As he climbed into Uckfield's BMW he wondered what was so urgent and sensitive that Uckfield wanted to relay it away from the station. Then his heart plummeted. Uckfield must have a positive ID on the body, and they must be on their way to break it to Cantelli. Agent Eames must have reported back from her conversation with Andreadis's skipper that Johnnie had a tattoo which matched the location and vague description Dr Clayton had given them. But Uckfield had said 'drink' and they were heading north on the motorway out of the city, the wrong direction for Cantelli's house, so it couldn't be that. Whatever it was that Uckfield had to say though, Horton wasn't sure he was going to like it, because it was clear that Uckfield had been looking out for him and that wasn't a good sign by any reckoning.

THIRTEEN

'**D**o you believe all that bollocks about international jewellery thefts?' Uckfield swallowed a large mouthful of his half pint of bitter and glowered at the city spread out before them as though it had done something to personally annoy him.

Horton eyed him closely. 'Do you?'

'No, I bloody don't.' Uckfield swivelled his gaze back on Horton. 'I didn't the last time Sawyer shoved his beaky nose into one of my cases and I believe it even less now.'

'Then what's he doing here?'

'I was going to ask you that.'

'How should I know?' Horton said, surprised, and yet deep inside him he thought of Zeus. He wondered what Uckfield had picked up from his sources. Sawyer was hardly likely to confide in Uckfield, but perhaps Sawyer had mentioned to Uckfield that he was interested in getting Horton seconded to the Intelligence Directorate. 'Detective Chief Superintendent Sawyer doesn't confide in me.'

'But Agent Eames might.' Uckfield eyed him pointedly with a grotesque leer.

'There's no reason why she should,' Horton said somewhat stiffly, keeping his gaze steadily on Uckfield. Just what had been said in Cowes on Monday night when Uckfield had been there? Or was Uckfield implying that Harriet Eames fancied him?

Uckfield sniffed, shrugged and let it go. After a moment he said, 'Funny how she's shown up with Sawyer twice and how she seems to be spending more time here than at The Hague where she's *supposed* to be working.'

Yes, wasn't it? Horton hadn't checked that she really was working at The Hague; maybe he should. Even if he did though, he guessed whoever he asked would be primed to confirm it. Unless he could find someone he knew personally who was working on secondment there and could pump them for information on the quiet. Perhaps she, like her father, was working for the intelligence services. Or perhaps she was working with the Intelligent Directorate. He said,

'Maybe there is some truth in these jewellery robberies, and maybe Johnnie Oslow is involved.'

'Yeah, and maybe I'm the fairy on the Christmas tree.'

The mind boggled. Any Christmas tree would buckle under Uckfield's weight. Horton suppressed a fleeting smile. 'The Andreadis family are very wealthy, and they're personal friends of Lord Eames. Xander's probably pulled some strings to bring in the big guns.'

'For a lad of twenty-three, only one amongst his hundreds of employees, who he'd normally think has gone off with a tart!' scoffed Uckfield.

He was right, but what was he driving at? 'Then why spin us this yarn about jewellery thefts if it's not true? We can easily check it out.'

'Trueman's working on it when the blonde beauty isn't breathing down his neck, and before you suggest it I've also got him checking out Masefield and his jolly jack-tar crew.'

Good. Trueman had contacts everywhere. Horton said, 'And that seems even more relevant now. Two of them sailed with the same charity as Johnnie.' He told Uckfield about his visit to Don Winscom and Dr Needham, adding, 'So if it isn't jewellery robberies or a woman, what do you think is going on, Steve?'

'Blackmail.'

'You're not serious?' asked Horton, surprised.

'Perfectly.'

'You think Xander Andreadis is being blackmailed?'

Uckfield nodded and swallowed his beer.

'By Johnnie!' said Horton incredulously.

'By someone who used Johnnie Oslow to get the information they need, and now they have it they've disposed of him.'

Horton considered this. Maybe it wasn't so far fetched. But would Johnnie have had access to highly sensitive information? He said as much.

'Why not?' was Uckfield's prompt reply. 'He's been working on-board that private yacht and racing with Xander Andreadis's team for some years. He's probably picked up a great deal, being a bright lad. There must be some shady dealings in Andreadis's past.'

Or a member of his family, thought Horton, recalling what Harriet Eames had told him on Saturday night about Christos Andreadis returning to Greece from England with enough money to kick-start his business fortune even though he'd only been barman, and Giorgio Andreadis's love of art, antiques and women.

Uckfield said, 'No one gets that rich without soiling their hands somewhere along the line.'

'Would Xander tell the police that he was being blackmailed? Surely he'd want it kept quiet if it was something illegal. Wouldn't he have paid up and then thought of a way to get even, or perhaps hired a private agency to handle it?'

'Maybe he struck a deal with Interpol: help me get this black-mailer off my back and I'll give you something you need on someone. Maybe Xander Andreadis has information on these jewellery thefts or some other villain, and the latter's much more plausible if you ask me.'

Zeus? Or was Horton just getting obsessed about him? 'And whatever Andreadis is being blackmailed over, Sawyer doesn't want us to know about it.' He wondered if Johnnie could have met this blackmailer or someone working with him on the sixteenth of July. Could he have been in on a cut? Or perhaps he had no idea that what he was handing over was so valuable and dangerous. He said, 'How are Europol getting on at digging deep into Xander's finances?'

'I'll ask Agent Eames,' Uckfield said in a manner that left Horton in no doubt that he didn't expect to get a truthful answer. 'We keep this blackmail theory to ourselves,' he added, tossing back his beer.

Horton had no intention of sharing it with anyone. 'If it is black-mail then we're not going to be told about it.'

'No. We follow up the leads we've got on Johnnie, of which there are none, and we carry on investigating the death at the Lines.'

'What did they tell you in Cowes last night? Don't play dumb, Steve. I know you were summoned there. To the Castle Hill Yacht Club, was it?'

Uckfield sniffed and scratched the inside of his thigh. 'Yeah. Sawyer just gave me the gen he spouted today about the thefts and Johnnie being involved, and then you phoned with news of the burnt offering.'

'Only Sawyer?'

'And the blonde beauty.'

'No one else.'

'No.'

Horton searched the craggy face to see if that was the truth. He thought it was. He tossed back the remainder of his coke and fell into step beside Uckfield as they headed to the car. 'So if the body hadn't been found, what were your instructions?'

'To sit on the missing persons report for the rest of the week and make sure Bliss did the same.'

'That stinks,' Horton said angrily, halting.

'Yeah, and I told the bastard that.' Uckfield zapped open the car but didn't climb in.

'But you'd have done it.'

Uckfield shrugged. 'That wouldn't have stopped you. And you don't report to me.'

Horton could read between the lines. Bliss would have obeyed without question, and his own continued investigations would have got him reprimanded unless he'd been pushed on to working on something else. Cantelli would have been ordered to take some time off. Would Uckfield really have done nothing? He valued his career. 'I take it that Dean was in on it.'

'Yes.'

Horton liked to think that Uckfield would at least have helped with the investigation into Johnnie's disappearance, but he wasn't certain. He felt bitter and sickened by the fact that the force wouldn't even look out for its own.

As they headed back to the station in silence he mulled over what Uckfield had said. It was another possible theory but it didn't get them any closer to finding out where Johnnie was or whether his was the body in the fire last night. They seemed to have a lot of theories and very little facts. And none of the latter seemed to be forthcoming either when Horton entered the incident suite some half an hour after Uckfield. Walters had left him a message saying he'd drawn a blank with trying to identify anyone acting suspiciously at the scene of the fire and the traffic cameras had come up with zilch. The house-to-house was progressing, and tomorrow Walters would begin checking out the vehicle licence numbers that uniform were collecting from the residents to possibly identify any vehicle that wasn't usually parked in that area. In the incident suite Dennings reported that Sergeant Winton and his search team had returned from the Hilsea Lines with twenty black bags of rubbish, which had pleased the lab no end but they'd found no evidence of any accelerants. And Agent Eames had contacted the skipper of *Calista* to ask if Johnnie had a tattoo, but reported that no one seemed to remember seeing one. Horton had rapidly scrutinized the photographs that Sarah Conway had sent over of Johnnie and couldn't see any tattoo. That didn't mean to say he hadn't had one done recently, though.

It was dark and raining by the time Horton climbed on his boat. He threw his keys on the table and ran a glass of water, drinking it while listening to the rain hitting the deck and the wind whistling around the yacht. No one had followed him and no one had been waiting for him. The pontoon was silent, no strange boats moored up close by and no one moored up for the night on the visitors' pontoon outside the Cill or waiting to enter the marina when the Cill gate opened on the rising tide.

He pushed aside thoughts of Johnnie and of what Uckfield had told him and plucked the Manila envelope from his jacket pocket. He stared at it, recognizing a reluctance to open it not because he was afraid of what it might contain but because of what it might not. Would this be another blind alley along which he was to stumble? He feared the worse, like some school kid anticipating his exam results and expecting them to be dire. But he could put it off no longer.

Sliding open the kitchen drawer he picked out a sharp knife and then, taking a deep breath, slit the envelope under the red wax and drew out the contents. There were two sheets of white paper, folded lengthways in three. He unfurled them, his heart beating fast, the sweat pricking his brow, hardly daring to hope that Dr Amos had revealed facts about Jennifer that would explain her disappearance.

'What the hell?' Quickly, he turned them over. He held them up against the light. There wasn't even a watermark. He was staring at nothing. Just two pieces of blank paper. He peered into the envelope, there had to be something. But there was absolutely sod all. Fury replaced his shock. Who was taking the piss – Quentin Amos? Or had someone intercepted what had been in this envelope and replaced it with blank pieces of paper? Were they laughing at him even now?

Disgusted, hurt, disappointed and angry he threw the paper and envelope on to the table. All that anxiety, anticipation, excitement for nothing. The belief that at last he might learn something about his mother had come to this. How could they do this to him? One fucking disappointment after another. It was a sick joke, and it was on him. How could he have been so naive as to think it would be so simple? That he'd only have to open the envelope and all would be revealed; the reason why his mother had left London, why she'd come to Portsmouth, who his father might be and ultimately why she'd vanished one November day in 1978, just like some sodding fairy tale. He was a fool. Memories of his childhood, spent in those shit, awful children's homes, flashed before him, tormenting him. His life destroyed because of what he'd experienced, because of her and because of Lord Bloody Eames and his stupid intelligence games. He wanted to lash out at someone, anyone. Lord Eames was top of his list, and if he had been anywhere near Cowes now he'd have stormed into that yacht club or Eames' house and shaken the superior little shit until he got the truth.

He rammed his clenched fist on the table. He wanted to get blind paralytic drunk, to sink into oblivion and forget his past, forget the bloody future. He could go out now and buy a bottle of whisky; the supermarket was open all night. He grabbed his jacket and swept up his keys but he got only as far as the cockpit. There he stood in the driving rain almost as though it had shocked him into reality. He let it pour off his face ignoring the fact that he hadn't even bothered to put on his jacket. What stopped him he couldn't precisely say, but a small voice inside told him that they would have won if he touched one drop of liquor, they would crow with delight if he got blind drunk, and through all this he saw in his mind's eye young Johnnie Oslow as he'd known him when he was sixteen: angry, hurt, bewildered, afraid. And then his transformation on that sailing course: confident, laughing, enjoying life. And finally he saw Cantelli's ashen, terrified face. How could he let Cantelli down? He couldn't. He had to find Johnnie or at least the truth behind his disappearance, otherwise Cantelli and his family would live with the uncertainty, just as he had, for the rest of their lives. It would destroy them.

And how could he let smooth bastards like Lord Eames win? He couldn't. That was what they wanted. As his fury ebbed, his brain began to function again. Had someone from the intelligence services broken into Teckstone's office in the last week, opened the safe, extracted the contents of the envelope, replaced them with blank paper and managed to reseal it? Or had it been a member of staff? Was Teckstone himself guilty? No, Horton didn't think so, and any break-in would have been reported. He would check with the local police just to make certain, but the one factor that dispelled that theory were those dates on the reverse of the envelope. He descended into the cabin and studied the back of the envelope. They had to mean something, especially if Amos had deliberately put blank sheets inside the envelope.

He sat down heavily and stared at the figures. Perhaps Amos was trying to tell him something and had made his message obscure because he knew the intelligence services were watching him and might discover the envelope. If so, then why hadn't they taken it and destroyed it? Or altered the figures on the outside? The figures didn't appear to have been tampered with. Had Amos been *instructed* to leave this cryptic message for him?

He rubbed his forehead. Did this have any link with Sawyer's theories about Zeus and his mother running off with him? How could it, though? Amos wouldn't know about that. No, he was way off beam there, but maybe he should talk to Sawyer, who so far had made no fresh attempt to talk to him about Zeus or try and persuade him to flush Zeus out. Why hadn't he? Perhaps he was waiting for the right moment. And perhaps tomorrow Horton would give him that.

He knew sleep wouldn't come easy, so he switched on his laptop and keyed in the dates, just as he'd done before with the thirteenth of March, 1967. The results were disappointing. They didn't refer to any significant event. No, that would have been too bloody easy. So what did they mean? Perhaps the dates referred to something that had only been newsworthy locally. He'd have to check with the newspaper archives. Or, he thought despondently, they could refer to something that had happened anywhere in the UK but hadn't warranted national media coverage. Perhaps added together they signified something, but what, for devil's sake? He again studied them: *01.07.05* and *5.11.09*. Why wasn't there a zero in front of the second five? Amos had put a zero in front of the other single numbers, so why not that one? Had it been just a simple omission?

His head ached. He was soaking wet, and he was weary rather than tired. It was clear he wasn't going to get much further forward tonight. He switched off the computer, showered and lay on his bunk with the envelope and its blank pages under the pillow. His ears were attuned for the sound of any unusual movement on the pontoon that suggested someone trying to break-in, because there was always the chance that the letter hadn't been tampered with and that the intelligences services didn't know its contents. His thoughts returned to Sawyer and then Agent Harriet Eames and finally to Johnnie. It was better to think of Johnnie than himself. He had time, Johnnie didn't. But even then his thoughts merely took him round in circles.

He must have fallen asleep at some stage because when he woke it was morning and it had stopped raining. The wind was still brisk though, which would please Masefield and Crawford, and his ex father-in-law Toby Kempton, who was teaching Emma to sail. Shit. He felt awful. He went for a run to try and stimulate his brain into action and to shrug off the weariness and despair he felt but the physical activity failed to conjure up the meaning of those figures and did little to lift his mood.

With the envelope in his jacket pocket, he was in his office, and ringing Woking police to ask if any break-ins had been reported at Teckstone's solicitors in the last week, when Walters lumbered into CID, eating a bar of chocolate, and settled himself at his desk. A dejected and drawn Cantelli followed. The answer from Woking was no.

With Cantelli and Walters, Horton headed for the briefing in the incident suite, but he might just as well not have bothered. There was nothing new to report.

There had to be something more they could do. That *he* could do. He couldn't just sit around and wait for all the statements to come in and reports to be checked!

Trueman's phone rang just as Uckfield was wrapping up the briefing. Uckfield paused as Trueman looked up and nodded at him while listening. 'OK, I'll tell the Super. That was the front desk,' he announced, coming off the line. 'We've got a visitor in the interview room. It's Darlene Chambers, Ryan Spencer's partner, and she'd very much like to know what we've done with him?'

FOURTEEN

'Well?' Uckfield demanded as Horton entered the incident suite forty-five minutes later and crossed to the water cooler.

'I'm ninety nine per cent certain the body we have in the mortuary is Ryan Spencer,' he answered, pouring himself a plastic cup of water and glancing at Cantelli. His expression of relief was almost instantly replaced with bewilderment followed by concern. Horton knew why. If it was Ryan Spencer who'd been killed at the Hilsea Lines, then where was Johnnie? And did this blow out Uckfield's theory of Andreadis being blackmailed and Sawyer's of Johnnie being involved in international robberies? That interview they hadn't had with Stuart Jayston was now looking much more relevant.

'Darlene has confirmed that Ryan has a tattoo of some kind of bird on his right arm. And she last saw him on Monday morning, when Cantelli and I interviewed him. A patrol car has taken her home, and she's given us permission to search Ryan's belongings on the understanding that if we find anything there that's nicked she knows nothing about it. They'll get something we can take a DNA sample from, but we won't get dental records because, according to Darlene, Ryan was so scared of dentists he wouldn't go within twenty miles of one. And we can't get DNA from the kids because they're not Ryan's. They've only been together for three months. Before then Ryan lived in a bedsit in the centre of the city.'

'What about Ryan's parents?' asked Bliss.

Eames, who had been with Horton during the interview on Uckfield's orders, answered: 'Darlene claims both are dead.'

'Did you tell her about the body?' asked Uckfield, scratching his crotch, which drew a pinched look of distaste from Bliss. A reason, Horton thought, for Uckfield to do it even more.

'Yes. But not how badly burnt it was,' Horton replied. 'She shed some tears but I got the impression they were for show rather than genuine sorrow, although that might come later.' Perhaps she really did love him? Perhaps the black eye she was sporting had been caused by her little boy bashing her in the face with a toy, as she claimed, but neither he nor Eames thought so.

Uckfield moved his hand from his crotch to run it through his short greying hair as Horton continued. 'She says she has no idea what Ryan was doing at the Hilsea Lines. She claims she didn't even know the place existed, and I believe her. She also says she doesn't know what time Ryan left the house. She took the kids for a McDonald's at twelve and then went shopping. She didn't get home until about three forty-five, and Ryan wasn't there.'

'Didn't she think it strange when he didn't return home on Monday night?' asked Walters.

Eames answered. 'No. She claims he often goes out on a bender and stays out, leaving her to look after the kids. After all, they're not his, as he keeps reminding her.'

'Only she expressed it more graphically and colourfully,' Horton added.

'I bet she did,' grunted Uckfield.

Horton said, 'If she complains she's told to shut her mouth, and we saw the evidence of that. She didn't have that black eye when Cantelli and I interviewed her on Monday, so they obviously had a row shortly after we left, and it could have been about why we were questioning Ryan. She says he went up to their room immediately after we left and she caught him texting on his phone. When she asked what was going on he told her to shut up.'

Frowning, Bliss said, 'So why report him missing if he knocked her about? I'd have thought she'd have said good riddance.'

Horton said, 'Some women want the bastards back no matter what they do. When he didn't come home Tuesday, she checked his clothes and belongings. He'd taken nothing with him except the phone, which she says is new. He'd only had it a couple of weeks, and before you ask it's pay as you go, so no chance of checking calls. Eames has tried the number Darlene gave us. There's no signal. When he didn't show up this morning, Darlene went down to the benefit office knowing he would be there to sign on, but he wasn't. She asked if he'd been in, they said not and that no one had seen him. That's when she began to worry. She got someone to look after the kids and got a taxi here.'

Bliss's keen gaze fell briefly on Cantelli before she turned it on Uckfield. Crisply, she said, 'Could this make Johnnie Oslow a suspect?'

Cantelli opened his mouth to reply but Horton got there first. 'If he did kill Ryan, which I doubt, then he's taken his time. If we'd discovered Ryan dead last Thursday morning or even Wednesday night and then Johnnie missing it might have made more sense, but the timing is wrong for Johnnie to be our killer. And where's the motive?'

Cantelli threw him a grateful look and said, 'I can't see Ryan Spencer being involved in these international jewel robberies, and I certainly can't see Johnnie having confided in him. There's no indication that he's been in touch with Ryan since that day in court seven years ago.'

Horton had been considering this while interviewing Darlene. 'Darlene doesn't know where Ryan got the mobile phone and he wouldn't say. I think she assumes it was stolen, but what if his killer gave it to him as a means of keeping in touch?'

'Why?' demanded Bliss.

Horton crossed the room to the map on the crime board that contained Johnnie's details. 'This is where the taxi driver saw Johnnie at the Hard, and Johnnie walked away in the direction of the entrance to Oyster Quays, where he never arrived. If he didn't turn right into Gunwharf Road, he could have crossed the road by HMS *Temeraire* and walked up Park Road.' He ran his finger along the road running in a south easterly direction. 'And if he crossed Anglesea Road and turned into White Swan Road, look at where he'd come out? Yes, Guildhall Walk and the White Swan pub, where Ryan Spencer spent that afternoon.'

Uckfield pulled a wooden toothpick from his trouser pocket and inserted it in his mouth where he proceeded to chew it. 'So who was Ryan getting his instructions from? And why lure Johnnie away?'

'In order to dispose of him,' said Dennings promptly, without any sense of feeling for Cantelli's nerves. 'Then, having done his bit, Ryan is killed.'

Cantelli blanched.

Uckfield rejoined, 'Which means we're back to DCS Sawyer's and Agent Eames' motive that Johnnie knew too much.'

'But why use Ryan?' Horton insisted. He was about to add *and how did the killer know about Ryan's connection with Johnnie?* but the words froze on his lips. There were two people who might have discovered that connection from the Go About sailing charity: Scott Masefield and Martin Leighton. Either of them could have gained access to Johnnie's file while there, especially once they knew he

worked for the billionaire Xander Andreadis. The plan to steal valuables on the sailing circuit could have been hatched years ago. They
hadn't killed Ryan, because they had been in Cowes, but again he
considered the possibility of them having an accomplice on the
mainland. Masefield, armed with information about Johnnie's past
conviction, had sought out the member of the gang with the most
criminal convictions and the one mostly in need of money. He'd
paid Ryan to get Johnnie somewhere and had given Ryan the phone
in order that he might receive his orders. Once Johnnie had been
lured away and probably killed, this accomplice had killed Ryan.

He said nothing about his suspicions regarding Masefield and
Leighton but added, 'Johnnie might have known he was meeting
Ryan. The killer could have made sure that Ryan contacted Johnnie
on his mobile phone, spun him a yarn about how he'd reformed, or
perhaps he threatened Johnnie that if he didn't show for a meet he'd
let on to his boss about the fire or some other misdemeanour they
hadn't got caught for. Whatever it was it was enough for Johnnie
to agree to meet him.'

'And then what?' Uckfield growled.

Trueman came off the phone. 'Stuart Jayston is on site at a
customer's house. It's on Hayling Island.'

Cantelli quickly caught on. Looking troubled, he said, 'They took
a taxi to Hayling Island to meet Stuart.'

But that didn't sound right to Horton, and there were other things
bugging him about his theory. 'Why would a gang of highly sophisticated thieves risk using Ryan Spencer and Stuart Jayston when it
would be much easier to deal with Johnnie directly and away from
his home patch, say in London?' It didn't add up, but then none of
it did.

Uckfield hauled himself up. 'Perhaps they decided to reform the
old gang and go in for a bit of business on their own account, with
Johnnie supplying information on some wealthy people for them to
target.'

Cantelli looked pained. Uckfield continued, 'They rowed; perhaps
one of them said he wasn't going to play ball, although I can't see
that being Ryan Spencer. But he ends up dead and they flash up his
body in the hope it will cover their tracks. They've been convicted
of arson before so they revert to their old methods. Yeah, I know it's
weak and we need some bloody answers to questions.' He addressed
Horton. 'Interview this Stuart Jayston.' To Cantelli, Uckfield said,

'Take Walters with you and talk to Tyler Godfray. If we don't get some straight answers bring them in.' Uckfield turned to Trueman. 'Get a team asking around the White Swan to confirm any sightings of either or both of them last Wednesday and get hold of the security camera footage from there and along Guildhall Walk. Get on to the taxi firms that work that area. Agent Eames, write up the interview with Darlene Chambers. DCI Bliss, DI Dennings, my office.' He stomped off leaving Bliss to strut after him and Dennings to swagger.

Horton studied Eames' expression as her eyes followed them. She looked a little irritated, Horton thought. He wondered if Uckfield had asked her to accompany him on the interview with Darlene just to keep her occupied afterwards in writing up the report from it. Perhaps. He was just grateful to get out of the station and to be doing something. Clearly, Cantelli felt the same although Walters didn't look too keen. Horton would have liked a quick word with Trueman to find out if he had been able to get some information on Masefield and his crew, but with Harriet Eames listening that was out of the question.

He headed for Hayling Island after exchanging a brief word with Cantelli in the car park. There was no need to urge him to go easy with Tyler; in fact, it was time to do the opposite. So, instead, he asked Cantelli to call him if he picked up any information that might help with the investigation and have an impact on him questioning Stuart Jayston.

Twenty minutes later Horton was turning into a winding leafy lane on Hayling Island and pulling into the long driveway of a large house that was in the process of being made even larger. He drew up behind a small white van with Jayston's emblazoned across it and several larger white vans beside it. One of the workmen told him where he could find Stuart. 'Round the back.'

Horton headed there. The expansive gardens backed on to a small inlet of Chichester Harbour, where he could see a number of dinghies, yachts and motorboats in the distance. There was also a boathouse and slipway, but he found Stuart Jayston pacing the edge of the swimming pool to his right, with his phone clasped to his ear. Horton eyed him with interest. Stuart Jayston looked as though he'd done very well for himself since that court appearance seven years ago. His clothes – smart jeans and an open-necked cotton shirt – looked expensive. There were no painter's overalls or grimy jeans and grubby T-shirts here. And he was sporting a lot of gold jewellery, along with

an expensive wrist watch. He'd filled out and grown flabby. His fair
hair was still cropped short but his face was more sullen, with a
mouth that turned down and eyes that were moody and suspicious.

'What do you want?' he demanded, coming off his phone as
Horton approached.

Horton eyed the petulant mouth and thought the same about Stuart
Jayston as he had about Tyler Godfray: spoilt, and most probably
by his mother. Jayston was also lacking in manners as well as intelligence because he hadn't even considered the fact that Horton could
be a relative or friend of the owner. He flashed his ID.

Jayston didn't even bother looking at it. 'Look, I don't know
where Johnnie is. I haven't seen him for years.'

'Why do you think I'm here to ask you about Johnnie?' Horton
asked smoothly against the backdrop of hammering and drilling
coming from inside the house.

'Well, you are, aren't you?' Jayston answered belligerently and
looked away.

So who had told him? Tyler Godfray or Ryan Spencer? Had Cantelli
been right in suggesting that Ryan and Johnnie had come here last
Wednesday afternoon? If a taxi had brought them then perhaps the
driver would remember them. And where had they both gone after
that? He could see that Jayston was uneasy about something.

'Have you *heard* from Johnnie recently?'

'No. I've got work to do.'

But Horton blocked his way. 'And what about Ryan Spencer?'

'What about him?'

'When was the last time you saw him?'

'Bloody years ago.'

Was that the truth? Jayston's eye contact was weak, but that could
be normal for him.

'Are you sure it wasn't Monday night?

'Course I'm bloody sure.'

It sounded and smelt like the truth.

'Where were you last Wednesday afternoon?' If Tyler had warned
him the police had been asking, or if he'd been involved with Ryan,
then he'd have his answer off pat.

'Here, I guess.'

'You don't know!' Horton eyed him keenly.

Jayston shifted under the intense gaze and was forced to add, 'Look,
I get around, I can't remember where I was exactly when. We've got

more work on than we know what to do with and you can't be slack
with builders and decorators, they need a kick up the arse now and
again. I have to visit them and make sure they're not slacking.'

Oh, I bet they love you. 'That must be tough.'

Jayston eyed Horton suspiciously. 'It bloody well is, and if you've
finished I'd like to get on with it.'

But Horton hadn't, not by a long chalk.

'Do you drive?'

'Course I do, how do you think I got here, by magic?'

'What do you drive?'

'A car,' Jayston sneered.

'So not always the works van.'

Jayston looked surprised and then wary, as though he'd been
caught out. 'No. Got an Alfa Romeo.'

'Were you out in it on Monday night?'

'No.'

'Maybe the works van then?'

'No. I was at home,' Jayston answered nervously.

'All night?'

'Yeah. Nothing wrong with that, is there?'

'Alone?'

'Yeah. Mum and Dad were away.'

'You live with them?'

'What's it to you if I do?'

'And Wednesday night?'

'At home.'

'Again?' Horton raised his eyebrows

'Yeah. OK?' he sneered. His phone rang he snatched it up.
'Finished?'

But Horton didn't move. He watched as Stuart registered the
caller before answering. Did he see relief cross his face? 'Yeah, the
job's going OK, Dad, only they haven't delivered that bloody wood.'

Horton left Stuart to his call. He didn't like him, and he was
betting the workforce and subcontractors didn't go a bundle on him
either, but that didn't make him a kidnapper or killer. But there was
something troubling Stuart Jayston. Behind the bluster Horton smelt
fear. Maybe Uckfield was right and they should get him down the
station, then the bravado might evaporate. And he found it curious
that Stuart hadn't demanded to know why Horton was interested in
his movements last Wednesday and particularly on Monday night.

It was possible that Tyler Godfray had told him about Johnnie's disappearance last Wednesday but nothing had been mentioned about Monday. He eyed Stuart's van. Could it have been used to take Johnnie away and Ryan to the Hilsea Lines? He noted the registration number. Or had Stuart taken his own car there?

Horton called Trueman and gave him the van's registration number. He also asked him to get hold of the vehicle licence number for Stuart's car and check for them both on the CCTV footage for Monday night. 'Anything on Masefield?'

'Still checking.'

That meant Harriet Eames was within earshot. He'd only just rung off when Cantelli rang him. 'Tyler Godfray didn't show for work this morning. We're on our way to Gosport to see if he's at home.'

Horton returned to Jayston. 'Thought you'd left,' he grumbled.

'Tyler Godfray hasn't come into work today. Why?'

'How the hell do I know?'

'Did he phone in sick?'

'Ask the office.'

Horton felt like shaking the little tyke. He made to leave, noting a flicker of relief in Jayston's eyes, and then turned back.

'Have you ever been on holiday abroad?'

'Course I have,' Stuart Jayston answered, clearly surprised at the question.

'Where?'

'What's it to—'

'Where?' Horton barked.

'France, Italy, Greece.'

'Get around, don't you?' Horton sneered. 'Ever been to Sardinia?'

'Might have been, yes, last year,' he added hastily at Horton's black look.

'See Johnnie there?'

'No.'

Horton left him, noting that Jayston looked troubled. In the lane outside the house he stopped the Harley and called Jayston's office to be told that Tyler hadn't reported in sick. They'd not heard from him. Horton felt uneasy. That jagged feeling between his shoulder blades was back. Stuart didn't have an alibi for the critical nights in question but that didn't mean he was involved. Perhaps his shifty manner was his normal personality.

He found a message on his phone. It was from Gaye Clayton.

Leaving the Harley where it was he walked along the road towards a footpath that led down to the shore and called her. She didn't waste time with small talk.

'The Odontologist has confirmed the body is not that of Johnnie Oslow.'

That was a relief, although it would be short lived. It had to be Ryan Spencer. Horton quickly relayed the news to her.

Gaye said, 'Has he any connection with Johnnie?'

'Yes.'

'Ah. Tell me how it's going when you have a moment, and give Sergeant Cantelli my love. If there's anything I can do, just ask.'

'I will.'

He stepped on to a narrow footpath that bordered the shore and headed west to the rear of the property where Stuart Jayston was working. It was only a few hundred yards and he passed a handful of exclusive properties on his way that appeared to be deserted. Perhaps they were all holiday homes inhabited by the rich who were on holiday elsewhere. Cowes, maybe? He stopped and eyed the boathouse and the slipway he'd seen earlier. There was no sign of Stuart. He continued onward but the house was the last in the row that backed on to the shore, except for the derelict one that faced on to a stretch of waste ground and an equally derelict former boatyard.

His phone rang. It was Cantelli. 'Can you talk, Andy?'

'Yes. What is it?'

'I'm at Karen Godfray's. She had no idea that Tyler didn't show up for work this morning. He's not here. She was out all last night and went straight to work at the Co-op this morning without coming home. She's a cashier. She last spoke to her son on his mobile at four thirty yesterday afternoon to tell him she'd left his dinner in the oven. He didn't say that he was going out. And she didn't call him again. I got the impression she usually runs around after him, but for once she didn't and she feels as guilty as hell. She was with a man overnight, a new boyfriend. It looks as though Tyler never came home last night. His bed's not been slept in, and she says he never makes it himself. His work overalls are still here, but there's no sign of him or his mobile phone.'

Horton cursed, while his head spun with this news.

Cantelli hastily continued, 'According to Les Batten, Tyler's boss, Tyler left work last night at five but they didn't give him a lift to the Gosport Ferry as usual. He said he had a date.'

With a killer? Horton hoped not. But why go missing? Could Tyler, like Ryan, be involved with Johnnie's disappearance? It was beginning to look very much like it.

'There's another thing,' Cantelli added. 'His mobile phone is dead.'

Ditched or broken?

Cantelli said, 'He's got a computer, and I asked Mrs Godfray if we could take it and have a look at it. She's almost hysterical and blames you and me for bullying her boy and driving him away. When I said looking at his computer might help us find him, she agreed to it, but she's adamant that she'll make a formal complaint against us for harassment.' That didn't frighten Horton and neither would it Cantelli.

'None of his clothes or belongings are missing. So it doesn't look as though he's gone on the run.'

Horton gave Cantelli Gaye Clayton's news. He heard him take a deep breath before he said, 'Could Stuart Jayston be behind this? According to Les Batten he was at the property in Old Portsmouth last Wednesday, but Les couldn't say for certain at what time.'

'I don't think he's bright enough. He and Tyler could have seen who Johnnie met, though. But where does that leave Ryan? Why is he dead if he wasn't there? It should have been Tyler or Stuart we found dead. Not Ryan.' But, as he was beginning to fear, perhaps Tyler was already dead, and if so that put Stuart in danger.

He did have another idea, though. Was it possible that the three of them had ganged up on Johnnie and kidnapped him to teach him a lesson? Maybe they'd seen him on the sixteenth of July and Johnnie had bragged about what he'd done with his life and who he'd met. Ryan had nothing and was a thief, Tyler was a painter and hated it and was firmly tied to his mother's apron strings, and Stuart liked expensive cars and jewellery and thought he was the big 'I am' . . . then along comes Johnnie and shows them all what the big 'I am' really is and tells them who he's met and how he's travelled the world. Stuart flips and says *let's get even*. But something went wrong? They met at the Hilsea Lines and argued. Stuart or Tyler lost it and Ryan was dead. Then, seeing what they'd done, they hastily tried to cover their tracks by setting the fire. And now, after the police had interviewed Tyler, he'd got scared and had gone on the run. But without taking his clothes or belongings? No, Horton didn't think so. And why was his phone dead?

He said, 'Ask Tyler's foreman if Stuart and Tyler were both at the property in Old Portsmouth on the sixteenth of July.'

Horton rang off and stared across the sea at the boats and yachts in Chichester Harbour. This wasn't making any sense. Mentally, he ran through all the scenarios they'd explored so far. That Johnnie had run off with a woman – then why was Ryan dead and Tyler missing? That Johnnie had simply done a bunk to change jobs – again, why were Ryan and Tyler involved and why hadn't Johnnie called his mother? Had Johnnie got involved in something illegal like drug smuggling and enlisted the help of one of his old school mates? Stuart, for instance – he could have seen him in Sardinia, or Tyler come to that, and one of them had roped in Ryan. Then Johnnie's paymasters had found out and were cleaning the trail. Stuart had looked uneasy but not scared, though, and Horton thought he would be very scared indeed if that were the scenario.

Then there was Sawyer's theory about the jewellery robberies and Uckfield's about blackmail, and the only way Ryan, Tyler and possibly Stuart could be involved was if they'd seen someone with Johnnie at the Camber and that someone had found out from Johnnie who they were. Yes, that was possible, because this person might have taken until Monday to extract that information from Johnnie, after which he'd killed Ryan. Horton shuddered in the midday sun. If that were so then Johnnie was most certainly dead too.

So he was back to Masefield, who had an accomplice in Portsmouth. Neither Sawyer nor Eames had categorically denied that Masefield was involved in the robberies, and there were several connections between him and his crew with Johnnie and Xander Andreadis's rich friends. Horton thought it was time he had another word with Masefield, and sod Sawyer's instructions to keep his distance. Besides, there was someone else he wanted to consult, and she was at Cowes. He rang Sergeant Elkins and gave instructions to be picked up from Oyster Quays.

FIFTEEN

'She won't be difficult to spot,' Elkins said ninety minutes later, on the launch heading for Cowes, when Horton asked if Sarah Conway was around. 'She and her mad helmsman, Duncan Farrelly, will be the ones impersonating Kamikaze pilots.'

Horton gave a brief smile as the launch headed towards the myriad of yachts and pleasure craft. His mind flicked back to Amos's envelope. He'd barely had time to consider it throughout the morning, what with Darlene's revelation and then the interview with Stuart Jayston. Were the figures on the reverse some kind of code? If they were, perhaps a code-breaker could help him – except he didn't know any. But surely Amos would have left a message that he knew he'd eventually be able to decipher? And if that was so, then anyone else would probably be able to as well, and maybe Amos hadn't wanted that. So their meaning had to have a significance for him personally, and yet they rang no bells. Could they be the code to a safe deposit box containing information about Jennifer and her past? It was possible. But where? Amos had given no indication to him regarding that.

'There she is.' Elkins interrupted his thoughts.

Horton looked up to see Sarah leaning almost over the side of the RIB, lying on her back, photographing a yacht they were perilously close to. It belonged to Rupert Crawford and it looked as though Roland Stevington had again taken Harriet Eames' place on the team.

'Has she ever fallen in?' Horton asked a little anxiously as Sarah Conway twisted and turned her lithe body in an attempt to get better and different shots.

'Not here, but she must have done somewhere.'

Ripley made for the RIB as quickly as he dared without endangering the lives of the other boaters. Sarah straightened up with a broad smile on her face and made an O with her finger and thumb to her skipper to indicate she had all she wanted. She looked up and raised a hand in a cheerful wave to Elkins. He made a sign for her to come towards them. She nodded and gave instructions to Duncan Farrelly, who swung the RIB round and came alongside.

'Can we talk?' asked Horton.

'I'll come on-board.'

'No,' he quickly added as she made to climb from the RIB to the police launch, but he was too late. She was already on.

Elkins shook his head, saying, 'You're going to kill yourself one day.'

'Better that than die a lingering death in old age,' she answered cheerfully.

Elkins rolled his eyes and gave instructions for Ripley to head back to Shepards Wharf at a sedate pace and within the regulation speed limits. Farrelly followed in the RIB.

Sarah sat in the cockpit. 'What I can do for you, Inspector?'

'Do you remember if Scott Masefield and his crew were here for the Cowes to St Malo race in July?'

'They were. I've got some great shots of them and of Andreadis's yacht; would you like to see them?'

'I would. When exactly were they here?'

'The same time as we were – from the tenth to the seventeenth of July. The race set off on the thirteenth, and Duncan I and followed it across to St Malo.'

'On the RIB!'

'No. Duncan hired a high speed motorboat, but it's not as good for taking shots as the RIB.'

'When did you return?'

'I can check the diary, but I'm almost certain it was the fifteenth. We got back just before the yachts pulled in. Then there was the party.'

'Have you photographs of that?'

'Of course.'

That meant Masefield was here when Johnnie had his day off.

'Do you remember seeing them on the sixteenth of July?' he asked.

'Not off the top of my head, but the photographs will give me the time and date.'

'Can you do that now?'

'As soon as I get back; everything's in the marina office.'

Ripley deposited them on one of the pontoons in the marina. Sarah went to have a word with Duncan, who had pulled up in the

RIB a little further down. The marina was busy, and Horton's gaze fell on a large motor cruiser and, on-board it, a man in his late forties who looked as though he could benefit from losing two stone. His suntanned face was a little too fleshy, his brown straight hair slightly over gelled and slightly too long, and his manner a little too over-confident, but then Horton guessed his view could be jaundiced because standing beside him was Catherine, so this had to be her new boyfriend, Peter. There was no sign of Emma. She must be with her grandparents. Catherine looked up. Irritation swept across her face as she registered him.

'Ready?' Sarah said, coming up behind him.

'Do you know that man?' Horton asked, indicating the cabin cruiser. Catherine's irritation turned to surprise and then to hostility.

'It's Peter Jarvis. He's some kind of businessman.'

Good, he'd got a surname. 'Married?'

'No idea. Not my type. Too old and too fat.'

Horton smiled. They headed towards the marina office. He wondered what Catherine was thinking. Would she wonder if Sarah was his girlfriend? Probably not. Catherine would surmise it had something to do with work, and she'd be right, he thought sadly. He said, 'How well do you know Masefield and his crew?'

'They don't mix much, but they're very serious about racing.'

'Has Masefield sailed many races for Andreadis?'

'Quite a few.'

'Do you know which ones?'

'I'll have it on the photo files.'

Their conversation had taken them to the marina office where she greeted the staff and made for a small room at the rear. A few seconds later she emerged with her laptop. Horton offered to buy her a coffee and a baguette, which she accepted with alacrity, and by the time he returned she had the photographs on the screen. Drinking his own coffee and biting into a ham and cheese roll he watched as she pulled up the various yacht races. She didn't ask why he wanted the information – perhaps because she knew he wouldn't tell her.

'Masefield and his team have sailed in nine races, ten if you include this week. Last year in July they were racing at Cork Week in Ireland, and then there was Cowes Week, followed by the Royal Dartmouth Regatta in Devon at the end of August. They were at Les Voiles de St Tropez in September; The Rolex Middle Sea Race

in October, from Grand Harbour, Malta; and the next time I photographed them after that was at The Heineken Regatta in February,
racing around the island of St Martin; then the Caribbean BVI
Spring Regatta in March; Antigua Sailing Week at the end of April;
and then the Cowes to St Malo Race here in July; and now again
this Cowes Week.'

Horton rapidly linked this volley of information with what Harriet
Eames had told them about the robberies. The first had been in an
exclusive villa situated near Port De Saint-Tropez on the twenty-
ninth of September, which tied in with the Les Voiles de St Tropez
race. The next had been in a property close to Grand Harbour, Malta
on the twenty-eighth of October, coinciding with The Rolex Middle
Sea Race. The third, again in a top market villa near Simpson Bay
Marina, St Marteen on the twenty-sixth of February, linked up with
The Heineken Regatta. The last, on the twenty-third of April, had
been just outside Falmouth Harbour, Antigua, linking with the
Antigua Sailing Week.

He asked her to call up photographs of the Cowes to St Malo
race in July and was soon looking at pictures of Masefield's yacht
in amongst several others, including Crawford's. He looked to see
if Harriet Eames was on-board, but she wasn't. Then he spotted
Andreadis's yacht. He asked if Crawford's yacht had been at the
same races as Masefield and discovered that he hadn't, but he had
been at all the races where the robberies had taken place. Interesting.
He asked her to email the pictures to him at work.

Sarah then called up photographs of the party on the evening of
the sixteenth of July. Again Horton spotted Masefield and all his
crew members, along with Rupert Crawford, and the crew he'd seen
on-board on Saturday.

'Have you got any pictures from last Wednesday and Thursday?'

'Only a few. There wasn't any racing, but Duncan and I went
around the Island taking shots of pleasure craft and working
boats.'

She didn't have any of Masefield's yacht. He asked if she had
any for Monday, and soon he was looking at Masefield's yacht
racing in the Solent, again alongside Crawford's, and they were all
at the yacht club for the presentations in the evening. So neither
Masefield nor any of his crew could have got to Hilsea, killed and
set light to Ryan Spencer. But they could still be involved if someone
else had done their dirty work for them.

Horton thanked her and headed for the pontoon, where he found Masefield and his crew. Judging by the joyous expression on their faces and the beer glasses in their hands they were obviously celebrating.

'Congratulations,' Horton said.

Masefield's expression slipped a little as he looked up and saw who was hailing him. The others eyed Horton curiously and, he thought, a little warily.

'Two more races and we'll win the class.'

'That will please Andreadis.'

Was this man Andreadis's blackmailer, Horton wondered, or were he and his crew jewel thieves? He studied Leighton, Weatherby, Saunders and Creed as they sat drinking. Fit, intelligent, fearless, organized. Yes, it was possible. He asked Masefield if he could have a word alone.

Masefield stepped off the yacht, calling out to the others, 'Won't be long.'

You'll be as long as I want, thought Horton, recognizing there was something he didn't like about Masefield, although he couldn't put his finger on it. Maybe that was how Don Winscom felt.

They walked along the pontoon in the opposite direction to the boardwalk. That was Masefield's choice and Horton was happy to go along with it, though he wondered why Masefield had decided to walk to the seaward side rather than landward. Admittedly, it was quieter here but only just. Crawford looked up as they passed and then away again, not even bothering to acknowledge them, but Roland Stevington called out a congratulations to Masefield, who smiled his thanks.

The narrow stretch of the Medina was swarming with pleasure craft, which were obliged to stop and wait for the clanking chain ferry to make its noisy and laborious way from East to West Cowes.

Horton said, 'I understand that you got your idea about sailing as therapy from your time at Go About.'

Masefield's eyes narrowed perceptibly. 'Yes.'

'You were referred there by the services' community mental health department.'

'So?'

'By Dr Claire Needham?'

'I thought you were interested in finding Johnnie Oslow.' There was curiosity in Masefield's tone, but Horton also caught a hint of hostility.

He said, 'I understand Martin Leighton was also referred to the charity.' Horton looked back and saw the broad-shouldered, fair-haired Leighton glance their way.

'And?' There was again a small flicker of annoyance behind Masefield's eyes.

'Did you know the charity also helped Johnnie Oslow?' He watched Masefield's reaction closely and saw only surprise. Perhaps it was genuine, or perhaps Masefield was good at feigning it.

'Did Don Winscom or any of the other volunteers mention Johnnie Oslow while you were there?'

'No.'

But Masefield or Leighton could have accessed the records.

Masefield said, 'Andreadis didn't mention him either when I floated my idea past him. Perhaps that was why he was so willing to help – he already knew what the charity did. I guess it must have helped Oslow. But he wasn't a serviceman, was he?'

You know damn well he wasn't. 'When were you at the charity, Mr Masefield?'

'I suspect you already know that. But if you're checking me out then I'll humour you. I was there three years ago. I stayed for a year.'

'And was this the same time as Martin Leighton?'

'No.'

Horton had known that from Winscom.

'I'm sorry I can't help,' Masefield said, making to leave, but Horton hadn't finished yet.

'How did you meet Andreadis?' He thought he caught a flicker of exasperation in Masefield's eyes.

'I was sailing with another team in the Round the Island Race in June two years ago, just after I'd left Go About. We did well. Xander and I got talking in the club after the race, and I mentioned my idea to him and it went from there.'

And from there Masefield had got himself a yacht, a crew and had begun competing in his first race, which according to Sarah Conway was Cork Week in July of the following year. Not bad going. Horton was betting that Masefield had singled out Andreadis and targeted him, and he'd probably got that information from the files or from a conversation at Go About. He asked him when he had competed in his first race under Andreadis's patronage, and Masefield confirmed what Sarah Conway had told him.

'With the same crew?'

'Yes.'

'Did you go on-board Andreadis' personal yacht *Calista* at any time it was here in the Solent for the Cowes to St Malo race in July?'

'No. We met a few times in the Castle Hill Yacht Club.'

'I'd like a word with Martin Leighton.' Horton made no attempt to move.

Masefield turned and walked briskly down the pontoon. Horton watched as he boarded the yacht and said something to the crew. Leighton's eyes spun to Horton's, but his expression was one of curiosity rather than concern. He headed towards Horton with an easy gait.

Horton didn't waste time with unnecessary words because he knew Masefield must have given him the gist of his questioning. 'Did you know Johnnie Oslow?'

'No.'

'Are you sure his name wasn't mentioned when you were with the sailing charity Go About?'

'Why should it have been? Did he work there?'

Horton felt certain that Leighton had known he did. He was equally certain he was going to get nothing of value out of him.

'Are you ex navy like Masefield?'

'Yes.'

'And the others?'

'Eddie is ex Royal Navy, Declan and Craig are ex Royal Marines.'

'How did you all end up together?'

'Scott called me and asked if I wanted to join him, just like he did the others.'

'Had you sailed before you were referred to the charity?'

'Only on big ships,' Leighton said with a slightly cynical smile.

'So you learnt while with the charity?'

'Yes. But Scott had sailed before then. Eddie, Declan and Craig were all experienced sailors when they joined.'

Horton left feeling uneasy. There was a lot they weren't telling him and had no intention of telling him. He diverted to the bar and asked if the manager or any of his staff remembered seeing Masefield and his crew in there a week ago, Wednesday evening.

'They've been in every evening for the last week, at least for a while,' the manager, a man in his mid-fifties with a slight squint, answered. 'So I guess they were here last Wednesday, but the days go so fast I can't remember.'

That wasn't a great deal of help, but one of the bar staff remembered they were definitely in the bar on Wednesday. 'It was my birthday, and Scott insisted on buying me a bottle of champagne. I told him I couldn't drink on duty, but he said I was to take it home and celebrate in my own time. I thought it was a lovely gesture.'

And an extravagant one at the prices the bar would charge. And was it done deliberately so that the date would stick in her mind? But Masefield couldn't have engineered her birthday. But if had been a deliberate act in case someone came asking then he'd have found another reason to make the date memorable. Horton asked if all the crew were there.

'Yes. They must have been.'

That wasn't the same as saying they were there.

He called Elkins and said he was ready to return to Portsmouth. As he waited for the police launch to come alongside he looked around for Peter Jarvis and his luxury cruiser, but he, Catherine and it had gone.

On the police launch he considered what he'd been told. The dates of the jewellery thefts fitted with Masefield's sailing itinerary, and despite what Masefield and Leighton claimed they must have known Johnnie. Masefield in particular because of his relationship with Andreadis.

By the time he returned to the station it was late afternoon, and he found Cantelli and Walters in CID. Cantelli reported that he'd assigned a female police officer to liaise with Karen Godfray, and Karen had asked if Tyler could have gone off with Johnnie – a natural assumption given their line of questioning on Monday.

'I told her we were checking every possibility. But I couldn't find any evidence in his room to suggest it. The high-tech unit might get something from his computer though. Neither Tyler nor Stuart were at the property in Old Portsmouth on the sixteenth of July because Jaystons didn't start working on it until the twenty-second of July, and the Gosport ferry staff don't remember seeing him crossing on Tuesday night.'

Horton addressed Walters: 'Anything from the CCTV footage?'

Walters shook his head. 'Can't see him on the Hard or approaching the railway station or ferry.'

Horton was about to relay what he'd discovered on the Island when Uckfield stormed in with a face like a constipated turkey. He jerked his head at Horton's office. Horton could guess what this was about. With glance at Cantelli he followed Uckfield in and closed the door behind him.

SIXTEEN

'I've just had my arse chewed off by Wonder Boy.'

One of Uckfield's more complimentary terms for ACC Dean. Horton walked around to his side of the desk but didn't sit and neither did Uckfield.

'Sawyer's complained to Dean, who wanted to know why I gave you permission to question Masefield.'

'News travels fast. Who told him I was there?'

'No bloody idea. He claims they won't attempt a robbery now.'

'That's one happy householder then who will keep hold of his possessions. Sawyer believes it *is* Masefield then?'

Uckfield threw himself in the chair the other side of Horton's desk. 'I don't know.'

Horton sat. 'His yacht was at all the locations where the robberies took place and on the relevant dates. Sarah Conway gave me photographic evidence. I know that's not enough,' he added hastily, stalling Uckfield's predictable reply, 'but if they are the culprits then me showing up asking about Johnnie isn't going to scare them off. There are too many connections with Johnnie to ignore the fact they could be involved in his disappearance. I believe they're working with someone here on the mainland, but don't ask me who because I haven't a clue.' An idea was forming in the back of his mind, though – one which he'd examine later. He also had an idea of who might have tipped off Sawyer about his visit to Masefield. Perhaps Rupert Crawford had rung Harriet Eames and told her he was over there nosing around.

'You're not to go near Masefield or any of his crew again.'

'Not even if they lead us to Johnnie, and to Ryan's killer?'

'*If* they do then *I* put it before Dean and he decides. Or rather Sawyer does and tells the gnome what to do.' Uckfield rose. 'I've got a press conference to give tomorrow morning. DCI Bliss will be on it with me.'

That would please her. 'Are you putting out an appeal for Johnnie?'

'You heard what Sawyer said earlier. No. We concentrate on

getting information that can help us with the inquiry into Ryan's death, which you're supposed to be working on.'

'Are you going to mention Tyler Godfray's disappearance?' Horton asked, ignoring Uckfield's jibe. He *was* working on it. If Godfray was mentioned alongside Ryan Spencer, then some clever dick journalist such as Leanne Payne would look them up in back issues of the newspaper and come up with a connection to Johnnie Oslow and Stuart Jayston.

Uckfield said, 'Just Ryan Spencer.'

Good, but Horton didn't think that would stop Karen Godfray from going to the press, especially as she'd be anxious to get as much assistance as she could in trying to locate her son. And no one could blame her for that.

After Uckfield had left, Horton shelved his thoughts on the case for a few minutes and looked up Peter Jarvis. He didn't have a criminal record, but then Horton hadn't expected him to have one. He probably had a big bank balance though, because according to the Internet he was chief executive of an international packaging conglomerate. Catherine was moving in wealthy circles, which would please her and her snotty-nosed parents no end. Jarvis was also divorced and had a son, aged sixteen. Horton hoped Jarvis was decent, honest and normal, whatever that was. He didn't care what Catherine got up to, but he was particular about who was spending time with his daughter. He thought the sooner she returned to boarding school the better.

He dealt with some messages and emails with only a third of his mind on the job; the other two thirds were occupied by thoughts of the numbers on the envelope, and of the murder of Ryan and disappearance of Johnnie and Tyler. Sarah Conway had sent over a whole swathe of photographs complete with times and dates on them, which Horton studied before sending them across to Trueman and calling him to explain what they were and why he'd asked for them. 'Anything on the crew yet?'

'No, but I might have something later tomorrow.'

'Is Agent Eames still there?'

'Left half an hour ago.'

To go where? wondered Horton. Back to the Island to spend the evening with Crawford and Stevington in the yacht club, or to join her father at his house? Or was she reporting to Sawyer? Or perhaps she'd returned to a hotel to spend the evening alone going over the case notes or the jewellery robberies. It wasn't his concern.

By the time he took a couple of telephone calls, both unconnected with the case, it was gone seven. Walters had left twenty minutes ago, bleary eyed, he claimed, from staring at the screen with zilch result. Cantelli came in to say that he and his brother Tony were going to ask around the shops, pubs and bars in Oyster Quays, Old Portsmouth and in Guildhall Walk to see if anyone remembered seeing Johnnie. At the same time they'd show Tyler's photograph. Horton doubted they'd get a result, and Cantelli knew that. 'I've got to do something, Andy,' he said before leaving.

Yes, thought Horton with frustration and agitation as he made his way to his yacht. And *he* should be doing something, but what, for Christ's sake? Poor Barney was growing leaner and more haggard by the hour. Cantelli had told him that Isabella was still working in the seafront café, to keep herself occupied, but Horton knew she must be wearing herself to a shadow with worry.

He changed into his running gear as soon as he arrived at the yacht and, after locking up, made for the promenade. He still favoured Masefield for playing some part in this and considered the idea that had occurred to him earlier, which he'd put to the back of his mind – could Masefield have recruited someone who had been at Winscom's sailing charity but who hadn't joined the sailing team for some reason? A former armed service colleague who had been referred by Dr Claire Needham, perhaps? He thought it was viable, and although Don Winscom had sent through the list of those who had been at the charity when Johnnie had been there, that had been before the community health department had begun referring service personnel and veterans. And the latter list was the one he wanted. Cantelli and Walters would start checking through the first tomorrow to see if any of the people on it had a criminal record, had been in touch with Johnnie or had visited any of the localities where he'd been.

He reached the old hot walls where he descended to street level and swung left, with the entrance to Portsmouth Harbour and Gosport on his right and Oyster Quays behind him. The seats outside the pub that faced on to the harbour were packed with people enjoying a drink and meal in the tranquil, humid night. He noticed a couple sitting close, their heads together over their drinks. His heart skipped several beats as the woman looked up, and Horton felt a searing surge of jealousy. Harriet Eames' blue eyes registered surprise. Roland Stevington followed her gaze. She waved a hand, gesturing him over, but Horton stabbed a finger at his wristwatch, smiled and ran off, the smile instantly vanishing when he was out of sight. His envy was irrational because he'd already acknowledged that he was never going to have a relationship with her, but he couldn't help feeling it nonetheless. And why shouldn't she be enjoying herself and carrying on as though nothing of importance was happening? He could hardly expect her to be stuck in some hotel room alone worrying about Cantelli's nephew.

He tried hard to get thoughts of her out of his mind but it was difficult, so it was with surprise and annoyance that on entering the marina car park he found himself facing DCS Sawyer. He'd been caught off guard.

'Have you thought any more about my offer, Inspector?' Sawyer asked. 'The chance to find your mother.'

'And Zeus.'

'Yes.'

How much did Sawyer know of his recent research? Was he in Professor Madeley's and Lord Eames' confidence? Were the intelligence services using Sawyer and the Zeus story to divert him from finding out the truth? Did Zeus really exist, and if so, had Jennifer had some connection with him? Horton couldn't trust anyone.

'Why do you think Jennifer ran off with Zeus?' he asked.

'I told you, we have certain information.'

'Yeah, from an informant who is now dead. Why don't you officially reopen the case into her disappearance?'

'You know why – it would alert Zeus, or certainly one of his operatives, who would report back to him.'

'And do you know who these operatives are? No, I thought not. So all you've got is the word of some toerag criminal that someone called Jennifer Horton once had an affair with this top guy codenamed Zeus. Not much, is it? But publicly putting around that Detective Inspector Horton, the son of Jennifer Horton, is now working for the Intelligence Directorate might provoke one of them out of the sewer and into the daylight, especially if you then leak that I'm engaged in looking into a series of jewellery robberies. Why not simply leak the information about who I am and hint that I'm working on the thefts anyway? Ah, but then you wouldn't be able to keep such close tabs on what happens as a result.'

'And I wouldn't want you to come to any harm,' said Sawyer smoothly.

'And Zeus might slip through your fingers. I'm happy as I am, sir,' Horton said, beginning to move away.

'You might not have a choice.'

Horton halted. He knew that Sawyer was referring to the fact that he might be forcibly transferred out of CID into the Intelligence Directorate, or possibly into a dead-end desk job that would positively make him beg Sawyer to take him on. 'There's always a choice,' he said evenly and walked away.

His phone rang as he stepped on-board his yacht. Tense and troubled by Sawyer's visit, he answered it. It was the station.

'Jean Jayston has reported her son, Stuart, missing,' the officer said. 'I thought you'd like to know.'

Horton glanced at his watch. It was a few minutes to ten. It was a bit early to worry about a grown man's absence, or rather it would have been in normal circumstances, but these were far from that.

'They called in five minutes ago, sir. I took the details and suggested that he might be with friends, but she's contacted everyone they know and no one's seen him. He was supposed to be meeting Gordon Jayston, his father, at a prospective client's house at seven o'clock, and he didn't show up. Mr Jayston called the men who were working on the property on Hayling Island with his son and they said he left there at four thirty, and that seems to be the last time anyone saw him. Mrs Jayston has tried her son's mobile phone several times and left messages but he hasn't called her back.'

That sounded more than just a lad going off with his mates. Horton relayed the registration number of the van and asked for an alert to be put out for it. 'Tell the Jaystons I'm on my way.'

Twenty minutes later Gordon Jayston, a short, stout balding man in his mid-forties, showed Horton into the lounge of the large modern house, situated on the main road that headed east out of the small town of Havant. Horton remembered him quite clearly now from the court appearance of his son. He'd lost a lot of his hair in the last seven years but he was still the same blunt angry-faced man.

'I'm pissed off with him, and he'll get a piece of my mind when he does come in,' Jayston declared. 'I told Jean not to call the police, but you know what women are like.' He darted a hot, angry glare at the listless woman sitting on the cream leather sofa shredding a tissue. Her streaked flat blonde hair fell around a lined, sallow face. Horton calculated that she must be a similar age to her husband, but she looked a lot older and indeed had aged since he remembered her from the court. Back then she was a much smarter woman, dressed fashionably and heavily made-up.

'He's probably with some tart and forgot he had to meet me, but I'm telling you that's it, he's out.'

'Gordon, he's young.'

'Young or not he'll get a piece of my mind and the sack,' Jayston declared, standing with his short legs astride and glowering at his wife. 'I'm sorry if we're wasting your time, Inspector.'

Horton didn't think they were. He'd noted Stuart's car on the driveway but not the van he had been driving that morning. But then he hadn't expected to see that there. He addressed Jean Jayston: 'Does he usually go off without telling you or stay out of contact this long?'

'No. Never.'

Her husband snorted. She flinched as though he'd physically hit her or personally abused her – maybe he had by slagging off her precious son. But her anxiety made her brave enough to say, 'He's never not shown up when he's meant to be meeting you, Gordon.'

'Too bloody right. I'll give him what for.'

'When did you last see your son, Mr Jayston?' Horton asked without his voice betraying any of his concern.

'This morning. He was lounging about in the kitchen drinking tea and fiddling with his bloody phone. I told him to shift his arse and do some work. I got a grunt for my troubles as usual. I didn't have time to hang around. I've got another big job on over at Cosham – we're renovating a garage, and we're running behind schedule. The small jobs I leave to Stuart, and he can't even handle them. I've had to pull everyone off that house on Hayling Island because the bloody wood hasn't arrived, which it would have done if he'd remembered to order it when I told him to.'

'And you, Mrs Jayston?'

'Stuart left here at about nine thirty.'

'Did Stuart tell you that I interviewed him this morning?' Clearly, by their shocked expressions, he hadn't. 'I went to the Hayling Island property to ask him if he has seen or heard from Johnnie Oslow.'

'Johnnie? No, of course he hasn't,' Jean Jayston replied.

Horton eyed Gordon Jayston carefully.

'That again!' Mr Jayston exploded. 'Don't you ever let it go?'

'Not when we have a suspicious death, sir,' Horton answered

evenly. Jean Jayston went paler and her husband glowered. Horton continued: 'Ryan Spencer is dead, and Tyler Godfray and Johnnie Oslow are both missing.'

'Well, Stuart has nothing to do with that or them,' Jean Jayston cried while twisting the tissue in her hand. It was almost in shreds. She appealed to her husband.

'He better not had. I gave him a right bollocking last time when I knew the kind of trouble he'd got into. I still can't believe that a son of mine could have done such a stupid thing like setting a fire. High jinks, yes, I can accept that. But arson, no. His mother spoilt him; he'd had too much of his own way and that made him weak. I hoped that he'd show a bit more spunk if I gave him responsibility. Huh, I might just as well have been pissing in the wind.'

Jean flinched again, and the tissue was now pulp in her skinny fingers.

'Why did you engage Tyler Godfray then?' asked Horton.

'That's a bloody good question! Why did I? Because Stuart asked me to and his mother *begged* me to. I thought OK, let's give him the chance, but he's lazy, arrogant and useless. I wouldn't be surprised if he just wants a couple of days' holiday.'

'He's done this before?'

'Yeah, phoned in sick with some illness that no bugger's ever heard of. A load of old flannel. This time he probably forgot to call in, or thought he could get away with it because he's Stuart's friend. Tyler's already had two warnings. He's late so many times with enough wild excuses that would make an adventure novel sound boring. Either the ferry's broken down, the skipper's had a heart attack and they had to be boarded by the Pilot, they had to wait for a battle cruiser to sail up the channel, or the Border Agency stopped them to search for drugs or a criminal. You name it he's claimed it. Lives in a ruddy fantasy world. This time he's out.'

'Was Stuart worried Tyler hadn't shown for work?' Horton asked, thinking he hadn't sounded worried when he'd interviewed him, but he recalled that he had been uneasy.

'No. I don't think he cares for him much now anyway.'

'Have you seen Johnnie Oslow in recent years?' Horton probed, in case one of them had come across Johnnie while on holiday. But they both shook their heads.

'You can't think that Stuart has anything to do with them missing and this . . . this death?' Jean Jayston asked, ashen faced.

'We're just gathering information, Mrs Jayston, but we do need to speak to Stuart again and we are concerned for him. We'll put out an alert. If you could let me have a recent photograph.'

She swallowed and grabbed her mobile phone. 'I've got one on here.'

Horton handed her his card and she sent the photograph across to his phone with fumbling fingers. Her nails were bitten down to the quick. 'I'll try Stuart's mobile again.'

Horton could see by their expressions that they were now far more concerned than when he had first arrived.

'I can't seem to get through to his number,' she said anxiously.

That sent alarm bells ringing through Horton, but he disguised his fears.

'I'll get this picture circulated. There's a chance that he's got held up drinking with friends you don't know and his phone battery's run down.'

It was bluff, and they both knew it.

'If you could give me his mobile phone number.' Jean Jayston relayed it. Horton said, 'Does Stuart have a computer?'

Gordon Jayston answered, 'Yes, a laptop.'

'Is it here?'

This time his wife replied. 'It's in his room. I'll check.'

She looked at her husband for approval. He gave a curt nod, and she scurried out.

Eyeing him with suspicion, Jayston said, 'Why are you interested in that?'

'He might have sent an email arranging to meet someone.'

'He'd have done that from his phone.'

'Possibly. But there's always a chance that he didn't.'

Jean Jayston hurried back slightly breathless. 'It's not there. He must have it with him.'

Horton's apprehension deepened. 'Is that usual?'

She looked confused.

'Did you see him leave with it this morning?'

'No. I don't think so.'

'Could he have returned home today when you weren't here?'

'I suppose he could have done. I had to go shopping. It didn't look as though he'd been home though. There were no cups of tea lying around. You think something's happened to him, don't you?' she added, her voice shaking. She dashed a glance at her husband.

Horton, following it, caught a flash of something in Gordon Jayston's eyes and it wasn't just concern. There was fear and suspicion. Despite his angry denials, Horton could see that Jayston was actually considering if his son *was* responsible for Ryan's death.

He said, 'Can you tell me where Stuart was last Wednesday afternoon and evening?'

Gordon Jayston answered promptly: 'Working on Wednesday and here in the evening.'

'You were here?'

'Yes.'

'Does he have a girlfriend?'

'No.'

Horton said, 'I'll keep you informed. Meanwhile if you hear from your son, please call me.'

Gordon Jayston showed Horton out into the hall. His voice hard he said, 'You're wrong, Inspector, dead wrong. Stuart was a bit wild in his youth thanks to being easily influenced and weak willed, but he knows better than to get involved in anything like arson again.'

'Does he though, Mr Jayston?' Horton said calmly, holding his gaze.

'I bloody hope so,' he muttered, miserably.

Horton called the station and asked someone to check with the hospital. He relayed the details the Jaystons had given him and emailed over the photograph. He didn't think there was any point in disturbing Uckfield or Bliss. It was now just after eleven thirty. He returned to the boat. There was nothing more he could do that night. But tomorrow morning was different. And he knew exactly who he was going to see. They needed help. He just hoped she'd be able and willing to provide it.

SEVENTEEN

Thursday

Horton was surprised when Dr Needham answered the intercom at the gates to her house. He had expected muscle man. He said he needed to consult her urgently, and without commenting she buzzed him through. He rode slowly up the gravel drive recalling his phone calls earlier that morning. The Jaystons had reported that there was still no sign of their son and no contact from him, while the station had confirmed no sightings of the van. Horton had then rung Uckfield and updated him but he'd said nothing about coming here. Horton knew that Uckfield wouldn't approve and neither would Bliss but he didn't need their approval. He just needed results.

'Come in,' Dr Needham said, opening the door to him, her tone a little more guarded than at their previous meeting. He suspected she was anticipating him trying to pump her about Masefield and Leighton. She was again wearing trousers, but this time they were a rose brown and complimented by a white cotton shirt that showed no cleavage or bra beneath it and which was tucked into the waist of her trousers. He thought of Harriet Eames' neat waist and shapely figure and tried not to think of Roland Stevington enjoying it last night.

'Coffee? It's freshly made.'

He could smell it. He accepted with alacrity and followed her into a bright, modern and spacious kitchen at the rear of the house, where the dark-haired man with muscles like Jean-Claude Van Damme was drinking from a mug. He eyed Horton without showing any emotion.

Claire Needham said, 'My brother, Art.'

Art nodded at Horton but didn't offer his hand. At what must have been a minute gesture from Dr Needham he left the room. Horton gazed around it. It was divided in half by a low-slung sofa which faced a row of built-in bookshelves and a large plasma television screen showing a politician pontificating about something.

Horton was about to mentally tune him out when Claire Needham stabbed a button on the remote control and the oily politician disappeared. In front of the sofa was a coffee table covered with paperwork. She crossed to it, retrieved the mug on it and, taking it to the coffee machine, poured herself a fresh cup and one for him. Handing it to him she said, 'Help yourself to milk and sugar.'

He took neither. She invited him to sit at the breakfast table in the middle of the kitchen and took the seat opposite him, sipping her coffee and studying him with her keen hazel eyes. The scent of the intoxicating perfume on his previous visit was absent. In fact he couldn't smell any perfume at all, but her make-up was again exquisite and there was still an erotic air about her that would have sent his blood pressure up if he hadn't been so worried.

He began: 'Everything I'm going to tell you is confidential.'

'Of course.'

'The press have some of the details and Detective Superintendent Uckfield will be giving a press conference in about half an hour, but a great deal of what I am going to tell you the media won't be told and I'd like it to stay that way.'

'If you don't trust me, Detective Inspector Horton, then I suggest you drink your coffee and leave.'

He took a breath. He almost called it off then, but he thought what the hell – Cantelli needed all the help he could get, and if this meant he'd get reprimanded then it was a price he was willing to pay. And what was one more reprimand to those he had already accumulated? Besides, he needed information desperately. He had to trust her for Cantelli's sake. He said, 'I apologize. I need someone unconnected with the case both professionally and emotionally and—'

'Your bosses don't know you're here.'

He nodded and swallowed some coffee. It was good.

'You're going out on a limb for this. Why? Because you're personally involved?' A small frown puckered between her perfectly shaped eyebrows as she studied him with interest.

He told her about Johnnie Oslow's background, the arson he'd committed with the other boys when they were sixteen, and how Johnnie had been rehabilitated by the same sailing charity as Masefield and Leighton, and no doubt others she'd referred there. That drew a slight look of surprise from her but no comment. He gave her the details of how and when Johnnie had gone missing but didn't mention Johnnie's relationship to Cantelli or Cantelli to himself.

She listened in silence without interrupting, giving only the occasional nod while keeping comfortable eye contact to show he had her full attention. Neither did she say anything when he relayed that Johnnie had been working for and sailing with Xander Andreadis, just as Masefield and Leighton now were, and that on the day he'd disappeared Johnnie had been due to be collected by them from Oyster Quays. He'd arrived in Portsmouth just over a week ago and had vanished. Now one of the boys who had committed the arson with him was dead and the other two were also missing.

When he'd finished she said, 'Hence your previous questions about Scott Masefield and Martin Leighton. You want to know if either man is capable of kidnap and killing. Even if I told you that they could be that doesn't make them suspects or killers. Many people are capable of doing vile deeds sometimes committed because of extreme provocation, other times the result of professional training or because the individual is disturbed and suffers from a personality disorder, as you in your job well know.'

He made to speak but she held up her beautifully manicured hand and continued. 'I know nothing about Johnnie, or the other boys, other than what you have told me, so let's explore the other possibilities and the one which is concerning you. Could Johnnie have returned to his old ways, killed Ryan Spencer and set the fire to cover his tracks?'

She'd gone right to the nub of one of the theories that had been espoused, which he should have expected because he hadn't mentioned Johnnie's possible involvement in the international jewel thefts or Uckfield's theory of Andreadis being blackmailed. So she had no reason to suspect Masefield and Leighton of any involvement. But he was dismayed and discouraged that she had so readily grasped at that theory. It confirmed to him what he had voiced to Cantelli, that if the press got hold of the connection between Johnnie and the death of Ryan they might hint at or print the same theory. And now with Stuart and Tyler missing they'd fairly leap to the same conclusion. There was no hard evidence to back this up, and there were several unanswered questions about how they'd got to the Hilsea Lines and where the remaining three men were, but when had facts got in the way of a good story?

He recalled the lad he'd taken sailing. He'd been consumed with guilt over what he'd done, and Horton remembered what Winscom had told him – that Johnnie had been determined to start afresh. He said, 'I just can't see him risking his job and his future.'

'Maybe he found he had no choice. Ryan, Tyler and Stuart were a threat from his past, about to ruin everything he'd fought against. He'd pulled away from them, probably told himself that it had never happened, or that it had happened to a different person in a different life. But he's met someone he is desperate to hide his past from. He's in love or infatuated with her.'

Christ, she was reading his thoughts! She'd put forward another of the theories he'd had but with a new twist. He hadn't put the woman that Johnnie might have fallen in love with alongside Tyler, Ryan and Stuart. But would Johnnie kill in order to keep his past from her? No, he still couldn't believe it. She eyed him carefully as she sipped her coffee. He heard a phone ringing but it was answered after three rings, presumably by her brother.

She said, 'Perhaps Ryan saw Johnnie with this woman and demanded money to keep his past a secret. Johnnie agrees but has no intention of paying Ryan. Instead he makes arrangements to meet him and kills him, but he believes, or is afraid, that Ryan has told the others so he has to kill them and wipe out the past.'

'But that doesn't answer why he'd wait four days to kill Ryan.'

She sat back looking thoughtful. 'You said Ryan's body was set alight?'

'Yes. And the fire service was called before the second fire was ignited.'

'To make sure you found the body.'

Horton silently groaned. God, they'd forgotten that. Or rather lost track of it. There were too many damn theories clouding this investigation. Without the fire Ryan might still be there rotting away, and he *needed* to be found. Why?

She said, 'You're fond of Johnnie. Is he a relation of yours?'

'No.'

'But there is a personal connection?'

He eyed her closely; she was getting at something. 'Yes.' He still wasn't prepared to tell her who Johnnie's uncle was.

'Then that could open up a new dimension. It raises other possible theories which could provide a key to the situation.'

Horton didn't know how. He was beginning to admire her

analytical mind as his own raced to put together the possible scenarios before she spelt them out. He sat forward as she continued.

'Johnnie is being used as a hostage, and the death of Ryan and the disappearance of the others is a message, which as yet hasn't been correctly interpreted.'

Horton eyed her with amazement. 'But Johnnie's family don't have any money.' And he couldn't see Andreadis coughing up for his release . . . or would he? Was that what this was all about? Uckfield had expressed his idea of blackmail, but could it be ransom money? But why no ransom note? Or was there one, which Sawyer had sat on?

'It might not be for money,' she answered slowly and let her words sink in. They did, and swiftly. Horton felt his nape hairs prick as he grappled with this new angle. Before he could air his thoughts though she pressed on: 'You say he went missing when he arrived here in Portsmouth, so the locality is important. It is more closely linked with his family than with Xander Andreadis, apart from the fact that Andreadis sails these waters occasionally.'

'But no demands have been made,' Horton said.

'Are you sure?'

Horton couldn't see Cantelli keeping silent; surely he would have confided in him. But perhaps he was too frightened. Even then Horton thought he would have detected something or picked up a hint of it from Cantelli's words or actions. 'I'm sure,' he answered.

'Then the kidnapper could be waiting for the right psychological moment.'

Suddenly, he understood perfectly what she meant. 'Because Johnnie's family haven't suffered enough yet. But why should they suffer? What could they have done?'

'They? Do you mean they?'

Then he saw it, and his expression gave him away.

'You understand, don't you?' she said.

'But it's mad.'

'Tell me what you're thinking and then I'll tell you if it's mad.'

'Before I do I can tell you that it's not me they want to make suffer. Johnnie Oslow is the nephew of the sergeant I work with in CID, Sergeant Cantelli, and his father used to have a unit that backs on to the Hilsea Lines where Ryan Spencer's body was found. You're saying that the kidnapper and killer want Sergeant Cantelli to know what it feels like to suffer, and he's chosen to do it through a member of his family.' Could it be true? His mind swam with the possibility. 'Why though?' he asked in exasperation, then posed an answer to his own question. 'Is it about revenge for someone Cantelli's helped put away?'

'Possibly. The kidnapper could have been deprived of someone he or she loves who has been incarcerated, so why not deprive Sergeant Cantelli of someone he loves by imprisoning him?'

It made some kind of sick sense. 'You said he or she. You think this could be the act of a woman?'

'Why not? A woman whose husband, lover, brother or father has been jailed. Johnnie could have gone willingly with this woman, quite unsuspecting. She could have been planning this for some time, tricked him into thinking she was in love with him, lured him away and then drugged him. She might even have accomplices, brothers or sons.'

Horton's head was pounding as he considered this.

'Or it might be a man who's been deprived of his mother, wife, son or brother.'

'Then whoever the kidnapper is trying to avenge must be alive and in prison.'

'That is one possibility, but he or she could be dead and the kidnapper now sees Sergeant Cantelli as the focus for all his hatred and thoughts of revenge.'

Her words struck a chord with Horton. Was he was seeing Lord Eames as the focus for all his hatred, and therefore wanting revenge on him for his part in his mother's disappearance, even though he had no proof that he had been involved?

She continued, 'If that's so, then the kidnapper will want Sergeant Cantelli and his family to suffer for as long as he did, or at least for some time, before he kills Johnnie.'

Dejected, he said, 'He *will* kill him then?'

'Yes.'

'How long have we got?'

She shrugged as if to say *who knows*. 'But this killer will find more ways to make Sergeant Cantelli suffer.'

'Another death.'

'Yes.'

Tyler's or Stuart's?

She said, 'Sergeant Cantelli and his family, and you, Inspector, have all wondered, even if it is fleetingly, if Johnnie could be involved in this willingly. Is he an accomplice to murder? It's what I also initially suggested, so others will think it. Has he conspired with someone to capture the other members of the gang, or is he doing this himself and intending to kill the others? The thoughts must be tormenting Sergeant Cantelli.'

She was right, of course. His coffee now lay untouched, growing cold.

'The killer has made it his business to discover what he can about Sergeant Cantelli's life and personality. He's found that he has a nephew with a criminal record, and his sense of injustice is heightened. The sergeant had the gall to help convict him, and yet someone in his own family got away scot-free, as he sees it. Now the killer wants to get even. But whichever scenario, whether justice for an incarcerated loved one, alive or dead, or revenge for himself for being imprisoned, the killer wants to make Sergeant Cantelli suffer, and so he devises a scheme that will put him through the hoops. Sergeant Cantelli will run a gauntlet of emotions starting with concern, developing into worry when Johnnie stays missing. Then comes disbelief and horror when he and others begin to think that Johnnie might actually be conspiring with the killer – or, worse, be the killer himself. And the longer it goes on and the more deaths there are the more anxious Sergeant Cantelli and his family will become. He'll see his family falling apart as the newspapers and media pick up the story and come to the same conclusion.'

Horton knew that. He felt sick to his stomach. 'The killer will make sure they do.'

'Yes. Sergeant Cantelli's work will suffer. He'll be moved to another department or go sick. And finally, when the killer thinks Sergeant Cantelli has suffered enough, Johnnie's body will be found. But even then the killer might make him continue to suffer.'

Horton's gut tightened. 'He'll make it look as though Johnnie killed himself, suicide, unable to face what he'd done.'

She nodded. 'The police and the coroner might not believe it, but the evidence will leave it open.'

And Horton knew that meant people would continue to ask questions for years to come. People would say *there's no smoke without fire*. And the Cantelli family and Isabella would suffer for the rest of their lives. This was one hell of an evil bastard.

Grimly, Horton said, 'What sort of person are we looking for?'

She considered this for a moment before answering. 'Someone

who is clever and very devious. A planner, not a person who acts on impulse; this could be years in the hatching. I would say a loner, or rather someone who feels alone inside even if they surround themselves with acquaintances and friends. They're still always alone.'

Her last words twisted inside him. That partly described him.

'Someone who's been damaged by the experience. He's deeply hurt and very angry. And that anger is blocking out all reason – or rather I should say the killer will provide reasons for what he is doing, believing them to be just. But of course they can't be.'

Horton felt uncomfortable with her analysis. It was a little close to him. Yet *he* couldn't kidnap and kill for revenge. That was the difference, he told himself, between his mission to expose the truth behind his mother's disappearance and the kidnapper of Johnnie Oslow. But then perhaps the kidnapper had set out not believing he would go as far as he had. Who the devil was it? A question they needed the answer to, and quickly, if they were to save the lives of three young men.

'You're probably looking for someone with a paranoid personality disorder,' she added.

'Explain that in English.'

'Someone who is extremely sensitive to insults and rejection. He's hostile and arrogant, with domineering behaviour. He needs to demonstrate his superiority, so the kidnapping and killing in this ritualistic way fulfils that need. It all helps to bolster his self image.'

And he and Cantelli had met plenty of them in their police career. Now all he needed to do was find the one Cantelli had dealt with. He didn't know how far back they should look, if, according to Dr Needham, this killer could have been planning it for years. But perhaps Cantelli would recall someone who fitted the profile.

He left after thanking her, feeling even more despondent than when he had arrived, and he hadn't even asked for the lists of those service personnel she'd referred to Go About as he had intended. But then even with her additional knowledge about the case he knew she would still have refused.

This theory opened up another line of enquiry, and they already had enough of those to follow up. Perhaps Uckfield's press confer- ence would result in some hard facts, some sightings of Ryan Spencer on the day he was killed.

He made to return to the station but was forestalled by a call. It was Uckfield.

'We've got another body,' he announced grimly.

Horton's heart plummeted. 'Where?'

'Same place as before, Hilsea Lines, but this time the body's in the moat at the Airport Service Road end. I'm on my way there now.'

'Who is it?' Horton tensed, preparing himself.

'Don't know, but the copper who is there says it's a young man, about early twenties.'

And that fitted three men who were missing: Tyler Godfray, Stuart Jayston and Johnnie Oslow.

EIGHTEEN

Horton threw a concerned glance at Cantelli as they climbed out of the car in front of bastion number five. Uckfield hadn't called through with an ID. Horton didn't know if that was good or bad news. The blue and white police tape left over from Ryan Spencer's murder was still in evidence, lying limp in the long grass to their left. Fresh tape was stretched across the entrance to the small car park where they'd been admitted by a uniformed officer. Along with two patrol cars was SOCO's white van, the forensic photographer Jim Clarke's dark-blue estate and DS Uckfield's silver BMW. Uckfield had ordered that the whole area be sealed off. It had only been reopened at nine o'clock last night, and the killer must have known this. He certainly hadn't wasted much time. A small group of workers from Alanco Aviation had come out to see what all fuss was about, and no doubt one of them would call the newspaper office. Leanne Payne and Cliff Wesley would be here soon.

Cantelli had insisted on coming with him and had been waiting impatiently in the station car park. Horton had said nothing to Cantelli about his visit to Dr Needham. It wasn't the right moment, and Horton wanted to digest what she'd said and see who they had in the moat first. If it was Johnnie then it blew her theories out of the water anyway.

Cantelli had spoken only once on their way here. 'I have to know if it's Johnnie,' he'd said.

Horton didn't say that if it was Johnnie then he might not be recognizable. If he'd been killed a week ago and his body dumped in the water then it would be a gruesome sight. But Cantelli would know that anyway. And Horton knew that Cantelli would scour the corpse for some evidence to confirm or deny it was his nephew, something in the physiognomy or in the clothing that would tell him the worst. At least, thought Horton, reaching the summit and staring down at the scene beneath him, they wouldn't be viewing charred remains, but a water-bloated body was little better.

As they descended he took in the scene spread out before him.

Directly beneath them was the salt water moat, where he could see Taylor and his SOCOs at work and Jim Clarke taking photographs. Uckfield, in a scene suit, was sitting on one of the three wooden picnic benches, his mobile phone clasped to his ear. A train screeched across the low railway bridge over the creek on their right where another police officer stood blocking the footpath. It was about an hour and a half to high tide. Horton caught a glimpse of cars on the Eastern Road to his right and beyond that Langstone Harbour and the flat landscape of the western shores of Hayling Island, which made him think of Stuart Jayston.

As they approached, Uckfield looked up with a grim expression on his florid face. One of the SOCOs handed them scene suits, which they rapidly donned before entering the inner cordon. The drone of the motorway traffic filled the air, and some short distance from where they were standing and to the left Horton could see the blackened grass and bracken on the bank from the previous fire.

Uckfield came off his phone and nodded a glum greeting at them. In silence they made towards the lifeless heap that lay under the black plastic sheeting. Jim Clarke stepped aside. The stench emanating from the body was overwhelming and sickening. It stuck in Horton's throat, almost making him want to retch. Cantelli, ashen faced, was rapidly chewing his gum.

'Ready?' Horton addressed Cantelli.

Cantelli nodded and tensed.

Uckfield pulled back the sheeting. Horton gave a sharp intake of breath and heard Cantelli do the same. Then he turned away. Horton heard him taking several deep breaths, which would be little comfort because the stench of the corpse was overpowering.

Quietly, Horton said, 'It's Tyler Godfray.'

'You're sure?' Uckfield peered at the distorted, dirty and sodden face.

'Positive.' Decomposition wasn't advanced, and the marine life in the salt water moat hadn't had time to make a meal of the face, but even despite that the whitened skin of the corpse, which was covered with silt and weeds, was disgusting enough to view. There was no doubting it was Tyler Godfray though. They also had a description from Tyler's foreman, Len, of what Tyler had worn into work on Tuesday morning before putting on his white overalls. They were the same clothes Horton could see now: jeans, a pale-blue T-shirt and white trainers.

Cantelli, clearly fighting to keep control of himself, turned back and confirmed it. There was no obvious sign of cause of death that Horton could see. The skull seemed to be intact, although he couldn't see the back of the head, and there was no blood on the clothes or any wound to indicate stabbing or shooting. God knew how Karen Godfray was going to take this news. Very badly indeed.

Replacing the protective covering, Uckfield said, 'Dr Clayton's on her way.' They stepped away from the corpse and returned to where Uckfield had been sitting, but they all remained standing. Horton relayed the outcome of his meeting with Dr Needham, drawing first a scowl from Uckfield followed by raised eyebrows and clear disbelief while Cantelli looked on as though in a state of shock.

'You believe that!' Uckfield declared, making it clear that he didn't.

Horton felt like snapping that he didn't know what the hell to believe any longer, but he said to Cantelli, 'Anyone spring to mind?'

'Not immediately.'

To Uckfield, Horton said, 'I think Sergeant Cantelli should return to the station and review his cases. He should also check with the prison service to see who has been released over the last three years and cross-reference them against his files to see if anyone fits the profile. We should also check if anyone has died in prison during that time, or possibly shortly after being released, who has a relative who might also fit the profile. Steve, we've got to consider every-thing. We might not have much time.'

After a moment Uckfield gave a curt nod. Horton felt relieved that Cantelli would be fully occupied and away from the scene. And Cantelli looked eager to start. He said, 'If this is being done to get at me, then how did the killer discover that Johnnie was my nephew? It was never mentioned in the newspaper reports at the trial, and he doesn't even have the same surname.'

Horton rapidly thought. He didn't think it had been recorded on the paperwork that the sailing charity had either, but he would check. 'Kyle Proctor was given a custodial sentence for the arson attack and sent to a secure centre for young offenders for eighteen months. Find out who he served with and if anyone has a connection with you, Barney, or your family, or if anyone who was serving time with Kyle has been convicted since and has a link to you. Also check out Kyle Proctor's family – find out who is alive, where they are and what they're doing.'

Uckfield scratched his leg and made to speak but Horton quickly continued: 'It could be someone on the sailing circuit, because that's how they would have managed to befriend Johnnie,' and that brought him back to Go About. He added, 'I still believe that Johnnie was with this person on the sixteenth of July and probably on several other occasions, and that Johnnie has been persuaded into keeping his meetings with this person secret so that the killer could execute his plan.' He recalled what Dr Needham had said. 'There could be two of them involved in this. A woman, who has lured Johnnie into a trap, and possibly lured Tyler and Stuart. And a man, to lug these bodies here and deposit them.'

Uckfield said, 'Unless Ryan and Tyler came here willingly because they thought they were on to a good thing with this woman.'

Horton agreed. 'I'd like to check the Go About files, to see if Johnnie's relationship to Cantelli is listed.'

'You're still after Masefield for this?'

Horton shrugged. 'I'll see if Don will give me a list of everyone who has been through that charity since Johnnie was there, including the service and ex service personnel, and then we can cross-reference it against Cantelli's list.'

They could apply for a warrant, but that would take time. And so would checking the lists. Horton just hoped they'd get a break-through before Stuart Jayston's or Johnnie's body showed up. And it wouldn't be here, because Uckfield would keep this area sealed off. The only problem was they couldn't keep it sealed off forever.

He looked up to see Dr Clayton heading towards them. Within minutes she was in a scene suit, and after giving them a brief nod and dashing an empathetic glance at Cantelli she began examining the body.

'Can I move his head?' she asked, bending down.

'You can turn him over if you like.' Uckfield nodded at one of the nearby officers also wearing a scene suit to help. Horton watched as she examined the back of the head and upper torso, and again she studied the victim's neck. Cantelli chewed his gum and kept his eye focused on the corpse.

'Where was he found?' she asked, straightening up.

Uckfield answered, 'Face down on the bank just in the corner of the moat.'

'Was the entire body submerged?'

'No, just the head and upper torso. His lower torso and legs were on the bank. The officer who was first on the scene checked for a pulse in the neck and then called in. Clarke's got photographs of the original position of the body, which he'll send over to you. He's only just been moved and turned over for ID purposes.'

'You know who he is?' She flashed a look at Cantelli.

He nodded and, with an edge of sharpness to disguise his pain, said, 'It's another of the lads that Johnnie used to associate with.'

'Just like the first victim.'

Cantelli nodded.

Gaye eyed him sadly before more briskly addressing them all. 'I can't give you an exact time of death or the cause but from my initial examination I'd say he's been dead about twelve to fourteen hours, but that is approximate.'

Which put it some time between five thirty and nine thirty last night. But Tyler had gone missing on Tuesday, so where had he been before showing up here?

Gaye said, 'Probable cause of death is asphyxiation, similar to your last victim, but this asphyxiation is most probably due to drowning. Until I conduct the autopsy, though, I won't know that for certain. I'll do it as soon as I have the body in the mortuary. There are no obvious signs of a struggle and no wounds, but he could have been drugged or intoxicated which would have made it easier for him to drown.'

Uckfield eyed her, frowning. 'You're saying he either drank or took drugs or both and then fell in and drowned? Accidental death?'

She narrowed her eyes at him. 'No, Detective Superintendent Uckfield, that is not what I am saying. I leave that to you to conjecture and investigate. But his killer could have drugged him and then left him to drown. I will give you my findings as soon as I have them later today.'

She again threw a sympathetic gaze at Cantelli before marching off.

Uckfield said, 'Want another look at him?'

They both declined.

As they divested themselves of their scene suits Horton watched Dr Clayton's slim, petite figure climb the steps to the top of the bastion. His gaze travelled from her to the large grass bank to the right and the mounds of earth in front of the bricked-up bastions. Something pricked at the back of his mind, but he couldn't grasp it. His thoughts turned to Karen Godfray. Someone was going to have to break the news to her, and in the circumstances he didn't think he'd be the best person to do so. With her already blaming him and Cantelli for her son's disappearance, she was bound to believe they had led him to his death. Uckfield agreed and said he'd send Agent Eames with DC Marsden.

'Will DCS Sawyer allow that?' Horton queried as they climbed the steps to the top of the bastion. He suspected that Uckfield wanted Eames out of the way so that Trueman could continue his researches into the jewellery thefts, along with Xander Andreadis and Masefield and his crew, without her knowing.

'I don't care what he allows. If she's part of the investigation then she can bloody well take the rough with the rest of us. All she's done is sit on her pretty arse and fiddle with her computer.'

Horton was almost stung to defend her but he knew that would only goad Uckfield into making cheap jibes about him fancying her. Uckfield wasn't strictly correct, because Horton knew that Trueman and Eames had been logging, analysing and filtering all the incoming enquiries from the house-to-house team, in addition to which she was still directing the investigations at Andreadis's end and examining evidence from the jewellery robberies . . . when she wasn't spending time with Stevington, he thought, roughly pushing that aside. But he knew that Uckfield viewed her as Sawyer's spy, and he didn't care for that or for being mistrusted. And Horton didn't blame him.

At the top of the bastions Horton turned back and surveyed the scene. He could see the undertakers moving towards the body. Suddenly, the thought that had eluded him a moment ago came to him. 'The bastions below us are bricked up, but perhaps our killer found a way in. If Ryan came here willingly, perhaps Johnnie did too. We need to search inside all the bastions in case he was brought here last Wednesday and is being held here.'

Surely the killer would guess they'd do a search? But they hadn't after Ryan's body had been found, and perhaps the killer was counting on the fact they wouldn't do so again.

Cantelli looked as though he'd like to volunteer for the job, but he said nothing. Horton knew he'd reckon that his time would be better spent tracking back through his cases.

As they began the descent to the car park Uckfield said, 'I'll get Dennings on to that and to organize a fingertip search of the area. Bliss can organize another press conference. The media are going to have a field day with this, and they're bound to make the connection between Ryan Spencer and Tyler Godfray and dig up the past.' He threw a look at Cantelli.

'I'll warn the family,' he tersely replied.

Horton saw that several of the media had already gathered beyond the cordon, and they began shouting questions at them as they reached the small car park. Uckfield growled that he'd make a statement at midday.

In the car on the way back to the station Horton rang Sergeant Elkins and asked him to find out where Masefield and his team had been last night. 'All of them,' he stressed. 'But try not to make it too obvious that you're interested.' He briefed him as to what had happened. 'I want to know who they mixed with, who they talked to. Find out if anyone went on-board their yacht when they returned from racing.' He hadn't seen anyone when he'd been there, but that had only been for a few minutes. Masefield could have given instructions to the killer by phone if this was down to him.

When he came off the phone, Cantelli said, 'I've never had any dealings with Masefield or any of his crew.'

Horton glanced across the creek and the moat to where Ryan and now Tyler's bodies had been found. He said, 'Get Walters to help you check through your case files. I'll call you if I get anything from Don.'

Collecting his Harley, Horton headed for Gosport and Haslar Marina.

NINETEEN

Don Winscom wasn't in his office, and it was locked. With irritation Horton hoped he wasn't out sailing or had decided to take a yacht with a team across to Cowes, because that would delay matters and he knew that time was fast running out for both Stuart and Johnnie. Perhaps it had already, just as it had for poor Tyler Godfray. He didn't envy Harriet Eames the task of breaking such tragic news to Karen Godfray. It wasn't exactly the news the Jaystons wanted to hear either. Bliss would appoint an officer to liaise with them.

He went in search of Winscom in the marina, heading for the pontoon where he knew the charity's two sailing yachts were usually kept, mulling over what he'd just witnessed on the bank of the moat. He wondered how Tyler had got to the area. Had his killer picked him up close to the property where he'd been working on Tuesday and taken him somewhere, and once there had kept him drugged until he was ready to kill him and transport him to the Hilsea Lines? Or had the killer arranged to meet Tyler at the place where he had kept him prisoner, which was where Stuart (and possibly Johnnie) were being held until it was time to dispose of them? Could Tyler have met his killer on a boat in the Camber? He rang Trueman and asked him to get a couple of officers down there asking around.

He felt an annoying niggle at the edges of his mind. Why that area? Was it because it was a good place to hide someone? Or did it have some other significance apart from the fact that Cantelli and his brother had played there as children? Could this vendetta against Cantelli go back years? He'd only asked him to look back at his cases for three years. What had Dr Needham said? *This could be years in the hatching.* And if that were the case, Horton didn't hold out much hope of coming up with the killer in time to save two more lives. He knew the thought was churning up Cantelli.

He turned on to the pontoon and headed in the direction of Portsmouth Harbour with a deeply troubled mind. Glancing about him he saw there were a considerable number of empty spaces on the pontoons, including those where both of Winscom's yachts were usually moored. He cursed softly. Just his luck. And he didn't have Winscom's mobile number; someone in the marina office might have it, though. He was about to turn back when he was hailed, and he looked up to see Roland Stevington on the deck of the large ocean-going sailing yacht moored at the end of the pontoon. He didn't want to speak to Stevington, or have time for it, but a grey head bobbed up from the cabin and Horton saw with relief it was Don Winscom. Both climbed off as Horton made towards them. Stevington stretched out a hand. 'Inspector Horton, isn't it?'

Horton found the grasp firm and dry as he expected. He stifled his unreasonable resentment towards the man and tried to blot out the pictures of Harriet Eames with him.

'Hattie told me who you were when we saw you running last night. She says you're a very good sailor.'

How does she know, thought Horton; he'd never been sailing with her. He didn't care for the fact they'd discussed him and wondered what else *Hattie* had said about him. He eyed the sixty-foot yacht, wondering if she'd spent the night on-board. Had the two of them cosied up together on it? It was none of his business if they had.

'Don, I wondered if I could have a word.'

'Of course. Thanks Roland.'

'Not at all. Anything I can do to help. There but for the grace of God and so on.' He smiled.

Horton drew Don Winscom down the pontoon. Winscom said, 'Roland's offered to donate a large sum of money to the charity and to take some of the lads and girls out on his yacht when he returns from the Velux 5 Oceans race.'

'That's generous of him. I hope he and the yacht get back safely.'

'So do I. Not everyone makes it. Any news of Johnnie?'

'No, but we have another body, one of Johnnie's former mates.'

'My God!' Winscom ran a hand over his grey hair.

'And the other member of that gang is also missing.'

'Surely Johnnie can't be involved in this?'

Horton winced inwardly. Now even Don Winscom had suggested it. He said, 'Whether he is or not I need your help. I need a list of everyone who has been referred to your charity by the police and any other organization, including the services' community health department, for the last six years, and I need it urgently.'

Would he quote confidentiality at him? Would Horton have to

return with a warrant, which would take time? He held Winscom's
stare, and after a minute Winscom said, 'I'm sorry, Andy, I can't
give you that.' Then he glanced at his watch. 'My goodness, is that
the time! I've got a call to make. I need to go back to the office;
perhaps you'd like to join me there for a coffee in, say, ten minutes.
I should be through by then.'

Horton got the message loud and clear. He breathed an inner sigh
of relief. 'Of course,' he replied with a flicker of thanks in his eyes.
As Winscom hurried away Horton turned back. Stevington was
on-board his yacht, and, filled with curiosity, Horton headed towards
him. He eyed the boat admiringly.

'Don got called away. He told me about your generous offer.
What did you mean when you said there but for the grace of God?'

Stevington straightened up. 'Sailing wasn't something that kids
like me got the chance to do, despite living so near the sea. Working-
class boy, son of a factory worker and a waitress, Mum died when
I was eight, Dad struggled on alone in a dead end job, incarcerated
in a steel shed, hating every minute of it but not having the guts to
break loose. It drove him mad. Not much money coming in. I was
left to my own devices. Didn't get up to anything illegal, but it was
only a matter of time before I would have done. I was restless and
high-spirited. I got bored at school, my mates bored me. I needed
action and activity, and then a friend at Dad's works suggested
sailing. I never looked back, did all my sailing exams, worked as
a crew member, raced, skippered yachts, and then went solo. Ever
thought about doing it yourself?'

Would he fancy solo racing around the World? Did he have the
balls for it, the skill, the passion and dedication to compete in
the race that Stevington had won, sailing thirty thousand miles
alone, battling against hurricane-force winds, mountainous seas,
coping with extremes, enduring both physical and mental stress? It
was gruelling, and yet it *was* the supreme challenge. With surprise
he found himself seriously considering it. There was no one to hold
him back. No wife, no parents, no lover, only the job. Perhaps he
could take a sabbatical. It would mean giving up on the search for
his mother. But by the time he'd be ready to compete in the next race
four years from now he might have discovered the truth about her
disappearance – always assuming he did find out the truth, and he
wasn't certain of that. Amos's envelope had led nowhere, although
he'd not had much time to consider it. Then there was Sawyer's visit

last night. Could he speed up his investigations by joining forces with Sawyer? Did he want to? Or would the quest for Zeus sidetrack him and slow down his investigations? Perhaps as someone intended it should.

'It must be tough getting sponsorship.' He wondered who the hell would sponsor him. He couldn't see his former father-in-law's marine company putting up money, not unless Toby Kempton thought he'd get rid of him permanently. Horton wasn't well connected, but Stevington had managed it, judging by the names on the hull, which he noted included Rupert Crawford's investment bank.

Stevington smiled. 'That's usually harder than the sailing.'

Horton doubted that, but he understood what Stevington meant.

'You make connections on the circuit, and if you're passionate about what you do it shows through. People begin to believe you and want to associate with success. Sailing around the world single-handed in the most challenging yacht race there is was my dream, and I was determined to make it happen, and because of that I didn't care who I approached or how many knocks I got, I just kept on trying. And then when you do well—'

'Or win.'

'It becomes much easier. People approach *you*. I'll be off to La Rochelle soon to give her a test before the start of the first ocean sprint to Cape Town.'

And that, Horton knew, was followed by four more sprints, the last an adrenalin-fuelled race across the North Atlantic and back into the Bay of Biscay. He thought of Sarah Conway hanging off that RIB. He was surprised she didn't go in for this. And him? The sailing he could do, the challenges he'd face at sea didn't scare him. He was attracted to the idea. So what was stopping him? The fact that he'd be alone, perhaps, cut adrift from the only family he'd ever really known – and he didn't mean Catherine and Emma, he meant the force. He'd miss Emma, and perhaps by being away he'd play into Catherine's hands and he didn't want that. But maybe soon it would be time for a change.

'We could go for a sail before I leave,' Stevington added, 'to see if you fancy handling one of these on your own some day.'

Horton found he'd like that very much. 'It's a deal,' he replied, shaking Stevington's hand and feeling less hostile towards him than he had. He headed for Winscom's office. He'd given him enough time.

Winscom looked up from his desk as Horton pushed open the door. 'Blast I've got to go out. Sorry, Andy, won't be a few minutes. Make yourself comfortable; help yourself to a coffee if you fancy one. Everything's over there, just to the right of my desk.'

Horton could see the cups and kettle on top of the small fridge. Winscom was performing like a bad actor in an old Ealing comedy, but he got the point and this was no laughing matter. It meant he'd have to walk behind Winscom's desk to get to the coffee, and on that desk would be the information he wanted.

As soon as the door closed behind Winscom, Horton made his way around the desk. He had no intention of making a coffee, but he flicked on the kettle for good measure and as he did he looked over a large picture of the marina on the wall above it and, to the right of it, a description of the marina's facilities and location. Suddenly, he froze. His heart stalled. He could hardy believe what he was seeing. Swiftly, he whipped Amos's envelope from his pocket and stared at the reverse of it, and then at the board. It wasn't possible. It couldn't be. He looked between the two sets of numbers on the picture. The top ones were identical to those on Amos's envelope – *01.07.05* – but the bottom set was different. On the picture the second set of numbers read *50.47.27*. And on the envelope Amos had written *5.11.09*. Was that why Amos had omitted the zero, because it wasn't *05* but *50*? Rapidly, he did some calculations. If he added the figures four and seven together he got eleven and if he added two and seven together he got nine. Was he simply too keen to find the meaning for Amos's figures that he'd grasp at anything?

He sat at Winscom's desk. His heart was going like the clappers. If Amos *had* given him the longitude and latitude of the marina, then why, for God's sake? What the hell was he trying to tell him? He could ask if Edward Ballard had moored up here recently or was here now, but Ballard might not have used that name and he could have changed his boat. So was he here under another name? Or was this place connected with one or more of the six men in that photograph from 1967? Lord Eames perhaps? He owned a boat. Did he keep it here? Or was this where Jennifer had come the day she had disappeared? But Amos wouldn't know that. Or would he?

Was Amos trying to tell him something else? But what, for Christ's sake? Had he completely misread this? No, he felt sure he was right. And, if so, he'd found the answer by a mere fluke. Would it have occurred to him eventually that he was looking at a location reference? Perhaps Amos had known he was a sailor so he might eventually make the connection. But it could have taken him months – years, even. So what did he do now? *Nothing* was the answer, he thought, stuffing the envelope back in his pocket, because he had something far more urgent to deal with.

He looked up to see Winscom slowly making his way back. Horton glanced at the desk. On it were several sheets of paper, each with a list of names, and swiftly he stuffed them into the pocket of his jacket before crossing to the door.

'I've got to go,' Horton said, 'but thanks.'

'Let me know how it goes.'

Horton promised he would and, despite his resolve not to follow up the lead that Winscom's picture had thrown at him, he found himself heading for the marina office. He thought there was little point in asking if Edward Ballard had moored his motor cruiser in the marina recently, but he did nonetheless and got the answer he had expected. No. Neither did Lord Eames keep a boat here.

Returning to his Harley he couldn't rid his thoughts of those figures. They just had to be the longitude and latitude of this place, but why? He found himself turning right out of the car park instead of left back to Portsmouth. As the traffic lights changed he crossed the single-lane bridge that spanned the harbour on his left and Haslar Lake on his right. Haslar Marina hadn't existed in 1978, it had been opened in the early 1990s; before then this had just been sea and shore and little else, so what could have drawn Jennifer here? Again, as he headed along a road made narrower by the high, barbed-wired topped red-brick walls either side of him, he considered the fact that she might have arranged to meet someone.

To his right he glimpsed the sign for the marine technology park and remembered that it had once been the Admiralty Experimental Works, and to his left he was soon passing the site of the former Haslar Royal Naval Hospital, now shut and due for development. He'd read that it had been built in 1762 as a dedicated military hospital for the Royal Navy, but that its Georgian Grade II listed buildings, set in sixy acres of parkland, would soon become expensive apartments. But in 1978 the hospital had been fully operational, so was it possible it had been Jennifer's destination? Could she have come here to see a doctor? Not for a medical reason but because she was having an affair with one. Or had she come to visit a patient who was serving in the armed forces? That was a possibility, except for the fact that the neighbour's statement in the very brief missing person's report had said Jennifer had been happy. But then she would have been if the man she'd come to visit had been recovering from a successful operation.

He swung off the road into a gravel unofficial car park that held only a couple of vans and one car. Climbing off the Harley, he removed his helmet and headed for the sea. Huge dark-grey rocks abutted the shore, and he could see no other people, apart from the lone figure of a man walking along the narrow footpath above the shore to his left, which led back to the marina and on to the Gosport ferry. No one could gain access to the shore from here because of the boulders imported as sea defences, and the area to his right, Fort Monkton, belonged to the army. It was sealed off with a high wire-mesh fence, barbed wire and security cameras.

If Jennifer's lover had survived a complex and possibly life-threatening operation then that would have been cause for celebration and for her to put on her best clothes and make-up. Staring across the Solent at the steeple of the church standing above the houses on the hill slopes of Ryde to his right, he considered the idea more fully. Perhaps she'd only just received the news that this person she cared for was at Haslar hospital, alive and recovering. Perhaps she'd believed him to be dead. A serving member of the armed forces didn't exactly fit with her involvement in the Radical Student Alliance, but that had been eleven years before.

He returned to the Harley and was soon passing through a residential area with no clear idea of what he was doing here. These modern houses certainly hadn't been built in 1978, but the golf club might have been here and the Forts, both Monkton and Gilkicker, certainly had been. They'd been around for centuries.

At the sign to the lifeboat station he turned off, parked the Harley in the official car park, paid for a ticket and headed down to the sea; this was too far away from the marina location for Jennifer to have come.

He applied his thoughts to the more urgent matter of Johnnie's disappearance and the deaths of Ryan Spencer and Tyler Godfray. There was something playing at the back of his mind, something he'd missed – that they'd *all* missed, he thought, ignoring the curious glances of the dog walkers and hikers as he trudged on in his biker leathers towards a mound of green earth rising from the pebbled beach. He stopped in front of it. Behind the earth, hidden from view at this angle, was Fort Gilkicker, an ancient monument that was about to be developed into more exclusive houses and apartments. He gazed up at it. There was nothing to see except the revolving coastguard radar on top of what had once been gun casements, but behind it, hidden from view, lay a row of derelict red-bricked barracks, stores and offices, which were to be converted to houses. The fort had originally been built in 1871 to protect Portsmouth harbour and to defend the deepwater anchorage at Stokes Bay. It had been abandoned by the military some years ago and left to rot by the council; surrounded by a wire fence, it was out of bounds to the public, and the builders had yet to move in. The deep throb of the hovercraft caught his attention, and he turned to watch it ride the tops of the small waves across to the Isle of Wight where he could see the yachts racing out of Cowes. It made him think of Catherine, with her new boyfriend, and Emma. He tried hard to push away his personal problems and willed his mind to concentrate on the matter in hand: Johnnie Oslow and the deaths of his old schoolmates. What was it that was bugging him?

His gaze fell on the Portsmouth horizon, taking in the council tower blocks one of which he'd lived in with his mother. He remembered how he'd look out of the window for hours watching the ships on the Solent. Perhaps he might have joined the navy if his young life hadn't been so disrupted. For a brief moment he considered what might have been if his mother hadn't vanished, but only briefly, because he knew those kinds of thoughts only led to bitterness. His gaze swept along the coastline of Southsea to the pier, and then the castle that Henry VIII had commissioned to protect the coast. More fortifications. That elusive thought niggled at him. He frowned in concentration, trying to grasp it.

He let his eyes look back westwards to the oldest part of Portsmouth. The cathedral rose behind the ancient walls of Old Portsmouth, with its Round Tower, originally built in the fifteenth century, and its Square Tower, built in 1494. More sea defences, like the fort behind him. Then it clicked. He spun round and stared at the fort and then back at the sea. Of course. What an idiot. It had been staring him in the face. He must have been blind not to see it!

His pulse quickened as he rapidly recalled what he'd seen that morning with Cantelli while climbing to the top of the bastion from the car park. Uckfield too had missed it, and he shouldn't have done because he was also a sailor. It was so obvious that he was furious with himself for taking so long to realize that the killer hadn't met Ryan at the ramparts, or driven Tyler's body there. No, he'd take them there by sea.

It was simple. The killer had made his way up Langstone Harbour and into the Hilsea Channel and along Port Creek. It must have been a small boat without a mast, because one with wouldn't have been able to get under the bridge that spanned the dual carriageway of the Eastern Road. It would have been dark on both occasions, but a small light on the boat would have helped the pilot to navigate. There were no houses overlooking the area, and the cars flashing past on the motorway wouldn't have seen it either. The creek was navigable at high tide.

Swiftly, he took his tide timetable from his pocket, although he didn't really need to consult it. Yes, high tide on Monday night, when Ryan had been found, had been at eighteen minutes past nine, and the fire had been reported at fifteen minutes past nine. The killer had carried Ryan's body from the nearest accessible point from the creek up to the tunnel, dumped it, and then set light to it. Then he'd called the emergency services from a mobile, which had now been dumped, before setting the second fire, and had then calmly taken the boat back into Langstone Harbour. Where he had gone or come from was another matter entirely. He could have travelled from so many points along the coast. But whoever the killer was he was fit enough to carry a body, unless there had been two or maybe three of them. Two to carry the body and one to remain in the boat.

High tide last night had been at eleven o'clock, so Tyler's body could have been dumped anytime between nine p.m. and one a.m. They hadn't had to carry him very far, just under the railway bridge and around to the far corner of the moat. Men trained to be super fit. Men who had been in the services. Men who knew about tides and navigating in the dark. Masefield and his crew. But they were all in Cowes. Or were they? And if it was them then Dr Needham's theory about Cantelli was shot to pieces. And Sawyer's theory was right back in the frame.

He reached for his phone and called Trueman.

'What have you got on Masefield and his crew?' Horton asked eagerly as soon as Trueman came on the line, hoping that by now he had something and that Harriet Eames was still out of the office.

'Not much,' Trueman answered. 'Scott Masefield and Craig Weatherby are both former Special Boat Service members.'

Masefield had said he'd been in the Royal Navy, and Leighton had confirmed this. Neither had made any mention of being in the Special Boat Services. A deliberate lie or just an evasion of the truth to avoid being asked further questions? Horton wasn't sure but he knew that the Special Boat Service was an elite band of men trained to carry out highly secretive and dangerous missions not only on sea and along coastlines but also on dry land operations, including those undertaken in Afghanistan and Iraq. Men more than capable of navigating a narrow creek in the dark.

Trueman continued. 'Eddie Creed was in the Fleet Diving Squadron, served in Iraq, Dubai, Malaysia and the USA; Declan Saunders was also Royal Marines but Commandos, and Martin Leighton was Royal Navy, Corps of Royal Engineers, amphibious engineer. I can't get access to their medical records, but all five men were discharged from the services on medical grounds.'

Horton explained his theory. 'They must have another boat at Cowes they are using to get across the Solent when it's dark. And while some of them are making an appearance in the bars the other two or three are slipping away. It's either a small high-speed motor-boat or a RIB.'

'Aren't they taking a chance on being seen crossing the Solent?'

'What's another RIB at this time of the year? There are hundreds of them, and especially around Cowes Week. And why shouldn't they be out on it? Masefield claims not to have met Johnnie at Oyster Quays, which I believe, but there's nothing to stop one of the others, or an accomplice, meeting him at the Camber on the RIB. And that's what Tyler and Stuart witnessed.'

'And Ryan Spencer?'

'Johnnie told whoever picked him up who the two lads he was talking to were and also mentioned Ryan Spencer. It took the crew a few days to track them down and plan how to kill them, but these are resourceful men and they'd manage it.'

But there was still that matter of Ryan Spencer having a phone. Then he saw it. Tyler and Stuart hadn't seen Johnnie meet Masefield last Wednesday week, but they *had* seen him with the crew, or one or more of them, on the sixteenth of July, and by then Masefield was already planning to dispose of Johnnie.

But although some of the pieces fitted there were still a lot that didn't. Maybe under questioning they'd get slotted in. The important thing was to find out where the crew were holding Johnnie and get to him and Stuart before they were killed.

He continued: 'Johnnie must have discovered or suspected that they were involved in these thefts that Sawyer and Eames have been investigating. They were racing in all the relevant locations at the time.' He silently recalled what Sarah Conway had told him. 'Every safe had been expertly blown using the latest in sophisticated explosives and the scene wiped clean, a neat and quick in and out job. In other words a highly professional operation carried out by a very specialized team which Masefield carefully put together for just such a purpose. They thought Johnnie knew too much. Maybe they engineered it for Andreadis to suggest Johnnie join them.'

But why had Johnnie asked the taxi driver for the fare to Hayling Island? Could the taxi driver have been mistaken?

'Is Uckfield there?'

'No. He's in with the ACC and DCS Sawyer.'

Horton cursed. He didn't have time to hang around waiting for them to finish their meeting. 'Tell Uckfield we need to bring them in for questioning and bugger what DCS Sawyer says. If it cocks up his operation then tough.'

But Sawyer might overrule Uckfield. 'Tell him I'm on my way over to the Island to apprehend and question them.'

'Andy—'

'I know. But I've got to force the issue. If Uckfield or Sawyer want to bollock me then tell them they'll need to come over and do it there.'

These were clever men though. Horton knew they wouldn't talk. And they had no evidence to charge them. All they had to do was remain silent and wait until the time limit for questioning them was up and then they'd be released. The minutes and hours would tick by and Johnnie and Stuart would be dead. He couldn't let that happen. He had to make one of them talk before Sawyer got there.

TWENTY

Horton called Elkins and asked him to collect him from Haslar Marina as quickly as he could. It took Horton eight minutes to reach the marina, and it took Elkins and Ripley another eight before they arrived in the police launch, which to Horton seemed like the longest eight minutes of his life. Finally, though, he was on-board donning a life jacket and Ripley was speeding across the Solent towards the mass of sails swarming around Cowes and out of Cowes.

'Where's Masefield?' Horton shouted above the throb of the engine. He'd already asked Elkins to locate him.

'Getting ready to race. His class start at twelve thirty,' Elkins replied.

Horton consulted his watch. Good, that gave them at least half an hour, which was enough time to prevent Masefield from competing, and that would hit him where it hurt.

'But, Andy, I've been checking him and the crew out like you asked, and they have good alibis for last night.'

'All of them?'

'Yes, they were in the yacht club receiving the trophy for winning their class and they didn't leave until gone midnight.'

That was worrying – or it would have been, except that Horton was now becoming convinced, beyond all doubt, that the crew had an accomplice. There was no other explanation. 'Did you notice if they made contact with anyone in particular?'

'Not really, but I wasn't watching them the entire time, and I wasn't at the yacht club.'

'And Tuesday evening when Tyler went missing?'

'They were all in the bar at Shepards Wharf until eleven thirty.'

And that ruled them out but not an accomplice. Someone outside the immediate crew, but who was working with them. Someone with a RIB who had been at all the locations where the robberies had taken place. Someone on the sailing circuit who cased out the properties, listened to the gossip in the marinas and knew Xander Andreadis's movements. But that accomplice wasn't Johnnie. Somehow Johnnie had stumbled on who it was, or the accomplice believed he had, and therefore Johnnie had to be disposed of. When the accomplice had picked Johnnie up in the RIB at the Camber at Old Portsmouth he'd seen Johnnie talking to Tyler and Stuart, and he could possibly be identified, so Tyler and Stuart had to be dealt with. And so too had Ryan because one of the lads could have spoken to him.

As Horton's brain raced to pull the remaining threads together he saw, ahead, just coming out of the Medina, Sarah Conway and her helmsman, Duncan Farrelly, on their RIB, making towards the buoy that marked the start of the race, ready to take photographs. They'd both been here during the Cowes to St Malo race in July when Johnnie had been on *Calista*. And Sarah Conway and Duncan Farrelly had been at all the other race events where those properties had been targeted. Now he knew who Masefield's accomplice was alright. Duncan Farrelly.

He reached into his pocket for the lists he'd picked off Winscom's desk, cursing himself for not looking at them earlier. With mounting excitement he rapidly ran his eye down the names until he came to one. He drew in his breath. There he was, Duncan Farrelly, another of Dr Claire Needham's referrals two years ago.

To Elkins he said, 'What do you know about Duncan Farrelly?'

'Not much. He hardly speaks, worships the ground Sarah walks on, which is understandable, and is an ex commando.'

That figured. He was strong and fit. Certainly strong enough to carry a dead weight up a bank and hide it in a bastion, and to carry another body from a RIB and place it in the moat. It was what he had been trained to do. That, and to kill.

'Head them off.'

'I thought we were after Masefield.'

'Sawyer can deal with them. Farrelly's in league with them.'

Elkins looked surprised but gave instructions to Ripley at the helm. Horton watched Sarah Conway's RIB draw closer. The broad shouldered helmsman's face was serious and set. Farrelly tossed something over his shoulder at Sarah, who was standing behind him, photographing the yachts in her wake and those just leaving the marina. She moved to stand next to him, then she pointed the camera at the police launch and kept clicking until the RIB was level with them.

Horton hailed them. 'Sarah, I want a word with Duncan.'

'Can't. Not now, Inspector, the race is about to start.'

'I don't think you'll be photographing this one. Or if you are then you'll need to do it without Duncan.'

'Why? What's he done?' she asked, smiling.

'We'll escort you back to the quay.'

'Don't be ridiculous, Inspector. This is my job.'

'And I'm doing mine.' And time was running out. Farrelly was their killer, and he would know where Johnnie was. And if he was still alive. He didn't have time to piss about.

'Duncan Farrelly, I'm arresting you on suspicion of the murders of Ryan Spencer and Tyler Godfray and the kidnapping of Johnnie Oslow and Stuart Jayston, you do not—'

'What on earth are you talking about?' Sarah bellowed, still smiling. 'Duncan hasn't killed anyone.'

Still Duncan didn't speak. Ripley had now positioned the launch alongside the RIB. In Farrelly's eyes Horton saw a wildness that sent a shudder down his spine and which jarred a fragment of memory that he didn't have time to analyse. He said, 'I'm coming on-board with a line. PC Ripley will take us back to Cowes.'

'Not bloody likely,' Sarah shouted. She nodded at Duncan, who thrust back the throttle and, in a roar and wash of sea, spun the RIB hard round. The wash caught the police launch on the side. It bucked and swayed, and Horton grabbed the rail to prevent himself from being knocked overboard. Elkins did the same while Ripley quickly turned the boat into the wash. Horton swore and roared instructions at Ripley to take after the RIB, which was already heading out into the Solent at a reckless speed, causing several yachts to sway in its wake. Horton saw two people fall in and others shouting and shaking their fists at the RIB. Ripley went after it as fast as he dared. The safety boat would help those who had gone overboard. Elkins was already on the radio calling up assistance from the Border Agency, the Coastguard and the Coastguard rescue helicopter. At this rate Horton thought they might need all three.

The north coast of the Island was speeding past them on their right as the RIB headed further out through the East Solent, towards Ryde on their right and Portsmouth on their left.

'They're going to kill themselves,' Elkins shouted as they raced after them. The police launch could easily match the RIBs maximum speed, which had to be about fifty knots, but Horton knew they couldn't chance that with so many yachts, pleasure craft and working boats on the sea, which Ripley was skilfully dodging.

The RIB skirted the end of the Ryde Pier and shot across the bows of the hovercraft coming out of Ryde. Ripley had to slow and detour around it.

'Bloody maniacs,' Elkins bellowed. 'How the blazes are we going to stop them?'

With great difficulty, thought Horton, unless they ran out of fuel – which they would eventually, but that might not be for some time. The Border Agency and Coastguard were on their way, and the RIB was being tracked. It couldn't escape. As the number of leisure craft thinned out behind them for a while Ripley made up some of the gap. Sarah turned to face them and began taking photographs.

Elkins said, 'I hope to God she's wearing a safety line.'

Horton couldn't see one. He squinted into the sun at her as she snapped away at them, completely oblivious of the danger she was in, and putting others in. He knew she was wild, but now he also knew she was mad, a complete adrenalin junky. Any sudden movement of the RIB caused by an unexpected larger wave or turn of the helm could throw her over. The sea state was slight, but as they headed further out it became choppier and he could swear the wind was rising. The wash from a container ship or large ferry in the distance could hit them at any time.

Duncan Farrelly glanced back at them. Did Sarah know what Masefield and his crew had been up to? Did she know what Farrelly had done? Of course she did. She was part of it, Horton realized. He guessed she had lured Johnnie into a trap on the Wednesday he had disappeared. Perhaps she was the one who had met him at the Camber on the RIB, or perhaps both of them had. Where had they taken him though? He had to find out.

The small yachts racing out of Seaview lay ahead. Farrelly manoeuvred the RIB further out to avoid them, and Ripley did the same with the launch. Horton thought he could hear the buzz of a helicopter somewhere and squinted up into the sky, which was beginning to cloud over. It had grown colder too, or was that just a premonition that was sending a chill through his bones? If Johnnie's life hadn't depended on catching them and making them talk he might have called it off and given instructions for them to be picked up when they came to shore, which they'd have to eventually, but he didn't have the luxury of time.

Next they were round Bembridge Point and heading out across the English Channel. Now Ripley could open up. But so too could

Farrelly, and he did. Horton could hear the throb of the coastguard helicopter overhead. Ripley's young face was focused ahead; his hands gripping the helm were white-knuckled. Elkins was grim faced and pale. Horton wanted to go faster but it was dangerous enough for them at this speed. They were in the sturdy launch, and he'd hate to be on the RIB, which was far more unpredictable and treacherous at this speed. He could see it pounding the waves, rising and falling alarmingly, slapping against the restless unpredictable sea, almost lifting Farrelly and Conway off their feet. She'd stopped photographing. The camera was around her neck, and she was holding on to the rail of the seat in front of her, looking at them with exhilaration not fear. My God, she's beautiful, thought Horton with a gasp of admiration and alarm. In the distance he could see a fishing boat, and beyond that a large container ship moving on the horizon; he could also make out one of the navy ships on exercise. There were a handful of yachts with their sails up but they were thankfully out of their line.

They'd head for France. They must know they wouldn't be able to escape. Even if the police launch pulled back, the RIB would be followed by the Border Agency. They didn't care. Neither of them. This was a game to them, but killing and kidnapping was not.

Farrelly looked back again, and as he did a larger than normal swell struck the side of the RIB which must have been caused by the container ship far out to sea. Horton hadn't seen it coming and neither had Farrelly, but Farrelly's reactions were quick: he made a tight turn to avoid it and then another tighter, harder turn, pulling the wheel hard over. As the RIB encountered the waves created by its own wake the hull dug in, causing a sudden jolt and change in direction, and in a split sickening second Sarah Conway was knocked off her feet and flung overboard. Horton watched horrified as her body was caught by the propeller. His breath caught in his throat as he watched her suddenly go limp. He didn't need to give instructions to Ripley, but instinctively he shouted for him to go rapidly to her assistance. Farrelly, sensing that the helm had momentarily slowed, glanced back. His face whitened as he saw what had happened. He spun the RIB round, almost causing himself to be knocked clear, and headed back towards Sarah.

The police launch was there first and Horton looked up to see the coastguard rescue helicopter throbbing overhead. Elkins was speaking into the radio, relaying what had happened, while behind them raced the coastguard RIB. Was she still alive? Horton stared down at the limp body kept afloat by her life vest. Her head was a mess of blood, which spread out in the sea like a red snake behind her. He felt the bile rise in his throat and heard Elkins gasp behind him. Farrelly had come alongside. Without a second thought he cut the engine and threw himself in before anyone could stop him and had Sarah in his arms. The Coastguard RIB was alongside, and the Lifeboat out of Bembridge was heading their way. Horton didn't know if Sarah was still alive. He hoped to God she was, but with that kind of head injury caused by the RIB's propeller he doubted it, and maybe Farrelly did too. Or perhaps he knew from holding her that she'd gone.

Within minutes Sarah had been strapped to a stretcher and was being winched up into the helicopter. They would take her to the neurological unit at Southampton Hospital. Farrelly let himself be taken on-board the police launch, where Elkins wrapped him in a silver thermal blanket. He sat huddled, silent under the awning, staring sightlessly at nothing.

Horton recalled the words that Elkins had uttered when he'd had first seen Sarah hanging off the side of the RIB: *Mad as a hatter . . . I warned her about being reckless.* Horton recalled her youth and beauty, her vibrancy, and the thoughts he'd had about her, that she would be fun to be with. Not any longer. He knew her words would haunt him for some time, maybe for always; Elkins had said: *You're going to kill yourself one day*, and she'd replied: *Better that than die a lingering death in old age.* Judging by Elkins' grim expression and Ripley's ashen face they were also recalling that.

Farrelly had been obsessed with her. He looked shocked and numb with grief, but Horton needed him to speak. He needed to find out what he'd done with Johnnie. 'We'll get you to the hospital, Duncan, to be checked over.'

That seemed to spur him into life. 'No hospital,' he snarled.

'Then tell me where Johnnie and Stuart are; don't add their deaths to the others. They don't deserve to die.'

Farrelly stared at him, confused.

'Sarah wouldn't want them to die, would she?' Horton pressed. But she had allowed Tyler and Ryan to be killed.

Farrelly was now shaking his head so violently, with a mixture of irritation and bewilderment, that Horton thought he'd give himself a haemorrhage. His dark eyes were full of pain.

'Tell me where they are,' Horton pressed. 'It's all over now, Duncan. We know about the jewellery thefts, we know Sarah phoned Johnnie and told him that Masefield wouldn't be collecting him from Oyster Quays, that you'd meet him instead at the Camber and bring him over to Cowes in the RIB. Only when you arrived at the Camber he was talking to two of his old mates, and you and Sarah thought he was telling them about yours and Sarah's parts in the robberies. You couldn't take a chance that he wasn't, which was why you had to silence him.'

But Farrelly was frowning and looking bemused.

Horton continued as Cowes drew nearer. He was running out of time. 'You took Johnnie somewhere and asked him who they were and what he'd been saying to them. Scared, he told you about Tyler Godfray, Ryan Spencer and Stuart Jayston, so you had to go after them. You had to make sure that none of them could lead us back to you, and of course you had to protect Sarah. I can understand that. You'd do anything for her, anything to keep her the free spirit that she is.' *Maybe was.*

'No,' Farrelly shouted. 'You've got it wrong. I never met Johnnie Oslow at the Camber. I don't even know him. I don't know what you're talking about.'

Was he going to continue to deny it? 'Is Johnnie still alive? Tell us where he is!' Horton said, forcing his voice to remain calm with difficulty while inside he was filled with desperation.

'I can't tell you because I don't know.'

Horton held Farrelly's stricken and confused expression. He'd listened to countless denials and false confessions in his career and was attuned to lies and deception. Was this another one? No, with a sinking feeling in his gut he knew that Farrelly was telling the truth. But how *could* he be? With a cold chill he realized that Dr Claire Needham had been right. This was nothing to do with the robberies. Duncan Farrelly was not their killer.

TWENTY-ONE

'What the hell did you think you were doing?' Uckfield snarled after Farrelly had been escorted away. He'd refused to be taken to hospital, but Horton knew the doctor would see him at Newport Police Station.

He sat down heavily in the cabin of the police launch. Elkins and Ripley were on the pontoon, as per Uckfield's orders. Horton felt sickened and saddened by what had happened and was filled with anxiety for Johnnie.

'Trying to catch a killer and save a life, two maybe,' he snapped.

'And it cost a life in the process.'

Horton winced inside. 'And Masefield and his crew?'

'Racing, where do you expect them to be?' Uckfield declared exasperated. 'DCS Sawyer does not take orders from you, and neither do I.'

'No, you're too busy covering your arse,' Horton snarled.

'And you won't have one to cover, never mind a job. Sawyer will see to that.'

'I doubt it,' Horton said in clipped tones. He'd given Sawyer a lever to use to get him to cooperate in the hunting down of Zeus. Stevington's suggestion of taking up solo round the world yacht racing was beginning to look very attractive.

'For Christ's sake, what have you got against Masefield and his crew?' asked Uckfield, still refusing to sit but looming over him in the cabin, his bulky presence filling it with aggression and tension.

I don't like them. But he could hardly say that. It didn't make them jewel thieves . . . and they weren't. Farrelly wasn't *their* accomplice, he was Sarah Conway's. He told Uckfield, who looked surprised then apprehensive, and finally a gleam appeared in his bloodshot grey blue eyes. Horton knew what was running through his mind. He'd got one up on Sawyer.

'You can prove this?' Uckfield said.

'No, but he'll talk now that Sarah is dead. It's my belief she cased out the properties. She knew a lot of people on the sailing circuit and probably personally knew each one of the victims who have been robbed. She got the security codes, found out when the residents wouldn't be at home, and then Duncan set the explosives and carried out the robberies with Sarah assisting him.'

'And the proceeds?'

'No idea. Probably just stashed away. I don't think either of them did it for the money but for the sheer bloody thrill of it.'

'Is he up to being questioned?'

Horton nodded. 'He denies having anything to do with Johnnie and the murders though.'

'We'll see if he changes his mind.' Uckfield made to leave. Horton knew he'd want to get in before Sawyer did and score one off him.

'I think he's telling the truth, and that means we'll waste hours questioning him while the real killer strikes again.'

Uckfield turned back. 'What makes you think he's not lying?'

Horton ran a hand over his face and took a deep breath. 'Gut feel. Yeah, I know you think that's a load of old bollocks. Go ahead and question Farrelly, and if I'm wrong then for God's sake break him quickly. But don't ask me to join you, because I'm going to look for the real killer.'

'But we've no idea who that is.'

'Then we'd better bloody find out,' Horton snapped, then took another breath. Losing control wasn't going to get them anywhere. He added more evenly, 'We need to get Winscom's list over to Cantelli in case he recognizes any names on it.' And he should have done that earlier. He'd wasted precious time. Oh, he'd got Sawyer's robbers for him – and in the process caused a death, he thought with bitterness, as Uckfield had so succinctly pointed out. And maybe his delay had caused two more deaths, Stuart's and Johnnie's. He'd been so sure it had been Masefield and Farrelly.

So who had Johnnie met on the Wednesday afternoon he'd disappeared? Again, Horton considered if the taxi driver could have been mistaken or lying. They'd relied a lot on his evidence. If he was mistaken then Johnnie could have headed anywhere, as they'd already hypothesized – perhaps to the centre of town where he'd met Ryan. But if the taxi driver was telling the truth and Johnnie had asked for Hayling, then he'd been instructed to do so by the killer. Why? To implicate him in a death, of course.

He sat up, alarmed, as the small fragments of information from the taxi driver clicked into place with what he'd seen recently – a long expanse of lawn that led down to an inlet of Chichester Harbour and the small sailing yachts off Hayling Island Sailing Club.

'Stuart Jayston!' he exclaimed, leaping up.

'Eh?'

'I know where he is or where his body will be.' He sincerely hoped it wasn't the latter, but he was very much afraid it would be. 'He's in the small boat house at the house on Hayling Island where I interviewed him, and that's why Johnnie was told to ask someone the fare there. To make us think he killed him.'

'But the workmen would have found him.'

Horton remembered what Gordon Jayston had told him. 'They're not working on the house. A delivery of wood hadn't arrived, and Gordon Jayston said he'd pulled them off and put them on another project. They had too much work for the workers to be idle.'

'The killer couldn't have known that.'

'He could if he contacted Stuart.' And Horton remembered Stuart being on the phone when he'd arrived. 'Or perhaps the killer thought he'd take a chance. He dumped his body there last night, either before or after dumping Tyler's at the moat.' And he could so easily have done that by boat, motoring around from Langstone Harbour into Chichester Harbour and to the house on Hayling. But perhaps Stuart had never left the area. He recalled the neighbouring property fronting on to the waste ground. 'The house Stuart was working on at Hayling is empty. The owners work and live in London. It's their weekend and holiday place. We'll probably find Stuart's van close by, and I think I know where.' He told him about the derelict house next door to the Hayling property. Uckfield was already on his phone ordering a unit over there immediately. Havant police, the nearest, would attend and call Uckfield as soon as they had news; it would take them, what, five minutes to get there on blue lights, as Uckfield instructed.

Horton's brain was teeming with thoughts. 'If Stuart is there, then obviously Johnnie's death is next and the last and it has to be made to look like suicide, even though we won't believe it. The coroner will give an open verdict, the press will speculate, and some will say that Johnnie did it to stop his old former school-mates from telling the sailing world he had a conviction.'

'But everyone knows about that.'

'Not everyone, Steve, only Andreadis, and he was good enough to give the lad another chance, just as Don Winscom was. *We* know that's not the real reason why these men have been killed, so there's another, and as Dr Needham said it's either revenge or some kind of warped justice against Cantelli or . . .' But Horton stalled. Was that just another blind alley? 'Or to stop Johnnie and the others from telling something they know.'

'If that's the case then they've had seven years to do it and seven years to be silenced. I can't see it being that.'

Uckfield must be right. Horton said, as though to himself, 'Where and how will the killer make it look like suicide?'

'A hose from the exhaust into a car?'

'Johnnie hasn't got a car.'

'The killer could steal one and make it look as though Johnnie had stolen it.'

'Possibly.'

'Drugs and drink administered to him under duress,' Uckfield said.

'Or put in his food and drink. Then he'll be taken out to sea, his shoes and some clothing, or perhaps most of his clothing, removed and his body thrown overboard. If his body is washed up along the shore the assumption will be that, disturbed by what he'd done, he got drunk, took some drugs and drowned himself.'

Even if his body was never washed up it would throw up enough questions and speculations to damage the Cantelli family. Had he killed himself? Did he kill the others? Where was his body? It would be a living hell. It would destroy them, and Horton wasn't going to allow that to happen.

'It's likely to be done tonight or tomorrow night, so where is he being kept? Where could the person who met him at the Camber have taken him by boat?' Horton said.

'It can't be the Hilsea bastions because he'd know we'd seal it off with the second death. We're still searching it. The killer won't be able to get Johnnie out of there if he's kept him hidden somewhere inside those tunnels.' Uckfield's phone rang, making them both start. Uckfield snatched it up, listened and then said, 'Seal it off. No one, and I mean no one, is to enter even the outer cordon until I get there. And if anyone speaks to the press I'll roast their balls over a slow fire.'

Horton didn't need to be told what the Havant police had found in the boat house on Hayling. Uckfield rang off and immediately punched in another number. Horton heard him relay the news and instructions to DI Dennings to meet him at the boat house and to mobilize the circus.

When Uckfield came off the phone Horton said, 'Do we know how he was killed?'

'Looks like strangulation, but they haven't disturbed the body just checked to make sure he is dead, although there wasn't any doubt. I'll call Dean.'

Horton went up on deck and beckoned Elkins and Ripley on to the launch. He told them to head back for Portsmouth. Uckfield had been brought over by a Border Agency RIB.

God knew how Cantelli was going to take this news, but Horton wanted to tell him before he heard it from Bliss or Dennings. He rang him. There was a moment's stunned silence before Cantelli, his voice tight with emotion and reverberating with desolation, said, 'I can't find anyone that fits the profile.'

'Keep looking, Barney. Elkins will make sure the list Winscom gave me gets to you at the station.' Elkins would drop Horton back to Haslar Marina where he'd collect the Harley and then the launch would take Uckfield on to Hayling. He was about to ring off when Cantelli said, 'I'm sorry to hear about Sarah Conway. That must have been tough for you.'

Even frantic with worry, Cantelli could think of someone else's loss. 'Not as tough as it is for Farrelly,' Horton answered. Coming off the line he instructed Elkins to get him a chart of the coast of Portsmouth and Gosport. They went below, where Uckfield stood red faced and tight-lipped. It didn't look as though his call to Dean had gone well.

'The bloody gnome thinks I can pull the murderer out of a hat. I've told him we need extra resources and bloody quick. He said he'll see what he can do. See what he can do! Anyone would think I'd asked him for a larger desk.'

Elkins, pretending not to hear this, spread the map out on the table. The three of them studied it as the launch made rapid progress across the Solent. Horton said, 'If we're right then the killer has taken Johnnie somewhere within easy distance of the Camber. A place where he is able to keep him hidden, alive, fed and unharmed until the time is right to dispose of him.'

Elkins said, 'He could have gone further up into Portsmouth

Harbour to Horsea Marina, or along the Portchester and Fareham coast.'

'Not the marina – that would be too restrictive because of the lock, and he'd be seen going in and out. He needs to be somewhere accessible and private.' Which could mean a house with a mooring, and they'd never be able to search all of them in time unless it was one that was vacant, perhaps on an estate agent's books. He said as much to Uckfield, who said he'd get Marsden on to it, and added, 'But if the owners are on holiday and haven't told the police there's not much chance of us knowing about it. He could have crossed Portsmouth Harbour into Gosport or Haslar Marina?'

'Too public,' answered Horton.

Elkins traced the coast of Portsmouth with his finger saying, 'Or along Southsea Bay to your marina, Andy, but that would mean he'd be restricted by the Cill and it wouldn't give him the flexibility he needs to come and go. So he could have gone anywhere along the coast of Langstone Harbour to Broadmarsh at the north where there's a public slipway, but I don't think there's anywhere to hide along there.'

'There isn't,' Horton answered. 'But there are a few houses with slipways on to Langstone Harbour, both on the Hayling Island side and on the Portsmouth side, not far from where the arson on the sailing club was.'

Uckfield said, 'I'll get uniform calling on them.' He telephoned Trueman and asked him to organize it and make it priority. 'Bugger what Dean says,' he added sotto voce to Horton.

Horton went back up on deck. Soon they were heading along Stokes Bay, past the Browndown Battery, which was built in the late 1800s and used by the army for training purposes; past Gilkicker Point, where he'd stood not long ago and had become convinced that Masefield and his accessory were their killers; and then past Fort Monkton, before the launch headed into the harbour and deposited him at the marina. He climbed on his Harley and began the journey back to Portsmouth, his head reeling with all that had happened and reverberating with so many questions that it hurt. Why had three young men died? What was this killer's motive? Was it revenge on Cantelli and the desire for a warped kind of justice? Or was it something linked to these lads, as he'd suggested to Uckfield? If the latter, the only thing they had in common was that arson attack seven years ago. Perhaps he should start there, and that meant going to the sailing club. He had no idea what he was going to achieve by viewing the scene of that long ago arson, but he headed there with a silent prayer that he'd find inspiration, because if he didn't the alternative was too horrific to think about.

TWENTY-TWO

An hour later – it was now late afternoon – he was standing on the shore by the sailing club and staring across Langstone Harbour. The clouds had joined up to form a blanket of oppressive dull greyness which the stiff warm breeze did little to dispel. He could smell rain in the air and feel the cloying dampness on his skin. To his right he could see the masts of the yachts in his own marina. Across the narrow stretch of water on Hayling Island, Uckfield and Dennings had already viewed Stuart's body. Uckfield had called him a few minutes ago to tell him that Dr Clayton's initial examination suggested the cause of death had been strangulation with a ligature, the same method as that used on the other two victims. She'd found evidence of it during the autopsy on Tyler Godfray. Stuart Jayston's estimated time of death she put between twenty-four and twenty-seven hours ago, which suggested to Horton that Stuart had been killed shortly after meeting the killer. Stuart's van had been found outside the derelict house where he'd been lured, possibly with the promise of a building contract. Taylor and his SOCO team were at the scene of crime on Hayling Island, and the derelict house and van would be examined for forensic evidence, but Horton wasn't convinced they'd find much.

He visualized the killer making his way to the creek under cover of darkness, showing perhaps just a small light on the boat, and dumping Tyler in the moat. Then he'd motored out of Langstone Harbour, along the Hayling coastline eastwards, and into Chichester Harbour, where he'd collected Stuart's body, slipped the boat on to the shingle shore and dumped him in the boat house. With just that handful of expensive large houses on one side of the inlet, and fields and horses the other side, no one would have seen anything.

Who had broken the news to Gordon and Jean Jayston? Perhaps someone from Havant police had been sent, or perhaps Uckfield had gone himself. They would obtain Stuart's mobile phone records, but Horton didn't hold out much hope of them getting a lead that way, or not before it was too late. His heart hardened as he thought of this cold calculating killer, and he recalled what Dr Needham

had told him: *the killer wants to get even.* With whom? If it was
with Cantelli then the killer had made his point. But he hadn't, not
yet, not until Johnnie was dead. Should he consult Claire Needham
again? Could she give him further information or insights into this
evil bastard that might help them apprehend him quickly?

He turned and surveyed the new sailing club building. Through
the windows facing on to the harbour he could see a handful of
people drinking and chatting, but there weren't many there; it was
low tide and getting late. He had found the secretary though on his
arrival and had asked him for a list of the members from seven
years ago, hoping it hadn't been destroyed. He'd been informed the
accountant would have it and the secretary would make sure it was
emailed to Horton first thing in the morning. That might be too late,
Horton thought gloomily, because even if they got it then it would
still take time to check out the names, unless one of them meant
something to Cantelli.

He called him. 'Anything?'

'Nothing,' Cantelli said mournfully. 'I've come across some scum
in my time but I can't find anyone who would do this. Are you sure
it's not Farrelly? If I pleaded with him would he tell me where
Johnnie is?'

Cantelli's despair and desperation gripped Horton with pain. For
a moment he questioned his judgement about Farrelly, but not for
long. 'It's not him.' He surveyed the dinghies and the club house
behind him. Horton couldn't see how anyone could kill three people
for setting fire to the club, especially when a new, better and bigger
one had been constructed in its place. No one had been inside at
the time, so no one had been injured or killed. Nobody had lost
anything of great value unless you counted a dinghy, but even that
would have been insured, and if it hadn't then replacing it would
only have cost a couple of hundred pounds – maybe less, maybe a
little more. It wasn't worth killing three people for. But people did
kill for less. They killed for the wrong glance or the mildest insult,
especially if they were unbalanced, drugged up or intoxicated. But
this was no random murder. This, as Dr Needham had said, had
been planned for some time. He recalled her words: *he's hostile
and arrogant with domineering behaviour. He needs to demonstrate
his superiority so the kidnapping and killing in this ritualistic way
fulfils that need. It all helps to bolster his self image.* That didn't
fit with getting even over losing a dinghy. And why wait seven

years? Maybe during that time this madman had brooded on it, it had festered and become a slight of huge proportions, a focus for all his problems and failures in life, just as Dr Needham had said. Cantelli had become that focus for hatred and revenge. And the killer wanted Cantelli to suffer. Well, the bastard was certainly succeeding there. And he wasn't the only one.

He said, 'Get hold of the insurance report on the arson at the sailing club. Find out who lost what in the fire.' He told Cantelli they'd have a list of the members from seven years ago in the morning and heard Cantelli's unspoken thoughts: *What good will that do when Johnnie might be dead?* 'Also get the case file on the arson. Go through it with a fine toothcomb, read all the statements, see if anything unusual stands out or if you recognize any names. I'm on my way back.'

There was nothing he could do here. He headed slowly back along the residential street where Johnnie and his mates had fled that night. The trees on his right signalled that he was passing the grounds of the psychiatric hospital. It was in there that Johnnie and his mates had run as the siren of the fire engines had sounded in the distance. Horton found himself turning the Harley into the long tree-lined driveway. He wondered how far they had run and in which direction. Had it been into the trees and across the grass to his left or into the thicker trees and shrubbery to his right? They couldn't have run as far as the roundabout he was now approaching, in front of the elegant brick building, because the security cameras would have picked them out. He drew to a halt in one of the parking spaces. Was it significant? Did it matter? He doubted it. What had Tyler Godfray said? *Haven't seen him for years. Not since he dropped us in it . . . He went squealing to the police.* Yes, Johnnie had been the first to own up after the patrol car had stopped them. And if they had stayed hidden in the trees and bushes they might have got away with it, or at least they might not have been apprehended so quickly.

Something stirred in Horton's mind. He continued to stare at the entrance to the psychiatric hospital, recalling more of what Tyler had said. *He got scared. Went running out of that mental hospital like a lunatic.* Like a lunatic. Was it just a turn of phrase prompted by the fact this was a psychiatric hospital? Why had he run out?

Horton's mind jumped to Zachary Benham, one of those six men in that photograph from 1967, and Horton recalled what he'd read online about the fire in which he and twenty-three other men had perished. They had all been locked in their rooms. But mental health patients weren't locked up any more, or were they? Yes, some were, but many weren't, and what if Zachary Benham had witnessed something and had died for it? What if Johnnie had seen something which had so scared him that he'd run out of the grounds and into the arm's of the police *like a lunatic*? The others had followed.

He felt a rush of adrenalin, sensing that he was on to something. If that was the case, then why hadn't Johnnie mentioned it when questioned? Had it terrified him so much that he couldn't bring himself to speak about it? Was it because he wasn't sure of what he'd seen? Or because if he mentioned it he'd be laughed at? Maybe he thought it was an illusion, his mind playing tricks with him; many people were frightened of the mentally ill. But he *had* seen something here, or rather someone, and the killer, fearing that Johnnie and the lads would talk about it, had silenced them because of it. But why wait seven years?

He made his way to the entrance, his mind working overtime. There was an answer to his last question. The killer had been admitted here and had stayed here until recently. On his release or discharge, whatever term they used, he'd gone to live or work abroad, and that was where he had suddenly and unexpectedly come across the young man who had seen him in the grounds one night seven years ago.

Horton stood in the entrance for a moment and considered it. The killer had made it his business to find out everything he could about Johnnie, and he'd watched and waited to find out if Johnnie would recognize him. Maybe he did. Maybe not. But the killer wasn't prepared to take that chance, because if it came out that he'd been here as a patient it would ruin him. Why? What was at stake here? His career? His marriage? Or was there no reason – the killer was mentally ill and viewed Johnnie as a threat for what he might reveal.

Horton made for reception and demanded to speak to the manager. She wasn't there, but the assistant manager was. Horton waited impatiently for her, only to be told that he couldn't have access to medical records or details of patients without a warrant. Horton felt like screaming, but she was adamant, and despite the fact that someone's life was in danger, which he told her, she dug her heels in.

He left in a temper. There might be another way. Dr Claire Needham. But as he headed along the seafront towards her house he suddenly realized that he didn't need the records or to talk to Dr Needham. He pulled over and removed his helmet, looking across the choppy Solent, which was growing steadily darker in the declining day. He just needed to put the strands of what he knew together. Think logically, he urged his tumultuous brain. Consider what you know, both the facts and the suppositions. The killer was a very competent sailor who knew the tides around Portsmouth and how to navigate narrow channels in the dark. How did he know that? Perhaps he had been raised here. He also knew the Hilsea Lines well enough to plant the bodies, so he could be someone who had either lived in the area, or who had worked in one of the units backing on to the bastions. Or perhaps, like Cantelli, his father had. Horton felt a frisson of excitement. This man had befriended Johnnie after coming across him while abroad. How had he met him? Through sailing, of course, either at a location where *Calista* had been moored or at one of the races Johnnie had participated in. He'd cultivated a friendship with Johnnie, who had been persuaded to keep it secret. Why? Because he had promised Johnnie something, a future racing with him, a special mentoring programme, oh yes, Horton was beginning to see it quite clearly. And on the sixteenth of July this man had met Johnnie and had taken him out sailing for the day – as a trial, he would have told him. But all the time he was pumping Johnnie for information about his past, his old school-mates, their names and backgrounds so that he could trace them and plot how best to deal with them. Then when his plan was complete he had suggested to Andreadis that he send Johnnie over to compete with Masefield to see how he shaped up with a new crew. Or perhaps he hadn't openly suggested it, perhaps he'd planted the idea in Andreadis's mind or in Johnnie's and it had somehow come up in conversation. Then Johnnie was here but was diverted to the Camber where the killer met him. Not on his yacht, that would have been too conspicuous, but on a borrowed RIB or small motorboat.

Farrelly's dark eyes swam before Horton's vision, and that pinprick of a memory he'd had when looking into them coalesced into recognition. He was looking for a fanatic. A man with passion, with a ruthless determination to succeed at all costs, a man who took risks and wasn't afraid of the consequences, a man who could plan in advance and for whom danger held no fear, just like Sarah Conway. A man who would cold-bloodedly kill.

Horton donned his helmet and swung the Harley round. He might already be too late, but he had to take the chance. How to get him to reveal where Johnnie was though, he didn't know, only that he had to try.

TWENTY-THREE

There was no sign of Stevington on-board his yacht. Horton's hopes were dashed only to be lifted a moment later when a voice called out, 'Looking for me, Inspector?'

Horton swivelled round to see Roland Stevington on the deck of a small hi-speed motorboat with a cuddy. 'I was,' he answered lightly, making his way towards him as casually as he could although his body was taut with anger and adrenalin.

Stevington said, 'I hear that Sarah Conway's been killed in a RIB accident. What a tragedy. She was a brilliant sailor and photographer; completely mad though.'

'How did you hear?'

'News travels fast on the sailing circuit. It's been on the Internet and the radio. I also heard that a man's being held for questioning regarding her death and that of the other lads who have died here recently. I'm assuming it's Duncan Farrelly. Is it true?'

'He denies having any involvement in the deaths of Ryan Spencer, Tyler Godfray and Stuart Jayston.' The last name hadn't been released, but Stevington showed no sign of surprise or puzzlement at Horton's mention of it. 'If he's telling the truth then we've hit a brick wall with the investigation, and there's still Johnnie Oslow to find.'

'No progress on that then?'

'None. But I'm not here about that. It's regarding what you were saying earlier, about single-handed yacht racing. I've been giving it some thought. It's been a hell of a couple of years for me, what with my suspension; Harriet might have mentioned it to you.' He knew he was fishing.

'She said something about an investigation that went wrong, but I don't know the details.'

Stevington might not, but Horton bet Harriet Eames did. She might not have heard about it from her father though; anyone in the station could have told her.

Stevington said, 'Still, you're back in the job now.'

'Yes, and I'm thinking of chucking it in. I've had enough, and now that my marriage is over there's nothing to keep me here. I wondered if you had a moment to talk.'

'Come on-board.'

Horton jumped on to the deck. 'Not your usual method of transport,' he joked.

'No, but it's useful for crossing to Cowes.'

And to the Hilsea Lines and the boat house on Hayling Island, thought Horton as Stevington added, 'The marina has loaned it to me.'

'I guess when you get to be famous you get quite a few things loaned to you.'

'And given to me. Clothing, equipment, just as long as I'm willing to be photographed wearing it or using it. Drink?'

'Diet Coke, if you've got one?'

Stevington slipped down into the small cabin and reappeared with a can unopened. Horton wouldn't have drunk from it if it had been opened.

'It's not very cold, I'm afraid. No fridge on this thing, very basic. Just a cool bag.'

'That's fine.' And in that cool bag would be food, drink and drugs for Johnnie. With relief, Horton realized he'd made it just in time. 'I'm not delaying you, am I?'

For a moment a flicker of surprise showed behind Stevington's deep brown eyes, before he smiled and said, 'Not at all.'

In that instance Horton saw that Stevington knew why he was here, and it didn't have anything to do with talking about single-handed round the world sailing. But they'd keep up the pretence a bit longer. Horton forced himself to appear relaxed although his body was filled with tension and his mind was working overtime on how to handle this.

'Did you belong to a sailing club when you lived in Portsmouth? Hilsea, wasn't it?'

'No, Cosham.'

'Not far from the Hilsea Lines then.' Horton took another pull at his Coke, keeping his eyes on Stevington, who was sitting opposite him. Cosham was across Port Creek to the north.

'My Dad worked at Alanco Aviation which practically backs on to it. Sometimes I'd meet him from work and play in the old ramparts and the moat.'

'Before you discovered sailing and competitive racing.'

'Yes.'

'But you were always best sailing on your own?'

'Yes. A bit like you, Inspector.'

'Why do you say that?'

'Because you're here on your own, and you're taking a chance. Hattie was right when she told me you would make a good single-handed sailor. You're like me: someone who prefers to be alone, without encumbrances.'

And did Harriet tell you that too? Is that her view of me?

Stevington continued: 'You like a challenge and you're prepared to take risks, just as you're doing now. No need to put on the bemused act, Inspector. You know I killed Ryan, Tyler and Stuart, and you want to know where Johnnie is and if he's alive.'

Horton wasn't surprised that Stevington had taken this stance; it was why he'd come here alone, without back up and without calling in, because if they had brought Stevington in for questioning he would simply have sat in the interview room, saying nothing and letting Johnnie die. Then they would probably have had to release him because of lack of evidence.

'Is he alive?' Horton asked almost casually, though his nerves were taut.

'I'll take you to him. It's what you want, isn't it?'

Horton saw the challenge in Stevington's eyes: duck out now and you might get to live but you'll never find out where Johnnie is, or come with me and take the slim chance that you'll get the better of me if it comes to a fight and you might get to save Johnnie.

'Thanks.'

Stevington cast off. As Stevington navigated out of the marina, Horton wondered if he could retrieve his phone from the pocket of his jacket and call in, but he wouldn't be able to do so with Stevington so close to him in the small motorboat at the helm. No, he had to go along with this and find a way out of it once he knew where Johnnie was. Once he'd seen him.

He didn't notice the drizzling rain now sweeping off the sea and blowing into his face as he sat close to Stevington under what little cover there was from the awning. He speculated on where they were heading, knowing it wouldn't be the Hilsea Lines. Soon Stevington was passing through Portsmouth Harbour and into the Solent, keeping the Gosport coastline close on their right. Old Portsmouth and Southsea receded further in the distance on their left.

Horton said, 'Why did you kill them?'

'I couldn't let them stop me from competing,' Stevington tossed over his shoulder, speaking as though Horton would understand.

'Would they have done that?' he asked, making sure to maintain a conversational tone.

'If they'd gone public with what they'd seen.'

'You in the grounds of the psychiatric hospital seven years ago, you mean?'

'Yes.'

And Horton knew that meant Stevington couldn't afford to let him live either. This was a man who would risk everything for his passion. A fanatic who would let nothing stand in his way, who had defied danger and cheated death so many times that he had probably come to believe he was invincible. He was fit and ruthless. He took chances, and so far they had paid off. If one day they didn't then maybe he would go out laughing – like Sarah Conway, Horton thought with a pang of sorrow. But however it ended Stevington certainly wouldn't go without a fight, and Horton steeled himself for it.

'But there's nothing shameful in mental illness,' he said.

'Isn't there? Don't you believe it! Once people know that they look at you more warily. No one will trust you, and they certainly won't give you money for sponsorship.'

'Scott Masefield seems to have done all right.' That earned him a glowering look.

'He and his crew are all veterans,' Stevington snarled with resentment. 'Everyone makes an exception in their case. Casualties of war, post traumatic stress disorder and all that. But it's different for everyone else.'

'Are you trying to tell me that you were a patient at the hospital?' Horton said, injecting incredulity into his voice, while silently thinking that Stevington should be committed and right now. He caught a flash of anger in the dark eyes.

'See, even you don't understand,' he cried, but his indignation didn't fool Horton. There had to be something more that Johnnie had seen, something that had really scared him, and it couldn't just have been a man, but a man doing something. Rapidly, he recalled what Stevington had said earlier. *Dad struggled on alone in a dead end job, incarcerated in a steel shed, hating every minute of it but not having the guts to break loose. It drove him mad.* And then he knew.

'Was your *father* a patient?'

Stevington eyed him keenly but didn't speak.

As the dark shadows of the buildings in the grounds of the former Royal Naval hospital at Haslar slid by on their right, Horton said, 'Your father suffered from depression and was admitted to the hospital. Johnnie and his mates saw you in the grounds with him.' But that wasn't enough to make Stevington kill them. Or was it? Not unless Stevington's father had killed himself in those grounds and Stevington had been there at the time.

Following Horton's train of thought, Stevington said, 'If the police had discovered that I had been there that night they would have jumped to the conclusion that I had something to do with his death. There would have been an investigation, media interest, I'd have lost my sponsors and I would have lost the chance of competing in the race because I'd have had to hang around and answer questions.'

'And for that three men have died!' Horton cried.

'They don't matter! What does is the race,' Stevington answered in earnest, almost beseeching Horton to understand.

'And winning it at all costs,' Horton said more calmly as he rapidly tried to assess how best to handle the man in front of him.

'Yes,' Stevington replied almost triumphantly. 'My father didn't want me to go. He thought I'd be killed. He begged me to stay.'

'And that meant making a commitment. You don't much care for those, do you, Roland?'

'No, and I don't think you do either.'

But Stevington was wrong about that.

'It means making sacrifices, compromising,' Stevington said as he slowed in an increasingly rough sea. Soon they'd be drawing level with Fort Monckton. 'I'd be trapped. He couldn't grasp what yacht racing meant to me. I was due to sail to La Rochelle the next day. I was getting the boat ready. I went to see him before sailing but when I got there he was dead, hanging from a tree in the grounds. There was nothing I could do.'

'You could have stayed and got his body down.' Horton didn't believe him. He knew what had happened. Stevington had killed his father and had made it look like suicide. Johnnie might not have witnessed that, but he'd seen the body swinging and a figure looming in the bushes. The tales of mad people haunting the grounds had assailed him. He thought he'd seen a ghost; he'd taken fright and ran out. The others had followed. Johnnie had been glad to be

arrested. It had shocked him, and he was too frightened to say what
he'd seen fearing he'd be ridiculed or haunted further. He put it out
of his mind and made an attempt to change his life. The nightmare
apparition of a man's body dangling from a tree and perhaps a
hunched figure beside it had receded. It had never happened.

'There wasn't time to get him down,' Stevington said. 'I couldn't
do anything anyway. I heard a noise, and that's when I saw them
run into the grounds. I stepped back behind the shrubbery but one
of them turned at the sound and looked straight at me. I heard him
tell the others that the place was giving him the creeps and to get
out. They didn't want to go. They argued. But he ran out into the
driveway.'

And the others had followed. Roland Stevington had escaped the
security cameras because he was already inside the grounds and
had been for some time. He'd also been permitted entry because
his father was a patient.

'But that's not how it happened, Roland. You killed your father
because you despised his weakness and you thought his dependency
would stifle you and prevent you from doing what you wanted, not
to mention that on his death you would inherit his house, which
would help fund your passion, sailing.'

He thought of Harriet Eames falling for this man. Was she in
love with Stevington? He'd seen them kiss, but that was nothing.
At least he hoped to God it meant nothing. Because the evening
he'd seen them together, Stevington had left her to dump Stuart's
body in the boat house and Tyler's in the moat. He wondered how
she was going to take the news and if she and Stevington had made
love before he'd done the deed. He said, 'Your determination and
bravery instil a kind of hero worship in others, which you used to
trap Johnnie.'

He thought with disgust how Johnnie had been duped by this
evil bastard. Curbing his fury as best he could and forcing his voice
to sound normal, he continued, 'You strangled your father, then you
took off into the night on your yacht. When did you hear the official
news about his death?'

They were rounding Gilkicker Point. Horton could just about
make out the curved mound of Gilkicker Fort where he'd been
earlier. But suddenly Stevington swung the motorboat shoreward,
and Horton, with a quickening heartbeat, realized this was their
destination.

'Days later, I forget when, but by then I was racing and couldn't come back. I left it to the lawyers to deal with, they were his executors. We had no family.'

It was dark, but Stevington, an accomplished yachtsman, had no trouble taking the small craft into the shore and up on to the beach. Silencing the engine and jumping off he said, 'My father was weak, ill and unhappy. It was a merciful release.'

'And you despise weakness. Yes, I can see that,' Horton answered thoughtfully, as though he was seriously considering and accepting this. And with his father dead Roland was free to pursue his goal. The winning of the Velux 5 Oceans race. And he did win it, and more in between, always sailing alone and making sure to guard against close commitments and to destroy anyone he thought would stand in his way.

Horton jumped off the boat but left Stevington to haul it further up the shingle beach on his own. He didn't need any assistance. Now that Horton knew Johnnie was inside the fort he could attempt to overcome Stevington, but he didn't know exactly where he was hidden. He could call in and get the huge ruinous building searched but that would take time and there was a chance that Stevington was decoying him here. He had to be certain. Stevington was counting on that.

He produced a torch. 'Shall we go?'

Horton noted Stevington didn't go back on to the boat to fetch the cool box. Perhaps he had decided he could give Johnnie what was in it once he had the young man on the boat, and that meant Stevington was counting on not having him along as a passenger. Horton fell into step beside Stevington, their feet crunching on the stones, the drizzling rain sweeping in off the sea behind them as they headed towards the looming dark curved structure.

'It's an amazing place,' Stevington said, as though he was a tour guide. 'Unique in defence fortification because so many important innovations in coastal defence were trialled here, including the use of electric searchlights for defence of the batteries at night. I'm glad it's going to be restored, even if it is for houses and apartments. They haven't got very far with it; it's costing an absolute fortune.'

Stevington veered to the left and began to climb the earth embankment that had been put in front of the fort in 1904. Horton followed, his mind racing. Wherever Johnnie was hidden in this edifice he hoped it wasn't underground, because in order to save him and get out of this alive he'd have to overcome his own dread of confined spaces.

'Did you promise Johnnie that you and he might join up to race together?' Johnnie would have looked up to Stevington. He suspected that Stevington had told Johnnie that he had the talent to become a world-renowned sailor. It would have been so simple; the lad loved sailing. And perhaps he craved the ultimate challenge, the danger and the exhilaration of pitting his wits against the most dangerous seas in the World. Stevington had offered to mentor Johnnie, but he'd told him it had to be kept a secret until they were ready to announce it to Andreadis and others when the time was right. When had Johnnie seen through this? When had the shock and then the bitter disappointment that he'd been duped dawned on him? Horton felt cold and sick with anger, but he couldn't let it show. Not yet.

He said, 'You saw Johnnie Oslow on Andreadis's yacht at Porto Cervo on the Costa Smeralda. You're well-known in the sailing world, a respected world-class hero, an accomplished yachtsman, and in front of you was a man who could possibly tell the world that you had been in the grounds of a psychiatric hospital one night seven years ago when your father had died. You couldn't be sure he hadn't recognized you. And you needed to know if he'd been in touch with the others and told them. But why did you have to kill them?'

'I couldn't take the chance. Besides, what does it matter? Ryan Spencer was a thief, a layabout, living off benefits and doing nothing with his life except fathering children and letting the state pay for them. He's no loss. Tyler Godfray was a mummy's boy who thought he was tough but blubbed like a child, just like Ryan.'

Horton stiffened. God, he'd like to make this tough guy blub, but he guessed that no matter what he did to him, if he ever got the chance, it wouldn't make the slightest bit of difference. 'And Stuart Jayston?'

'The same. Flash little tyke who couldn't even wipe his nose without running to mummy and daddy.'

Horton's fists clenched. He wanted to smash them into Stevington's face, but he couldn't. First he had to be sure that Johnnie was safe. He said, 'But Johnnie was different.'

'I knew the boy had something because I've watched him racing. He reminds me of myself when I was his age,' Stevington tossed

over his shoulder. They were almost at the top of the earth embankment now. It was slippery underfoot because of the rain.

'He's got guts. Even when I told him he'd never get out alive he
didn't plead or cry. He just nodded and said, "I guessed as much."'

And that was what had saved him thus far. That and the fact that
Stevington wanted him as a scapegoat for the murders.

Stevington peeled back a large piece of wood resting against the
wire fence at the top of the embankment and stepped through a gap
in the wire he'd probably cut himself. Horton slipped and quickly
recovered himself as Stevington turned at the sound. The rain was
driving off the sea in greater force now, chilling Horton to the bone
despite his leather jacket and it being August. Beneath him was
what appeared at first to be a large semicircle of blackness but in
reality was a courtyard, or rather a parade ground. To the right was
what remained of the gun casements, facing the sea, and underneath
them were ruins that had most probably been the ammunition stores.
To the left he could see the row of derelict houses that must have
been the barrack rooms and offices and an entrance to the fort from
the northern side. Stevington descended, and Horton followed.
Crossing the courtyard Stevington paused at a flight of stone steps
that led up the three-storey building, most of which was open to
the elements. To the left of the steps though was a green door, which
was padlocked. Stevington retrieved a key from his pocket and
opened it.

Horton had a moment's doubt that Johnnie was here. He said,
'You were taking a chance that the builders wouldn't want access.'

'I checked. They've postponed the work for a few weeks. Run
into some trouble on the development.'

He gestured Horton inside. Stevington's torch picked out a large
empty room with a gaping hole of a fireplace on Horton's right. As
Stevington led him further inside, Horton's eyes restlessly swept
the area. There didn't appear to be anything left inside this part of
the building that he could use as a weapon. They turned into a small
room before stepping through what must have been a corridor into
another largish room. The blackness was oppressive. Horton felt it
clawing at his throat. His fists clenched, and he could feel the sweat
on his back.

Stevington stopped. His torch beam swept the room, and Horton's
gaze followed it eagerly. There was a rusting chain on a wheel, a
kind of pulley mechanism, but it was too far away and he didn't

know if the chain would be easily dislodged from the pulley. Quickly, he looked back at the beam of the torch, which was now shining into the hole of the fireplace. And there huddled in it was Johnnie, his feet and hands bound and his mouth gagged with black tape. His eyes were closed, and they didn't open even when Stevington's torch beam alighted on his face, which was lean and filthy but unbeaten.

Horton controlled his fury sufficiently to say, 'Is he alive?'

'He was yesterday.'

And now that Horton had seen Johnnie, what was Stevington going to do with him? 'I want to check.'

'Please yourself.'

Horton stepped forward, holding his breath; he was giving Stevington the perfect opportunity to bring the torch crashing down on the back of his head and knock him unconscious; then Stevington would strangle him, just as he had Ryan, Tyler and Stuart. Horton had a fraction of a second to act. He held his breath and steeled himself for the attack. He leaned forward and, sensing the movement behind him, quickly dashed to his right, fell to the ground and rolled over, reaching inside his leather jacket for the large stone he'd grabbed from the top of the earth embankment as he'd slipped. It wasn't much, but it might buy him time – that, and the handful of grit he scooped from the floor with his other hand.

Stevington lunged forward. Horton threw the grit in his face, rolled over and jumped up as Stevington faltered, his hands flying to his face. But only for a second. Quickly recovering, he hurled himself at Horton. But Horton stepped aside, wrong footing Stevington, who stumbled. Horton lashed out with the rock on the back of Stevington's head, drawing blood. He staggered. As he drew level with the fireplace Johnnie threw his body forward, causing Stevington to crash to the ground falling over and on to Johnnie. Horton didn't waste time: he lunged forward, thrust his forearm around Stevington's throat and hauled him up.

But Stevington was strong. He rammed his elbow into Horton's midriff. Winded, Horton lost his grip. He staggered back, and suddenly he was down. He sensed rather than saw a boot come up and in a split second rolled away, preventing it from coming into contact with his side, while managing to grasp it and twist the leg. It took all Horton's strength to bring Stevington down. His heart was heaving fit to burst as he hurled himself on Stevington's back and, sitting on him, grabbed his hair and smashed his face into the ground not once but three times, and then because he felt like it he did it again. Then he reached into his pocket for his cuffs, pulled Stevington's hands behind his back and slapped the cuffs on him. Pushing a hand into Stevington's sailing jacket he retrieved the line he'd brought ready to strangle him with and fastened it as tight as he could around Stevington's ankles.

Straightening up, Horton went to Johnnie and swiftly untied him. Stripping off the gag he said, 'Are you OK?'

Johnnie nodded and after a moment grinned, and in that instant Horton saw Cantelli's smiling face. He reached out, took Johnnie's right hand firmly in both of his and clasped it tightly. 'I'll get help.'

TWENTY-FOUR

H e watched as the paramedics took Johnnie away strapped into a stretcher chair which he'd tried desperately to refuse. He'd wanted to walk out but he was too weak despite his determination. After calling for the ambulance Horton had rung Cantelli and had broken the news to him.

'He's dirty, cold and hungry but he's unharmed,' he'd added.

'Thank the Lord.' Cantelli's voice had shaken with relief and emotion.

'He's a plucky lad. And that's what saved him from being killed instantly by Stevington. If he'd grovelled and pleaded for his life or broken down, Stevington would have had nothing but contempt for him and would have disposed of him as soon as he could. But then a better idea occurred to him and that was to frame him for murder and then cover up his death by making it look like suicide, something Stevington has specialized in. Johnnie's on his way to hospital, just for a check-up.'

'I'll tell the family and get up there at once. Andy, I can't ever thank you—'

'Then don't,' Horton cut off his gratitude, then added more gently, 'There's no need, Barney. He helped save me.' Johnnie had sensed there was more than one person heading towards him; perhaps he'd caught the sound of their footsteps in that echoing empty building and had pretended to be unconscious in the hope that help might be on its way and he could seize whatever chance presented itself. And he had.

Prison would be another challenge for Stevington, which he probably believed he'd be able to conquer, just as he'd conquered treacherous seas, and maybe he would but Horton knew that being confined would be a fitting punishment for him. He'd miss the wide space of the sea, although there would be danger enough to overcome inside prison walls. He'd be psychiatrically assessed and with his background would most probably end up in a secure mental institution anyway.

'He's inside,' Horton said to the uniformed officers. A few seconds later they led out a bloodied and stunned Stevington. 'He cut himself shaving,' Horton tossed at the enquiring glances of the officers. Horton refused a lift, saying he'd take the boat back to Haslar Marina where he had left the Harley. He had called Uckfield immediately after breaking the news to Cantelli. Uckfield said he'd get Stevington brought round to Portsmouth and they'd question him there, but Horton was certain that Stevington wouldn't say anything until his lawyer showed.

He walked down the shore and to the boat. The Fort had been sealed off with police tape and an officer posted until Taylor and his SOCO officers could go over the place where Johnnie had been kept and Jim Clarke could take photographs. That would be in the morning; they'd need them to present the case against Stevington.

The sound of the sea washing up on the pebbled shore helped to soothe Horton's ragged nerve ends. The drizzling rain had turned into a soft mist but through it Horton could make out a few lights on the hilly streets of Ryde on the Isle of Wight, where he guessed Stevington had dropped Johnnie on the sixteenth of July in the motorboat. And it was in the motorboat that he must have collected Johnnie from the Camber on Saturday. Horton didn't think he would have risked taking Johnnie back to Haslar Marina or Gilkicker Fort in daylight, so he'd probably taken him out into the Solent and drugged him, just as he must have done Tyler Godfray. He'd then kept Johnnie hidden in the small cabin until it was dark, when he'd taken him to Fort Gilkicker. Johnnie would be able to fill the details in later.

The tide was coming in, and Horton only had to push the small motorboat a little further before it was bobbing on the sea. He started the engine and watched the lights on the Wightlink ferry as it sailed past on its way to Fishbourne. His mind was churning over all that had happened in the last six days and how Stevington's obsession and passion had led him to kill so many times. What was Harriet Eames going to think about Roland Stevington now? And what would Stevington's sponsors do? Easy, they'd pull out because there would be no yacht to sponsor. Maybe he should approach them and ask them to sponsor him to sail in Stevington's place. But he wasn't ready for that yet. Maybe in a few years' time, and before then he could compete in other races as a team member. With Scott Masefield? He smiled at the thought. He didn't think Masefield would welcome him with open arms. And in the meantime he could attempt to get sponsors. Andreadis might give him a start, and Lord Eames might even throw money at him to get him off his back. But then that might not be what Eames really wanted . . . which brought him back to thoughts of his mother and the code that Dr Amos had left for him on the back of that envelope.

He surveyed the Gosport shore on his left. Looming in the mist was a fort built to defend Portsmouth Harbour during the war of American independence and remodelled in the 1880s by Lord Palmerston. He'd stood next to it earlier, fenced off from prying public eyes by security wire, cameras and lighting because it was still in use by the military . . . Suddenly, his nerve ends jangled, and he slowed the boat to a crawl as he studied the dark shape on the shore. Was this the reason Amos had given him those location references, either of his own free will or because he'd been instructed to do so by someone? Amos hadn't been steering him towards Haslar Marina or even the hospital but to Fort Monckton, because it wasn't only used by the army but it was also reputed to be a training establishment for the intelligence services.

He stopped the boat and considered this further. Had Jennifer been heading there on the day she disappeared, or had she been waylaid from her rendezvous with someone and had been taken here? But by whom and why? Had it been used by the intelligence services in 1978? If so his chances of discovering who had been at Fort Monckton then were nil and perhaps the person she had met had only been there temporarily, or simply visiting. Maybe she'd never reached there. Maybe Amos's reference had nothing to do with Fort Monckton or the marina. Perhaps it wasn't a location at all. But somehow Horton felt it was. Or was that because he *wanted* to believe it?

He'd been fortunate to find its meaning so quickly. Maybe too fortunate. Amos couldn't have known about Johnnie being missing and that his inquiries would lead him to Go About, and neither could Lord Eames, not at the time when Amos had called his solicitor and given him the envelope to deposit. But if he hadn't made the connection between the numbers on the envelope and the location would Eames, or someone else who knew about Amos's envelope, have devised a way to get him to discover what the figures meant?

He sighed heavily and throttled up. Perhaps the location was only an obscure reference to his mother. But if he put it against everything else he'd discovered and speculated about in the last few months then his conclusions were simple. Everyone was pushing him to find someone, and it wasn't Jennifer Horton. It was someone that the intelligence services, with all their resources, couldn't find, so what hope had he? The answer slapped him in the face. Because they didn't know who it was but if *he* made enough noise this person would show himself or make contact with him, *because* of Jennifer. And why were they so keen to find him? Because whatever this man knew it was dangerous. Whether that was dangerous to an individual or a country, Horton didn't know; maybe it was both. They were running scared. They had used Sawyer and the Zeus story to tempt him to cooperate, but that hadn't worked. So they had used Ballard and his photograph, leading him to Professor Madeley and Dr Amos. And they were using him. He didn't much care for that. And he didn't like the game he was being made to play. So did he play it? Or did he quit? Could he quit?

He headed into the mouth of Portsmouth Harbour and then into the marina, tying up where he and Stevington had left two hours ago. It was quiet. Across the water he saw the lights of Oyster Quays where the restaurants, bars, nightclubs and the waterfront were buzzing with life. His mind turned to thoughts of the deaths of Ryan, Tyler and Stuart and of Sarah Conway. He recalled her laugh, the tiny piece of pastry lodged in the corner of her mouth that had seemed so seductive, her smile, her passion, her wildness and her love of danger, and suddenly the words Amos had spoken to him a week ago about Jennifer came to him. *She didn't like towing the line. Keeping silent and being a good little girl wasn't her style. She was too radical, too involved with the students . . . Jennifer liked living dangerously . . . She liked action . . .* Just like Sarah Conway.

And did that action mean Jennifer was directly involved with the intelligence services? Horton stood on the pontoon, surveying the boats but not seeing them. Could she have been working for the intelligence services? Was that why Amos had given him the location reference?

Swiftly, he remembered what else Amos had said: *She never mentioned him and I never saw her with him, but there was definitely someone . . .* Someone she was in love with. Someone she got pregnant by, his father. Someone from the intelligence services she was working for? Her control? Was that who she'd been coming here to see the day she disappeared? Was he being fanciful? Could it really be possible? Could he trust Amos's words?

He walked slowly down the deserted pontoons toward the car park. What else had Amos said? *Secrets and lies. Someone's kept silent for a long time. They might want it to stay that way.* He'd thought that was Lord Eames and his cronies in British Intelligence. He was wrong. *You might think the days of spies and the Cold War are over and that I'm an old man seeing shadows across every ripple of the sea, but they're not over, there is always evil below. Be careful, Andy Horton.*

At last he was beginning to understand. He was beginning to pierce the murky waters and see the evil below. As he crossed the road and headed for the Harley he knew that he was close to the truth and that he would do what Lord Eames and his cronies wanted. He'd play the game. He'd find this man for them. He had no choice, because he knew that only then would it end, one way or another.